TWINKLE TWINKLE

AU

REVOIR

TWINKLE TWINKLE AU REVOIR

A MERMAID BAY CHRISTMAS SHOPPE MYSTERY

HEATHER WEIDNER

LEVEL
BEST BOOKS

First published by Level Best Books 2024

This novel is entirely a work of fiction. The names, characters and incidents portrayed in it are the work of the author's imagination. Any resemblance to actual persons, living or dead, events or localities is entirely coincidental.

Author Photo Credit: Joy Pfister at Studio FBJ

First edition

ISBN: 978-1-68512-532-5

Cover art by Level Best Designs

This book was professionally typeset on Reedsy.
Find out more at reedsy.com

To Stan – Thanks for all the love and support along this bumpy writing journey.

Praise for the Mermaid Bay Christmas Shoppe Mysteries

Sticks and Stones and A Bag of Bones

"Another fun and interesting installment in an already popular cozy mystery series. Mystery and scandal rule this charmer. With main characters you feel like you know, twists and turns keep you reading."—Heather Douglass, NetGalley Reviewer

"Heather Weidner has everything I like in a cozy mystery. Good characters, charming town, and a bag of bones washing up on shore. Plus, a local murder. Jade Hicks the owner of a Christmas shop, and Christmas shops are always popular in beach towns, looks into the crime and hopes to save the town's Christmas in July festival. This is a terrific start to the Mermaid Bay Christmas Shoppe Mystery series."—Jackie Layton, Author of the Low Country Dog Walker Mysteries

"I enjoyed this light and fresh whodunit that kept me on my game. The author did a great job in presenting this well-written and fast-paced drama where mischief and mayhem was afoot where scattered notes and bits of voodoo seemed to plague the residents of Mermaid Bay. Who wanted the bookstore owner dead? There's a town full of potential suspects and I had a great time following along with Jade as each clue gathered took us closer to the killer's identity. What drove this tale was the visually descriptive narrative, the engaging dialogue, the small-neighborly atmosphere and the likeable cast of characters that includes Jade, Nick and Chloe. Overall, this was a great read and I look forward for more exciting times in Mermaid Bay with Jade and her friends."—DruAnn Love, Dru's Book Musing

"*Sticks and Stones and a Bag of Bones* by Heather Weidner is the first book in the Mermaid Bay Christmas Shoppe Mystery series. This is a good beginning to what looks to be a fun series. I really like amateur sleuth Jade Hicks, who owns the Christmas Shoppe, "Tis the Season in Mermaid Bay. She is very personable and intelligent. The secondary characters are quite likable too. I especially like Sheriff Nick Driscoll and Jade's new friend Amy. This was a fun read and I look forward to the next book in the series."—Margey Hager, NetGalley Reviewer

"Very entertaining cozy mystery with a bunch of fun characters. I knew I would like it from the title and cover, and the story was a smooth read start to finish. The motive was obvious to me almost from the start, so I was surprised that the investigation did not move along more logically and quickly. The spark between Jade and Nick is sweet, and the two seem well suited to each other. Nick may be the cop, but Jade is a bonafide sleuth in her own right. And the recipes at the end are quite a bonus!! Fun read!"—Autumn Danner, Goodreads Reviewer

"What a pleasant surprise. This is a new to me author. I came across this book on a New Release page and added it to my TBR list. Because of the series name and cover, I was just going to add it to my Christmas TBR list (because I never read the synopsis). Then, this showed up in the Recently Added list at my library, so I figured what the heck. I'm so glad I borrowed it.

"This book starts off like a traditional Cozy Mystery but it really doesn't follow the typical footprint, which was fun.

"No spoilers; however, the murder happens early but it's almost an afterthought throughout the rest of the book. Yes, it's mentioned but there are other mysteries to be solved that may or may not be connected (you'll have to find out for yourself).

"I really enjoyed the cast of characters and beachside small town they live in. I'm really looking forward to more books in this series."—Debra Jo Burnette, Room of Required Reading Bookstagrammer

"On a cold and dreary January weekend I took a virtual vacation to sunny, summer-y Mermaid Bay, thanks to the wonderful writing of Heather Weidner. *Sticks and Stones and a Bag of Bones* celebrates Christmas in July in a fictional beach town, which not only brought a favorite holiday into play, but was accompanied by peaceful and relaxing strolls on the beach. Oh, and did I mention murder? Yes, the main character Jade Hicks is in a perfect position to help solve the untimely death of a local store owner, along with the unfunny pranks that plague this small town. From the get-go when a suitcase of bones washes up on the beach, until the exciting ending when the mysteries (plural) are solved, well, what's not love about this well written, character-drive, fast-paced cozy mystery? Only downfall is that it will be a YEAR before I can make another visit to Mermaid Bay!"—Jayne Ormerod, Author of *Goin' Coastal*

"Good start to a new cozy series! I was approved for this one after it was already released and I listened to the audiobook. The narrator was delightful-entertaining, different voices for each character and emotions thought out. I loved getting to know these easy to like characters and look forward to reading the next one in their series!"—Anne Edester, NetGalley Reviewer

"This was a really good start to a new series! The characters were so much fun and I can't wait for more of them in the future books! The mystery itself was also entertaining and interesting and kept me reading. Definitely a quick read too!"—Tiffany Newton, NetGalley Reviewer

"I loved the range of characters, some quirky, others annoying, and some I'd like as friends. The relationships between the friends were warm, and I wondered if or when the sheriff would move into the love interest column."—Cynthia Smith, NetGalley Reviewer

"This is a really good mystery very well written with great characters I highly recommend for all mystery lovers."—Shelly Meyer, NetGalley Reviewer

"First in a new series. I found it highly enjoyable. Mermaid Bay sounds like a fun town. With Christmas in July comes a bunch of trouble ensues ending up in murder. Jade, the owner of the Christmas shop sets out to find the murderer. A good solid mystery with characters that are wonderful."—Renee Winter, NetGalley Reviewer

"The first book in the Mermaid Bay Christmas Shoppe Mystery series is *Sticks and Stones and a Bag of Bones* by Heather Weidner. This is a strong start to what appears to be an entertaining series. I liked the small-town seaside location, the Christmas store, and the cat and dog's role in the narrative."—Jody Joy, NetGalley Reviewer

"If you love starting cozy mystery series with book one, read this! *Sticks and Stones and a Bag of Bones* has so many of the elements that make a cozy mystery enjoyable: a diverse batch of characters, an adorable small town, a dog and a cat, and a perplexing mystery. I highly recommend that you read this charming cozy mystery!"—Christy's Cozy Corners, Book Blogger

"If small-town mysteries are what you enjoy, *Sticks and Stones and a Bag of Bones* won't disappoint."—Lori Van Buren, Novels Alive

"This is a "feel good " story, great for a beach visit or travel. Don't expect page-turning action. Do expect likable characters in an adorable village by the sea. I would definitely visit Mermaid Bay myself."—Beth Youngblood, NetGalley Reviewer

"I am not new to Heather Weidner's writing so I will say this: I knew this was going to be a brilliant series debut. I enjoyed reading every bit of this book. There were plenty of red herrings, an interesting set of characters and side stories, a couple of furry babies—a dog and cats, and, not to forget, a dash of romance.

"The mystery kept me guessing till the end. I loved the characters and their side stories. Apart from Jade, the one other character that I liked the most is that of Amy. She's so energetic, enthusiastic, and full of ideas— I would love to see a cozy series featuring Amy as main character.

"If you are looking for a new cozy series, love year-round Christmas shoppes and furry babies, and excellent storytelling, you might want to give *Sticks and Stones and a Bag of Bones* by Heather Weidner a try."—Rekha Rao, NetGalley Reviewer

"She pens an intriguing tale of the lengths a shady character might go to. It is engrossing."—Amary Chapman, NetGalley Reviewer

"*Sticks and Stones and a Bag of Bones* combines Christmas and beach living in an enjoyable start to a new series."—Cozy up with Kathy, Book Blogger

"I absolutely loved *Sticks and Stones and a Bag of Bones*! It's the first book in a brand new cozy mystery series by Heather Weidner called the Mermaid Bay Christmas Shoppe Mysteries. The series takes place in Mermaid Bay, Virginia which is a small town with lots of eclectic small businesses. The main character, Jade Hicks, runs 'Tis the Season, a shop dedicated to Christmas, of course! It's not just a tiny place either; it has different rooms with different themes and lots of Christmas trees filled with themed decorations. I love Christmas, and I want to live in this make believe store! In fact, I'd love to live in a place like Mermaid Bay. It's by the ocean; it has that small town vibe that I love in cozy mystery books; there are characters (though much younger than I!) with whom I could be friends.

"I like being surprised and unable to uncover the killer until near the end of the cozies I read. This one fits the bill. Like I said, you'll find lots of characters who jump on and off of your list of suspects. If you love starting cozy mystery series with book one, read this! *Sticks and Stones and a Bag of Bones* has so many of the elements that make a cozy mystery enjoyable: a diverse batch of characters, an adorable small town, a dog and a cat, and a perplexing mystery. I highly recommend that you read this charming cozy mystery!"—Christy's Cozy Corner, Book Reviewer

"Great book by Heather Weidner. I'm really liking this series, and its characters. This was a fun cozy. I liked trying to figure out who done what. I'll definitely be reading more from this author."—Valerie Blankenship, NetGalley Reviewer

"I enjoyed this first in the series book. Lovely characters, fun to read and a great mystery. I can't wait for the next book."—Stacey Bradley, NetGallley Reviewer

"An entertaining and compelling cozy mystery I thoroughly enjoyed. Well plotted, likeable and fleshed out characters, a lovely setting. The mystery is solid and kept me guessing. It's the first I read in this series and won't surely be the last. Highly recommended."—Anna Maria Giacomasso, NetGalley Reviewcr

"Quick, easy, entertaining and a year-round Christmas shop. What's not to like about that?

"A good cozy mystery that takes you one a ride, entertains you and as it isn't too long you can read it quickly and easily. I love a book like that. Great characters, a bit of fun and of course a good old bag of bones!

" I enjoyed this one and recommend as a fun, easy reading book."—Donna Robinson, NetGalley Reviewer

"I enjoyed the characters and the realistic problems of any town dependent on tourist dollars and the ever present problem in beach town areas of development vs. keeping a smaller town feel. There were plenty of twists and turns in this mystery to keep you guessing until the end. Of course, I loved the furry friends and the touch of romance. A good read when you are looking for a light cozy or longing for a beach getaway."—Juliane Silver, NetGalley Reviewer

"I enjoy my visits to Mermaid Bay. I like the characters and enjoy the dialog between Jade and Nick."—Dawn Tarrant, NetGalley Reviewer

"The quiet beachside community was thrown into disbelief by the murder of one of their own. Jade couldn't help being curious about the strangeness happening in their community, so she put on her sleuthing cap and began searching for answers. She was a businesswoman with a penchant for investigating crimes. This cozy was an intriguing and entertaining one."—Cherry-Ann London, NetGalley Reviewer

"Fine start to a brand-new cozy mystery series! Mermaid Bay is a tourist town in coastal Virginia and has a bunch of small shops with Christmas themes. The first sign of trouble is a suitcase found on the beach with a collection of bones in it. Then there are the threatening notes, voodoo dolls, and finally a murdered (unpleasant) bookseller. Jade does her part to help solve the crime even though no all of her efforts are appreciated by her good friend Sheriff Nick."—Jan Tangen, NetGalley Reviewer

"Nothing ruins a good walk on the beach like finding a mysterious suitcase full of damaged bones and a skull. The discovery rocks the peaceful community of Mermaid Bay, known for its historic beach cottages. The gruesome find is nothing like the usual summer ills of litterbugs and teens drinking under the pier for the idyllic seaside community, located a few miles from Virginia's historic triangle of Jamestown, Williamsburg, and Yorktown.

"This was a fun start to a new cozy mystery series, and I would definitely pick up the second! I enjoyed the cast of characters and the beach town setting. The story is as much about the relationships of the town residents as the mystery, making it a very enjoyable read."—Amanda Waggoner, NetGalley Reviewer

"I recently discovered Heather Weidner and was really intrigued to read this book, the first in the series. I might be a little biased as I live in Virginia, but I enjoyed this book and hope to see more in the series. There's never a dull moment in this town…a suitcase of washed up bones, voo doo dolls, threatening letters and smashed windows…oh my!"—Kim Schade, NetGalley Reviewer

"I really loved this book in a new to my series and author. I can't wait to read the next one. The characters and location really add to the plot. This book keeps you guessing until the end."—Lori Ruth, NetGalley Reviewer

"This was a light, fun cozy with some great characters. I love Chloe."—Lisa Garrett, NetGalley Reviewer

Chapter One

"Jaaaaaaaade," echoed through the store. "I may never wash my hand again. Love is in the air. Dee dee dee dee dee deeeeeeee."

Jade Hicks, owner of 'Tis the Season Christmas Shoppe, paused from filling online orders and stepped into the lobby. She pulled the Dutch door closed behind her to keep her French bulldog Chloe from joining in the excitement.

Jade's part-timer, Patti Hall, fondly known around the small beach town as "Peppermint Patti," waltzed around the space between the two large Christmas trees and the counter. "I got to meet Raphael Allard this morning, and he kissed my hand. I am so excited that the Love Channel's TV crew is here. I adore their shows, and now *My Coastal Valentine* will be my favorite since it was filmed here in Mermaid Bay. He is smoking hot and sooo exotic with those smoldering looks and hair. And that beautiful French accent. And those blue eyes. Ooooohlala." Patti continued to flit around in her red sweater with giant pink hearts that matched her leggings. "I pulled out all my Valentine wear for the occasion. This is sooooo exciting."

"I'm not sure the town will be the same," Jade said.

"Your empty lot next door looks like a pop-up town with all those campers and trucks," Patti said. Her blond curls bobbed as she danced.

"The RV company brought them in and did the setup, and the crew moved in within hours. And thankfully, the TV crew hired people to take care of the water and all the other stuff. Who knew we'd have people camping next to the store."

"Who knew where I work would be home to a TV crew and all the

Hollywood fun? We have front-row seats to all the behind-the-scenes action. And did you see that big food tent? I need to bring a pair of binoculars, so I won't miss anything. It looks like a beehive of activity out there."

"The bigwigs are staying over with Ruby at the Pearl. The staff and the crew are in the campers."

"The bed and breakfast will be the perfect setting. I hope they use it in the filming, too. Ruby's blue Victorian looks like a dollhouse with all that gingerbread work. All the Love Channel shows have some kind of quaint house. Mermaid Bay is a perfect setting for their audience. As you know, our streets haven't changed since 1950," Patti said.

Before Jade could comment, the front door flew open, and Bernie Nash barreled in. Jade's part-time handyman and Santa waved his cell phone. "Hey, gals. I need some help. How do I send a picture to the guys? That cute little movie star said hello and gave me a peck on the cheek." He handed Jade his phone to show her the photo of him in his flamingo print shirt with Elle Valentine, the Love Channel's darling and star of almost every show.

"Email or text?" Jade asked. "Or do you want to post it somewhere?"

A puzzled look crossed his face. "I can do email, I guess."

Jade stepped through how to attach a photo. Bernie nodded a lot and then called out the long list of his fishing buddies that he wanted to include.

"Nice picture of you and Elle," Jade said.

A flush made Bernie's cheeks rosier than normal. "Thanks. I knew you could help me out with this new-fangled stuff." The Santa-look-alike saluted and trotted out the door.

"If you're okay here. I'm going to run over to Ruby's and drop off the welcome gifts for her guests from 'Tis the Season," Jade said.

"No problemo. Chloe and I will have a dance-off or something while you're gone. We can handle the store. And maybe we'll see some stars. We've got this," Patti said.

"I pulled all the heart and Valentine decorations I could find for the two big display trees. You may want to check the storeroom to see if there are any I missed."

"I'm on it," Patti said with a twinkle in her blue eyes.

Jade gathered the red and purple gift bags full of sparkly tissue paper and set them in two large boxes. Throwing her purse strap over her shoulder, she balanced both boxes on her hip and opened the back door.

Traffic on Neptune Road had been diverted to the side streets, and the TV crew had surrounded Jade's side lot with plastic hurricane fencing. The quiet beach community looked different with all the traffic barriers and cordoned zones. Normally, everyone in town took a deep breath after Labor Day, but this fall, the business council contracted with a popular cable network to film a show in and around town. Everyone wanted to get close to the action, and many were vying for roles as extras. Mermaid Bay was ground zero for the Love Channel action.

Jade hustled to her lime-green Jeep Wrangler and loaded the boxes in the back seat. Normally, she walked everywhere in town, but with road closures, a vehicle would be a better way to navigate.

After dodging tourists and police barricades, she made it to the Pearl, a tall Victorian mansion that Ruby Ellis and her daughter Josie lovingly turned into a bed and breakfast. The house, originally built for a wealthy banker from Richmond and his family, was an escape from the city heat in a southern world without air conditioning.

Finding parking on a side street, Jade hurried around the block and up the oyster shell pathway to the kitchen door. Ruby flung the door open before Jade had a chance to knock.

"Thanks for bringing those over. I'll have Josie put them in the rooms this evening. Come in." Ruby reached for one of the boxes, brimming over with welcome gifts.

"How are things going? Everyone settled in?" Jade asked, placing her box on the large island in the industrial, white-tiled kitchen.

"Filming starts tomorrow, and everyone from town is buzzing. I can't tell you how many calls I've received about people wanting to volunteer to do things or visit the Pearl. Everyone's trying to get close to the actors. I don't need any more offers for casseroles or people wanting to work part-time here." Ruby rolled her eyes. "It's been fun to meet everyone, but it's been a tremendous amount of work. I'm not used to such high-maintenance guests. I've got the two stars Elle and Raphael, Brian Michaels, the director, Ezra Hopkins, the producer, and Olivia Morton as guests. The worker bees, including Olivia's assistant, are staying at your place."

Before Jade could respond, a loud crash and breaking glass echoed from the hallway. Jade followed on Ruby's heels to see what had happened. Ruby stopped suddenly in the doorway to the parlor, and Jade almost ran into the back of her. What was left of a large white vase and its pink roses lay scattered next to an overturned side table.

"I will not be talked to that way, Raphael. You are crude and a brute." Elle Valentine, a petite blond who resembled a Disney pixie, turned and stomped up the stairs.

"I was only kidding, Elle," he yelled at her back. "But Brian, I do need more lines. She always dominates everything. That is a fact, and she's a tad touchy about it," Raphael Allard whined, looking down at the mess on Ruby's area rug. He glanced around the room, trying to drum up support for his cause.

Olivia Morton, the tall production manager with long dark hair, scowled at him. "Paige, get this cleaned up now." She turned toward Ruby and said, "Please add this to our bill. We'll ensure that you're reimbursed for the vase. I need to go check on Elle."

"Of course," Raphael muttered, running a hand through his overly styled hair. "Go see how the princess is feeling."

Ezra and Brian continued their conversation like nothing had happened while Olivia's assistant, Paige Wilson, made a face as she bent over to pick up the larger pieces of the vase.

"Here, I've got this. I don't want you to cut yourself," Ruby said. "Y'all can move over to the couch while I take care of this mess."

Raphael followed the small group to the pale-yellow couches near the center of the room as Paige righted the side table.

Ruby returned a few minutes later with a whisk, broom, and trash can. While she took care of the mess, Jade leaned further into the doorway to try to hear the conversation. She caught several snippets of the discussion about tonight's rehearsal and tomorrow's filming.

"I'll run the vacuum when they're done," Ruby whispered. "This will have to do for now." She motioned for Jade to follow her.

When the swinging kitchen door closed behind Jade, Ruby plunked the trashcan in the corner and washed her hands. "This group is full of drama llamas. The producer and director are polite. Elle and Raphael are demanding. Nothing meets their standards, and I'm constantly trying to fill requests for avocados, vegetarian bacon, designer waters, and Vitamin D lightbulbs. And I've never seen so many people opposed to carbs. Sheesh. And I haven't even served a good ol' southern breakfast yet."

Ruby's phone buzzed. She pulled it out of her pocket and glanced at the screen. "I've got to run. Her Highness isn't pleased with the thread count in my towels. There is always something. I'm getting my exercise with this crowd." Ruby let out a heavy sigh. "Thanks again for the gift bags. Wish me luck. I hope I can survive the filming." Ruby hurried up the back staircase.

Jade let herself out the door and returned to her own store, where, hopefully, things were quieter.

Chapter Two

J ade and Chloe took the long route to work. They walked down the beach and over the dunes near the pier. Eventually, they would cut over Neptune Road by Mermaid Books and approach her store from the other side. Tourists and paparazzi, hoping to get a glance at one of the stars, staked out every spare inch of space on the sidewalks and in the sand, and the little dog had to greet everyone she met.

Chloe and Jade crossed the street and paused near the plastic fencing that surrounded her lot. People in black buzzed around the trailers and trucks, and the crowd stared intently and snapped pictures of the crew moving boxes and equipment.

After what seemed like hours of waiting for something to happen, Jade finally coaxed the butterball of a dog to head to the office, where Jade made a beeline for the coffee maker. While the machine chugged and spurted out steam, Jade pulled up the online orders from the previous night. Eight pages, a new record. Jade smiled to herself. She was pleased that the investment she put into the store's website for easy online orders was paying off. When Jade took over the shop after her grandmother's death, sales were dependent on summer beach traffic that wasn't all that consistent from year to year. The new website saved the store during the pandemic and now provided over half the store's annual revenue.

Jade's grandparents had purchased this building and a bungalow down the street in the seventies. As a little girl, Jade had many fond memories of summers here in Mermaid Bay. Thoughts of the car accident that killed her parents in her teen years caused her eyes to well up with tears. After the accident, Jade took up permanent residence in her grandparents' spare room until she left for college. Wiping her eyes with the back of her hands, Jade took a deep breath and concentrated on filling and packaging the orders.

When she had finished the labels, her aunt Lorelei sashayed in through the front door with Neville the Devil cat. The tuxedo cat, a stray that her grandmother had adopted, fancied himself as the store's mouser. A few months back, her single aunt asked to take him home for company. Neville, who now visited the store part-time when Lorelei worked, still acted like he owned the place. He hopped up on the ledge of the dividing door between the store and the office area and was greeted by a low growl from behind the door. Chloe, his nemesis, yipped and growled again.

"Perfect timing on my part," Lorelei said to Jade. "Looks like you've filled a ton of orders." She dropped her purse and red coat on the spare desk near the counter. "I see the TV crew made itself at home next door. They've taken over most of the town, too. See anybody famous yet?"

"I went over to Ruby's yesterday and saw Raphael and Elle. Some of the actors and the crew are staying in the trailers next door."

"Raphael is dreamy, and that accent is to die for. And those blue eyes make him dominate any scene he's in. Elle is adorable. I love the shows they're in together. And yes, I watch way too much TV. But that pair has such chemistry," Lorelei said.

Jade nodded and raised her eyebrows. "You can say that again. They had a little tiff while I was at the B and B. A table got flipped, and one of Ruby's vases didn't survive."

Lorelei's eyes widened and stopped in mid-step. "Raphael had an outburst?"

Jade shook her head slowly. "No, Elle did. Then she stormed up the stairs. Ruby was fussing that they're demanding guests. I didn't get the sense that she was as excited as the rest of the town is have them here."

Lorelei's mouth formed a small "o" as she stirred creamer into her coffee. "Interesting. But I still can't wait to meet them."

Jade's phone buzzed on her desk. "Hi, Ruby. What's up?"

"Can you come over to the Pearl? I'm having an issue with some social media comments, and I was hoping you can help me. I know you helped Todd that one time. And I was kinda hoping you could do the same for me. I'm at my wits' end today. And we're missing two of your gift bags. I know I counted them when you brought them over. Could you bring two? Elle is fussing again."

Jade's thoughts flashed back to last summer when someone flooded Todd Brickman's social media sites with thousands of bad reviews. A mystery troll kept harassing him to sell Hot Diggity Dogs, the beachfront property that had been in his family for years.

"Jade, did you hear me?" Ruby asked.

"Sorry. I was thinking about something. Lorelei's here. I can be over in a bit."

"See you then. Gotta run." The owner of the Pearl disconnected.

Jade buzzed around the back room, trying to remember what she put in the first set of gift bags. She pulled out items, hoping the contents were comparable. Lorelei breezed in the back as she was fluffing the tissue paper stuffing. "I'm headed to Ruby's. I should be back soon. I have my phone with me if it gets busy here," Jade said.

"We'll be fine. I'll work on inventory, and Neville, Chloe, and I will stalk the actors' social media accounts to see what they think of Mermaid Bay and to figure out where they'll be next."

Jade slipped on her parka and grabbed her purse from the drawer in her desk. She trotted down the back steps and threaded her way through the crowds that had taken over town since the word got out about the filming. She cut down an alley and through a neighborhood of vintage beach homes. Mermaid Bay, which prided itself in its historic district, did everything in its power to keep out the chain stores and kitschy beach attractions.

She dodged traffic and zipped through the iron gates in front of the Pearl. Following the shell path, Jade circled the house and knocked on the kitchen door of the B and B. Fall flowers bloomed in the neat beds that lined both sides of the path.

Ruby opened the door a crack. "Oh, hi. Thanks for coming over. I don't know what I'm going to do." She swung the door open and lowered her voice. "That woman! She is never satisfied. Elle tweeted or facegrammed this morning that my accommodations don't have room darkening shades and that the birds are too loud outside. Yesterday, she didn't like the quality of the sheets and towels. And Josie told me a minute ago, that she did a snarky post about the chocolates I left in her room. But she did like the Christmas gift bag you brought over. Kudos, she shared that with her three million followers." Ruby let out a puff of air. "I can't let that little so-and-so ruin my reputation. And I certainly can't afford to lose reservations because we don't meet her Hollywood standards." Ruby huffed and planted one hand on her hip.

Jade handed her the two bags.

"Thanks, you're a peach," Ruby said, letting out a puff of air that fluttered her hair.

Josie, with her long hair twisted in a messy bun, breezed in the kitchen. "Are you still talking about Her Highness?"

Ruby nodded. "This has got to stop. She has an opinion about everything. This filming was supposed to help me promote my business. I'm planning a 'stay where the stars of the Love Channel stayed' promotion for the winter and spring. But no one will want to come if she keeps bad-mouthing us. Jade, you helped Todd. What do you suggest I should do?"

"Todd made an effort to flood his sites with his own message. He created a bunch of posts and videos to show how great his place was. He shared positive reviews and ensured that his story was out there. And it seemed to push down some of the negative posts in the search results. Plus, people are fickle. They move on to the next big story in the blink of an eye, but you have to endure the mess until that happens. You can dominate the search results. People often don't go past the second page of the search results when they're looking for something."

"Josie, can you spend some time on our sites and keep the happy posts flowing? I don't have the time or know how to bother with it." Ruby sighed loudly and tucked a stray silver stand that had escaped from her bun.

The twenty-something nodded and pulled out her phone. "Of course. I love getting paid to do social media. My dream job. I'll get my friends to help, too. It's way more fun than running up and down the stairs fifty times a day to see what Elle wants, which is for me to wait on her hand and foot."

"Have you talked to Elle about her comments? Maybe she doesn't realize that it's affecting your business." Jade said.

"I've tried. She's as sweet as candy to your face, and then her evil side blasts you with snarky posts when you're not looking," Ruby said. "It's like she can't help herself. She has to comment in detail about every single thing."

"What about Olivia or Paige, her assistant? Maybe they could help?"

Ruby shook her head. "I'll try to catch Olivia away from the executives. She's always following either Ezra or Brian around like no one else exists. It's hard to get her attention, and Paige is a grumpy Gus. Olivia is my best bet. I'm desperate enough to give anything a try. Elle has got to stop with all the bad posts."

"Operation Good News has begun," Josie said, doing a fist pump and pulling up a stool to the island.

"I'll make sure to like and share them," Jade said.

"Elle is pretty cool, though," Josie muttered. "She has some amazing things in her room. She collects Victorian doodads like perfume bottles and hair combs. She has this gorgeous letter opener that looks like a dagger with a dragon on it. She showed it to me when I brought her some mineral water last night. And you know what else? She likes to have fresh flowers in her room every day."

Ruby's eyes widened, and a panicked look crossed her face. "Josie, no posts about the stars and their private rooms."

"Of course not. But I do know some secrets now, but I promise to keep them to myself. Though we could make some money with those online gossip sites." Her mother frowned, and Josie quickly added, "I'll only take pictures of our guests in the common areas, and I won't write about anything personal. And I'll get their permission before I post anything. I know your standards."

"We'll work on our social media posts. Thanks, Jade, for the help. I hope this works," Ruby said.

I hope I helped. On the way back to the store, Jade dodged spectators on the sidewalks. Word had traveled fast about the filming, and the crowd size rivaled the ones on Fourth of July weekend.

"So, what exciting things are going on?" Lorelei asked when Jade closed the door behind her.

"Oh, there's lots of drama at the Pearl. Elle's not too happy with the accommodations or the amenities. She's driving Ruby bat crazy with all the comments and posts to her social media sites."

A wry smile crossed Lorelei's face. "I'm sure Ruby's beside herself. She's overly protective of her business. And this younger generation feels the need to share and comment on everything."

Before they could continue, the bells on the front door tinkled, and Olivia Morton strode in carrying a black leather portfolio. "Hello. Thanks again, Jade, for letting us rent your lot for equipment storage and our portable kitchen and craft tent. You're a lifesaver. I had no idea where to stash our stuff. Let me know if you need anything or have any issues. Here's this week's filming schedule. We'll be in and out at different times, so maybe we won't cause that much disruption to your business."

"We're glad to have you all. This is the first time I've seen a show filmed, so I'm excited. And we can't wait to see the final product."

"The town is perfect for our audience. We don't have to do much to it. We'll be in a variety of different locations, so you all will recognize places when you see the show. Our audience will love it," Olivia said.

"This is my aunt Lorelei."

"It's nice to meet you. My numbers are on the schedule. Text me if you have any questions."

"Uh, one thing. Did Ruby get a chance to talk to you?"

Olivia paused. "Not really. Is this about the vase? We'll take care of it." Olivia brushed back her straight dark hair and frowned.

Jade shook her head. "Elle's not too happy about her accommodations. She's posting so many comments about the B and B."

Olivia waved her hand. "She's active on social media with her fans. She likes to share everything." Olivia's countenance hardened. "I certainly hope the owner and her daughter aren't posting stories about the actors. I told

TWINKLE TWINKLE AU REVOIR

her that privacy was imperative. They signed the agreements."

"No, they wouldn't do that. Ruby is the consummate professional, but she is concerned about her reputation. She's worked really hard to convert that Victorian home to a beautiful B and B. And she wants the actors to feel welcome and to enjoy their stay. Some of the comments aren't, uh, flattering."

"Elle is open about her feelings. That's just the way she is. I'll try to talk to Ruby. Her place is cute and, uh, charming. She shouldn't be offended. Elle doesn't mean anything by her comments. She should be grateful for the mention to Elle's vast fan base."

Lorelei coughed to cover up her retort.

"Let me or my assistant Paige know if you have any questions." Olivia turned on her three-inch boots and marched out the front door.

When the door closed, Lorelei said, "Not to be Captain Obvious here, but it's okay for the Hollywood folks to overshare and criticize, and us townies need to stand there and applaud them. And be quiet when we've been offended or abused." One of her aunt's eyebrows shot up and almost touched her hairline.

"I hope that this is the worst thing that happens as a result of the filming, and better yet, all our businesses get a boost in profits. The Love Channel should put Mermaid Bay on the map. But if we get a bad rap, it's going to be the longest two weeks ever," Jade said. "I don't think any of us had a plan for damage control. It was supposed to be all love and roses."

Chapter Three

The bells jangled on the front door, and Chloe scurried to the lobby before Jade could close the dividing door.

"Who are you, cuteness?" A tall woman with long hair leaned over to pet Chloe, who danced a jig on her hind legs.

"This is Chloe. She runs the place. Hi, I'm Jade Hicks."

"I'm Lexi Armstrong. I'm the stylist for the cast, and the crew bugged out this morning with all the generators for today's location filming. Could I bother you for an outlet to plug in my curling iron before work? Nobody wants a stylist with bedhead."

"No problem. You can use the bathroom. It's back here." Jade walked down a narrow hallway past the workroom and storage room.

"I love your store. I'll come back when I get a moment to shop. You've got some great stuff here," Lexi cooed, popping her head into the doorways of the display rooms they passed.

Jade smiled. "And if you like to shop in your PJs, we have a website, too."

"Thanks so much. The first day of filming is always exciting in a new place. I'm hoping we get some time to explore. We're outside today near the pier, and it feels like a perfect fall day. I haven't experienced all four seasons in a long time. L.A. isn't known for its fall foliage and snow." The woman stepped in the tiny bathroom and put her oversized purse on the sink.

"It's pretty moderate here in coastal Virginia, but we do get a taste of all the seasons. Can I get you some coffee?" Jade asked.

"No thanks. I'm good. But I do want to see some East Coast sights before we leave. This area and the next town overlook fun. I haven't been to Virginia since an eighth-grade band trip to Williamsburg."

"They call this area the Historic Triangle because of Jamestown, Williamsburg, and Yorktown. Lots of cool stuff to see."

"I'm loving the quiet walks on the beach. This town is the perfect setting for a Love Channel show. Maybe if it does well, the execs will come back to film other things here."

Jade smiled and waved over her shoulder. "Sounds great. We're excited that y'all are here."

About twenty minutes later, Lexi zipped into the lobby with her hair transformed into long corkscrew curls. "Thanks for the southern hospitality."

"Sure I can't get you some coffee or something to drink?"

"No, thanks. I have to get a move on. Dante and I need to get rolling on the hair and makeup, and I don't want to face the wrath of Ezra or Olivia if we slow down the schedule. See ya." Lexi shifted her bags on her shoulder and slid out the front door.

Lorelei and Neville waltzed in moments later. "Who was that?" her aunt asked.

"Lexi. One of the show's stylists. She needed a place to plug in her curling iron."

Lorelei nodded and headed for the office. "You'd think Hollywood folks would plan for things like electricity."

"She said they took the generators for outdoor filming."

Distracted by her phone's alert, Jade scanned a text from her friend, Amy Pemberton. **You won't believe the sights. Can you come over?**

What's up? Jade tapped into her phone.

I've never seen this many people in my parking lot. I have the best view of all the action.

Be there in a bit.

Come to the back door, Amy replied.

"I'm headed for the bookstore to see some of the filming. Do you need me to bring you anything?"

"Nope, I'm good. I've got my tea and my cat and dog friends," Lorelei said.

"Cool. Be back as soon as I can." Jade pulled on her parka and slid out the door.

Throngs of spectators lined the sidewalks and blocked part of the street near the dunes next to Mermaid Books. The bookstore, a fixture in town for years, shared a building with the town's coffee shop, the Busy Bean. Above the crowd's heads, Jade could see long booms with microphones and cameras. She made her way to the front for a glimpse of what everyone was watching. People in black moved around, adjusting equipment and yelling. They had fenced off the area around the front of the store and part of the beach area near the pier.

She moved through the people, dodging elbows and trying to keep from being stepped on as the crowd pushed forward to get a glimpse of the action. Jade scooted around the side of the building to the wooden staircase to Amy's apartment.

The door at the top burst open, and Amy waved her inside. "Hurry, I've got front-row seats. I should set up a book table outside, but I'm having too much fun watching everything from the window. Who wants to work while all of this is going on?"

Jade scurried up the wooden steps, worn by years of wind and sand. "Hey," she said after Amy shut the door behind her.

"Come on down into the store. We have a great view from the front windows. Not sure how long they'll let us stand here, especially if they figure out we're in the shot." Amy led her down the interior stairs into the darkened bookstore. The morning sun streamed in through the big display windows at the front, highlighting the reading nooks and the murals that Jade had helped Amy paint on the walls near the children's section. Jade's smile faded slightly when she thought of the reason for Amy's arrival from Massachusetts. Someone murdered her Aunt Emory, the previous store owner. Amy's takeover of the town's books store thwarted the plan the killer had to ruin the business. In the short time she had been in town, she had turned the shop's bottom line from red to black and offered all kinds of book events that attracted readers from all over. But despite all the progress, Jade still missed her friend, Emory.

Something scurried across the floor, and Jade let out a little squeal. "Mr.

Darcy, you scared me." The long-haired Persian hopped on the counter and licked his front paw.

"Look, look, the actors are getting out of that big, black SUV," Amy said, bouncing up and down in front of the door. "There's Raphael. He is such eye candy and my favorite. I wish they were filming in the store so I could get to meet him. What a cutie." Amy snapped pictures through the window. "I stocked up on the Love Channel books that accompany their shows. And they seem to be a hot seller with the tourists who've dropped in so far. I may put in another order. Oh, and I'm working with your web guy to help me fix the store's site. Aunt Emory wanted nothing to do with technology. Thanks for the name of your guru. I think he'll have to redo the site from scratch, but I can't wait to see it after he works his magic."

"What's going on out there? It seems to be a lot of movement, but no filming," Jade said.

"I have no idea. None of what I've watched makes that much sense. Let's go back to the apartment. I have drinks and snacks there. And my guest window looks out over the parking lot. Maybe we can see Raphael better from up there. You know, a bird's eye view." Amy giggled. Trudging back up the stairs, Amy asked, "Want something to drink? I've got Sprite, coffee, and beer. Oh, we could make mimosas. Want one?" Her voice echoed through the empty store.

"I'm fine for now."

"Make yourself at home," Amy said, pointing to the window seat covered in pillows.

The crew looked like ants moving around in hundreds of different directions. Jade snapped a couple of pictures as they continued to mill around near the pier while the audience grew by the minute.

A roar from the crowd caused both of them to press their noses up against the glass. Raphael and some men walked out from under the tent. The actor raised both arms and fist-pumped the air. Thunderous applause and hoots erupted when Elle and Olivia made their way to the grassy area. The diminutive actress waved at the crowd, and the applause seemed to go on forever.

Jade stood and stretched. She was tired of watching the crew set up a scene and the actors saying a few lines. This had repeated ad nauseam for about an hour. "This has been a different experience, but I need to go check on Lorelei and the critters. Though it looks like everyone within a hundred-mile radius is in front of your store and not shopping at mine."

"I'll text you if anything exciting happens. So far, this has been kinda boring. Maybe something exciting will happen. We can only hope," Amy said, following Jade to the back door. "Next time, we'll make a drinking game out of every time they repeat the same scene. We can spice it up a bit."

Amy waved as Jade jogged down the outdoor steps. The wind from the bay whipped around the building and caused her long, red curls to fly in all directions. She brushed her bangs out of her face and decided to head down the beach instead of trying to fight the crowds on Neptune Road.

As she approached 'Tis the Season, the lot next door looked like a camper ghost town. When she turned to punch in the code for the back door, Jade noticed movement near the fence and the oleander bushes. The purple fall blossoms were pretty against the wooden privacy fence.

Nell Jones, the gossip reporter for the *Beach Comber*, tiptoed toward the hurricane fencing. She leaned over and pressed part of the orange plastic to the ground, so she could step over it.

As she trotted toward the campers, Jade yelled, "Hey, Nell. How are you?" She waved both arms to get Nell's attention.

The pudgy woman in yellow Crocs hesitated. She looked toward the field and then waved like she wanted Jade to go away.

Jade stood and stared for several heartbeats. "Whatcha up to? All the action is over at Amy's store with the filming."

Nell waved one arm dismissively and disappeared between a row of campers.

Jade snickered to herself. Nosy Nell was at it again. Always looking for that one big story. Jade couldn't remember when the local paper had had a real news story. The tourists picked it up for the coupons, and the locals wanted to see if they appeared in any of the gossip columns. Maybe the Love Channel's presence would be Nell's big break.

Chapter Four

The next day, Jade printed four pages of overnight orders and busied herself with tracking down the items from the displays and her storeroom. Chloe, not interested in the increase in sales, did a series of circles in her bed and settled down for a mid-morning nap.

Halfway through the list, Patti strolled in. "I brought cookies. I was trying out some Valentine's recipes in honor of the filming. Wanna try them?"

Jade snagged one off the plate. "Mmmm. Yummy. And they look pretty."

"I call them my Cherry Sparkles." Patti set the plate on the counter and popped a coffee pod in the machine.

"Send me the recipe, and I'll add it to my special edition newsletter on all things Love Channel. Themed cookie recipes would be good for my picture collection. I think I'll add a new section called 'behind the scenes' where I show what's going on." Jade snapped a couple of pictures of Patti's cookie platter and then several of a beaming Patti, doing her best Vanna White impersonation with the red heart-shaped cookies.

Jade's phone dinged with a text alert.

Can you come over ASAP?

What's up? Jade tapped in as her reply to Ruby.

That woman is at it again, and my head is going to explode.

Be there soon, Jade replied. She changed her mind about adding a bomb emoji. Ruby was too stressed at the moment for jokes.

"I need to go see Ruby. Can you keep things humming here for a while?" Jade asked Patti, who added creamer to her mug.

"I can finish that while you're gone." Patti reached for the order report.

"I'll have them all boxed and ready for Simon." A slight blush blossomed on her cheeks.

"And how is your favorite delivery driver these days? Oh, wait, so that's the reason for the cookies. He'll love them." Jade teased.

Patti smiled and picked up a basket to gather the ornaments in the display rooms with the themed Christmas trees. "I'll update the inventory when I'm done," Patti yelled, changing the subject. "Hey, these kitty cat decorations are cute. They must be new. I don't remember seeing them before."

Outside, crowds lined the sidewalks around her lot as far as the eye could see. Deciding it would be easier to hoof it, she jogged down the street and behind the strip mall next door. She wended her way through the neighborhood of bungalows on her way to the Pearl. Scads of people with cameras and phones surrounded the front of Ruby's place. They spilled out into the street, blocking traffic. *So much for a quiet neighborhood.*

She ducked into the yard next door and cut through the small break in the hedges that separated the Pearl from its nearest neighbor. Ruby's well-tended flower beds overflowed with fall blooms of oleander, mums, pansies, and encore azaleas.

After a series of sharp knocks on the kitchen door, Ruby opened it. "Jade. I am beside myself. That woman is impossible," she hissed.

Jade inched up to the giant kitchen island where Ruby had a variety of fruit strewn out on a cutting board.

"I'm almost at a loss for words. She posted pictures of the inside of her bathroom. It seems my accommodations don't have the proper shower heads, and I don't offer spa services. And my cucumber soaps are irritating her skin. She's trying to ruin me. Each one of these snarky posts goes out to her bazillions of followers. I don't know what to do. I read through some of the comments that people made to her posts, and I shouldn't have. It's like she has this cult following. Oooooooooo!" Ruby's knife clattered on her cutting board, and she put the mango in a storage container with a little more force than needed.

"Have you tried talking to Olivia? She seems to have a relationship with Elle. Maybe she can convince her to post beach pictures or something else, not related to your place."

Before Ruby could respond, the back door flung open, and two burly guys in what looked like tactical gear dragged a man in jeans and a flannel shirt into the kitchen. The bald security guard in black slammed the door, and then they hauled the man through the swinging door to the foyer.

Jade opened her mouth, but no sound came out.

"Part of the security detail," Ruby said, rushing after them.

Jade dashed behind Ruby to the house's massive foyer that opened up to the three floors above.

The other security guard said, "We caught this reporter climbing up your trellis and trampling your rose bushes. Call the cops." He shook the thin man's shoulder. The reporter glared at Ruby and Jade but didn't respond.

After Ruby stood there for a few beats, Jade pulled out her phone and dialed the non-emergency number.

"She's dating the sheriff," Ruby whispered to the security detail.

"Hi, this is Jade Hicks. I'm over at the Pearl, and the TV crew's security guards caught a guy trying to climb up Ruby's trellis to get in one of the rooms. Can you send someone over? Thanks." Jade disconnected. "They're on their way."

"You know you're trespassing," the guard said.

The reporter continued to stare without a response.

"They'll do anything for a story," the bald guard said.

After glaring at each other for what seemed like forever, a whoop whoop outside broke the silence. Peering out the front windows, Ruby and Jade watched two police vehicles crawl through the crowd. Sheriff Nick Driscoll and Deputy Sebastian Sanchez parked and made their way up the steps.

Ruby pulled the big oak door open before they could knock. "Thanks for getting here so quickly." She turned her head and nodded toward the burly guards and the reporter.

"Hi, Ruby. Hey, Jade. Gentlemen, why don't we step in here, and we can sort this out." Nick pointed to the parlor and winked over his shoulder at Jade.

A tingle of excitement started in her stomach and traveled up her spine.

She had known Nick since middle school, and they had drifted apart during their college years. He returned to Mermaid Bay to replace the retiring sheriff at about the same time she took over the store after her grandmother passed away. The spark of a teen friendship kindled into a romance, and it was kind of fun to see him in action.

Ruby and Jade strained to hear what was going on in the parlor as the security guards and reporter talked to Sebastian and Nick in low tones.

"Any idea what they're saying?" Ruby whispered.

"Nope. I catch every fifth or sixth word," Jade said as she and Ruby inched closer to the doorway.

After what seemed like forever, Sebastian guided the handcuffed reporter out the front door. Nick shook hands with the guards, and the trio followed the deputy and his charge outside. The TV news crews that had descended on the bed and breakfast's front lawn like gulls after a food wrapper called out questions and snapped photos of the perp walk to Sebastian's vehicle.

Ruby shut the door behind them and leaned against it for a few seconds like she was trying to keep the chaos at bay.

Floorboards creaked above them on the landing to the second-floor guest rooms. Elle Valentine softly closed the door to Raphael's room and tiptoed across the hall, carrying an armload of clothes and a pair of stilettos. She paused and looked down at the women and the guards in the foyer. Without acknowledging them, Elle, in a man's white shirt, turned and climbed the steps to the third floor. The shirt that looked like a dress on the petite actor flowed behind her as she zipped up the stairs.

I thought they didn't like each other. Hollywood definitely brought some drama to our little beach.

After dinner, Jade and Chloe took a walk by the bay. The sandpipers and the seagulls outnumbered the humans, mostly locals strolling, jogging, and walking their dogs. The waves brought a sense of calm to Jade's life, and she stood for several minutes, letting her hair blow in the breeze and tasting the salty tang of the sea on her lips. The day's stress seemed to melt away.

Chloe pounced and chased a sand fiddler to the edge of the surf. After much digging and no success at finding the tiny crab, Chloe plopped down in the sand. Jade tugged on the leash to guide the small dog back to the bungalow.

As they approached the dune, Chloe spotted two figures sitting nearby. The smaller person sat between the legs of the tall man who had had her in a bear hug. Chloe yipped and tore off toward the couple.

The man let go of the woman who reached to pet the rollie pollie dog. Chloe couldn't resist finding new friends, even if it meant interrupting a moment.

"Hi, Elle," Jade said. "It's nice to see you again."

The actress nodded. "It's quiet out here. I like the smell of the ocean." Elle rose and brushed sand off of her leggings. The man, one of the security guards, rose and stood behind the diminutive actor. "I guess we better head back before someone misses us." She pulled her hood tighter around her head and took the guard's hand. "Remember, what happens on the beach, stays at the beach," she said softly.

Jade picked up Chloe and nuzzled the soft fur on her neck. When Elle and her friend were out of earshot, Jade whispered in the dog's ear, "The Hollywood folks have a lot going on in their lives. I need a dance card to keep up with all the partners."

Chloe snorted, not interested in the actors' love lives.

Chapter Five

J ade, craving a coffee treat with lots of whipped cream, slipped out her store's back door for a quick trip to the Busy Bean. Near the temporary fencing, Lexi Armstrong struggled with two bins and two oversized gym bags. "Can I help you with that?" Jade asked.

Lexi dropped the bins and blew a stray curl off of her face. "Thanks. Dante took the golf cart this morning, and I can't find anyone else headed over to that bed and breakfast."

"I can drive you. Come on." Jade took the containers, and Lexi picked up the bags.

Unlocking the passenger door for the stylist, Jade put the bins in the back seat of her Jeep Wrangler.

"Cute license plate," Lexi giggled. "NO GRNCH is perfect for your store." She tossed the bags on the top of the bins and hopped in.

Jade turned down the radio and drove slowly toward the road. The police had barricaded off the main thoroughfare, so she ducked down a side street and dodged wooden sawhorses, photographers, and fans. Taking the long way, she drove through a warren of side streets and alleys.

"This is about as close as I can get you to the action," Jade said as Lexi hopped out. "Let me help you carry those."

Jade hustled around to the passenger side of the Jeep as the crowd moved toward them to see what was going on. After hip-checking the door, Jade followed Lexi up the front sidewalk.

Before they could knock, the bald security guard with the mirrored sunglasses opened the door. "Dante is setting up in the office near the

23

kitchen," he said.

Lexi nodded, and Jade followed her down the hall. Dante had converted Ruby's office into a makeshift beauty parlor. Blow dryers, curling irons, and makeup bags covered every flat surface.

"'Bout time," Dante said with a smile that lit up his face. "Just kidding. Missed you. But I do need your help. The actors are chomping at the bit to get in here. And I need one of those multi-plug extension cord thingies. Got one?"

Lexi nodded and rummaged through one of the bins.

"Can I help with anything?" Jade asked.

"Thanks again for the ride. You're a lifesaver," Lexi said, handing Dante a cream-colored surge protector.

Jade stepped out into the hall and almost bumped into Olivia.

"Oh, sorry," the production manager muttered. "Have you seen Raphael? He's late again." She gritted her teeth and made a low growl that sounded like Chloe.

Jade shook her head, and the woman hustled toward the staircase. Jade followed voices to the end of the hall. Inside the bright kitchen, Josie pointed at something on her tablet, while her mother poured tea into china cups lined neatly on a tray.

"Morning, Jade," Ruby said, setting the teapot back on the stove. "What brings you over? Can I get you some tea?"

"Oh, no thanks. Lexi needed a chauffeur. She had lots of stuff and no transportation."

A scream echoed through the downstairs, and Ruby spilled some of the tea on the tray. The three women rushed to the foyer as another piercing scream came from the second level.

Rushing up the stairs, Jade almost slid into the back of Josie and the bald security guard when they stopped suddenly in an open doorway. Ruby, close on Jade's heels, peeked through the crowded doorway as Olivia pointed to the man curled up in the fetal position on the floor.

"Is he still breathing?" Ruby asked, barging into the room behind the security guard. She grabbed a shoulder and moved the injured man on his back. Blood had started to congeal on his white shirt and the area rug. The man, barefoot and in jeans, had a long, bejeweled dagger wedged in his neck.

Jade pulled out her phone and punched in 911. "Hi, this is Jade Hicks. I'm at the Pearl, and we need the police and an ambulance. There's a man in one of the guest rooms who's been stabbed." Jade paused. "Is he breathing?" she asked Ruby and Olivia.

Olivia shook her head.

"He's not breathing, and there's a puddle of blood. Please send help," Jade said, disconnecting.

"Josie, go wait for them out front," Ruby said.

"I'll go," the guard said, lumbering toward the doorway.

"Who is it?" Ruby asked, pointing at the body on the floor. "And where are his shoes?" She paled and grabbed the doorframe to steady herself.

"Thank goodness. It's not Raphael." Olivia let out a long puff of air like a balloon with a slow leak.

"It's the reporter the guards found trying to climb your trellis," Jade whispered. *And what was he doing in the actor's room?*

Jade's glance darted around the room. Nothing looked amiss. A pile of dirty clothes covered the chair next to the window. Six pairs of shoes littered the floor near the dresser, and a stack of notebooks and a spy novel sat on the nightstand. Thundering footsteps up the stairs interrupted her inventory of the room. Sebastian made his way inside as two EMTs followed closely behind him.

Sebastian shooed the women out in the hallway. "What happened?" he asked.

"We were in the kitchen, and we heard a scream. Jade, Josie, and I rushed up to see what was wrong with Olivia," Ruby said.

"Raphael was late for this morning's shoot. I came in to wake him up. When I opened the door, I found that guy." Olivia pointed to the reporter. She pulled out her phone and launched a fury of texts.

"Where's the room's owner?" the deputy asked.

Olivia shrugged and replied without looking up from her phone. "I have no idea. The door was unlocked. When I knocked, it opened."

It took almost an hour for Sebastian to collect the women's names and any details they could remember. It felt like they had been standing in the hallway forever. She shifted her weight from side to side. The bald security guard led a state trooper and two younger officers in black jackets with "forensics" emblazoned on their uniforms up the stairs.

"The team'll be here for a while. We'll have to cordon off this area, but your guests should still be able to get to their rooms," Sebastian said.

Ruby wrung her hands and stared at the body still on the floor of the guest room. This time, the body was covered in a white sheet.

Elle drifted down the stairs to the second floor and hesitated near the banister. "What's the delay with today's shoot? I got your text. And is there still time for breakfast?" She looked at Olivia.

"I went looking for Raphael this morning and found him." Olivia pointed to the floor in the bedroom.

Elle's sunny countenance darkened as she stared at the covered body through the doorway. Blood spatters and the congealing pool where the body had lain made it look like a set from a horror film.

Heavy footsteps on the wooden stairs caused heads to turn. Raphael, in a gray sweatshirt and shorts, bounded toward the landing. "What's all this? I'm just a few minutes late. Fifty texts from Olivia and a welcoming committee at my room? And who called the cops? It was a quick jog. It's not like I was kidnapped or anything." Even sweaty, the actor exuded charm with his quick laugh and pearly smile.

When Elle spotted Raphael, her hands flew to her mouth. She let out a little squeak and zipped up the stairs.

"What's wrong with her? Looks like she's seen a ghost." Raphael said.

Olivia grabbed his elbow and escorted him to the edge of the landing, where she whispered something and waved her arms around.

"But I need to get my stuff. And I need a shower. How long is this going to take?" Raphael asked loud enough for some of the bystanders to turn their heads.

"What do you need?" Sebastian asked.

"A shower." Raphael rolled his eyes.

"How about you go downstairs and get some coffee or something, and when forensics has processed the room, we'll get you what you need and find a place for you to take a shower," Sebastian said as several state troopers stomped up the stairs.

"Like I have all day," Raphael huffed.

"They need to be able to do their job," Sebastian said, guiding the actor into the hallway.

Olivia took Raphael's elbow again and pushed him toward the steps. "Do as the deputy says. I'll be down to check on you in a minute. But first, I want to see about Elle."

Before Jade could follow, Ruby pulled her aside. "I have no idea what I should do. This was supposed to be a big boost to my business. So much for capitalizing off the show's fame. Now, I'll be lucky if the rest of my reservations don't cancel. Jade, can you see what you can do to get to the bottom of this? I don't need to be known as the B and B with the dead body."

Jade patted her on the arm. "I'll see what I can find out." *It's probably better if I don't mention that having a notorious establishment also generates a buzz in certain circles. I'm sure Ruby doesn't want the Pearl as a stop on a true-crime tour.*

Chapter Six

Jade walked Chloe on the beach to soak up some early morning peacefulness. For the past twelve hours, neighbors and friends had blown up her phone with questions about the dead reporter. Taking a deep breath, Jade let the ocean breeze wash over her. The sun peeked over the pine trees across the street. The light announced the start of a new day and an opportunity to find out more about what happened to that reporter. Her phone vibrated in her pocket and broke the serenity of the waves lapping against the shore.

"Hi, Ruby. What's up?"

"It has been a zoo here since yesterday. They're back to filming today, so I was hoping you had some time to come over and help me with my plan to flood my social media sites sometime. Josie's been plugging away at it, but I think we need a theme or something. Sorry to call so early, but I wanted to catch you before you got busy. Could you take some photos of Josie and me in action? I want to step up my campaign and try to tamp down some of all this negativity. Plus, I did my hair and makeup this morning. And we've had a little bit of good news, if there can be any with a dead body in your place. All this chaos has slowed down Elle's online complaints. I guess that's some progress. I'm trying to get my mind on something else except the poor, dead reporter."

"Small miracles," Jade said. "Are they still having the meet and greet tonight for the town dignitaries?"

"Yep, at breakfast, Olivia and Ezra held a meeting and expressed their condolences for the loss of the reporter, and then in the next breath, they started barking out orders for things everyone had to do to catch up on the missed day yesterday and the party tonight."

"Once Lorelei arrives for work, I'll hop over to your place."

"Thanks, Jade. See you then."

"Come on, Chloe. Let's go start this day." The little round dog hopped through the sand like she was galloping.

After Lorelei and Neville settled in at the front counter, Jade hurried over to the B and B to help Ruby. She found the proprietor and her daughter in the kitchen, prepping for tomorrow's food service.

"Oh, hi, Jade," Ruby said, closing the door. "Thanks for coming over. I never have any pictures of Josie and me together. One of us is always the photographer." She pulled off a white apron and dusted her hands. "Where should we do these?"

"How about a couple in here, and then we can move to the parlor, library, and steps."

"And don't forget the garden," Josie said. "The trellis makes a great backdrop."

And a ladder for nosey reporters.

After some shots in the kitchen and parlor, Jade positioned the mother-daughter duo on the stairs with the banister as a backdrop. "You all look mah-va-lous. Let's do some outside."

"That looks nice. Let me get some up close and then some of the front of the building."

Jade paused when Josie scowled. "What is that?" Josie pointed across the street.

Nell slunk down in the front seat of her red Fiat. Only the top of her head and a huge pair of military binoculars appeared through the window.

"Hi, Nell. How's it going? Whatcha doing?" Ruby yelled, waving her arms in large, exaggerated circles.

The binoculars slowly dipped down. Then the engine started, and the tiny car tore around the corner.

After a giggling jag, Jade composed herself. "She's dogged. I'll give her that. I guess she was in stealth mode, and we blew her cover. I think we have some good shots of you two we can use. I'll upload them to the cloud and send you a link."

"Thanks, Jade. You're coming to the party, right?" Josie asked.

"I'm Nick's plus one, and I'm looking forward to it. See you all tonight."

Ruby paused, and a dark look crossed her countenance. "See what you can find out about that reporter…I don't want the Pearl to be known as a murder site."

"But, Mom. That could be fabulous. Places with creepy reputations or horrible deaths are always a magnet for the curious. Maybe they'd do a true crime documentary on us?" Josie's eyes sparkled at the thought.

"I want to promote a happy, relaxing place. Not something that shows up on true crime podcasts and documentaries." She turned on her gum-soled shoes and headed inside.

"I still think it would be cool. We'd have stories to tell besides those of a rich banker who moved his family here to escape the summer heat." Josie rolled her eyes and followed her mother.

Time for me to check on the team. On her way back to the store, lots of people wandered up and down the town's main drag. Inside her empty store, Neville stretched out on the front counter while Lorelei flipped through a fashion magazine. *Hordes of people out and about, but not much shopping going on.*

"I'd like to say you missed all the excitement," Lorelei said. "But you didn't." Her aunt stifled a yawn. "Anything going on at Ruby's?"

"Not really. I took a bunch of pictures of them for their flood the net with great stuff about the Pearl campaign."

"You headed to that shindig tonight? I heard it was for all the bigwigs in town." Her aunt set her magazine down and scratched Neville behind the ears.

Jade nodded. "I'm going with Nick. He and the town council folks were invited."

"Let me know if you uncover any secrets. And try to sneak in some pictures." Her aunt winked.

"I have to behave if Nick's in his sheriff mode." Jade stuck out her tongue and made her aunt laugh. Chloe trotted in with her jingle ball for a round or two of toss.

Tiring after three or four throws, the pudgy dog took the ball to her bed for a rest. Jade settled in her chair, too, and searched local news sites for information on the dead reporter. "There you are, Seth Davis. What does the big wide web say about you?"

She pulled out a notebook and started listing facts about the gossip reporter until she got lost in a string of his posts on all the latest Hollywood tales. *Lots of troll comments. Seth seemed to be able to always dig up the dirt. Do you have any connection to Raphael besides being a gossip reporter? And what were you really doing in his room?*

About four o'clock, Lorelei dug her purse out of the filing cabinet and touched up her lipstick. "I'm gone unless you need anything. It's paint party night with the gals. We'll see how well my work turns out after a couple of glasses of wine." She finger-waved over her shoulder, and Neville strolled out behind her.

"Have fun," Jade yelled to her back. "Chloe, we should lock up. I have no idea what I'm wearing tonight. Hey, this is my first boyfriend work function." She smiled to herself as she checked windows and doors and set the alarm. *It's nice to have a permanent plus one.*

Chloe decided to dawdle on the walk home. The flutter of activity in the lot next door became the dog's focus, and the grilled meat scents wafting from the large tent caught her attention. "Come on, pup. I need to get ready for tonight." When Chloe boycotted the attempt to leave the fabulous smells, Jade gently tugged on the leash. Chloe went prone on the sandy soil, and Jade picked her up and carried her across the street. More than the typical number of seasonal fall visitors still milled around the sidewalks and the barricades, hoping to get a glimpse of something Love Channel-related.

After feeding Chloe, Jade tried on four dresses. Finally settling on a black sheath with a beaded bolero jacket, she tried on a variety of shoes. Nick was over six feet tall, so there were no worries about heels. Settling on a pair of black ballet slippers for comfort, Jade heated up her curling iron.

A knock at the door sent Chloe into a barking spell. The round dog rolled on her back for a tummy rub when Nick stepped over the threshold.

"You have to pay the toll," Jade said.

Nick, in his dress uniform, laughed and reached down to pet the dog. "Chloe, you're always a star. And you look great." He smiled at Jade.

"You, too. Fancy duds. Come on in. I'll be ready in a sec."

Jade breezed through the house, turning off lights and double-checking that her curling iron was unplugged. She flipped the chain strap of her party purse over her shoulder. "'Bout ready?"

She patted Chloe, and Nick followed her out the door to his truck.

Hiking her dress up, she did a hop to boost herself up. Nick extended his arm to steady her as she climbed into the behemoth vehicle that he called a truck.

Nick roared out of her driveway, and downtown Mermaid Bay flashed by her window. A few minutes later, he parked on a side street and jumped out to help her exit. She took his arm, and they strolled up the sidewalk, lined with paparazzi and news crews.

Ruby, dressed in a long black skirt with a satiny red top, held the door for them. Her gray hair pulled back in a trendy twist, sported a gemstone clip that sparkled under the chandelier in the high-ceilinged foyer. "Welcome, Jade and Nick. Make yourself at home."

Nick glad-handed everyone standing along the path through the foyer into the parlor. When he was swallowed up in a conversation with Tom Berryman, the town councilman, and three of the movie executives, Jade made her way to the library.

Snagging a flute of champagne from a tray Josie offered, Jade said, "Thanks. Quite a crowd here."

"Oh, everybody and her brother in town has been wheedling for an invitation to get close to the TV folks. They hired extra security that set up an outer perimeter to keep people from trying to sneak in." Josie rolled her eyes. "They should have done that before you-know-what happened," she whispered.

Jade greeted friends and maneuvered her way to the corner where Paige Wilson, the tall production assistant, slouched next to a leather wing chair.

"Hi. It's nice to see you again."

Paige smoothed her rumpled gray blazer and searched for some imaginary bit of fluff. "Another work event," Paige finally replied.

"It must be a great job. You get to hang out with celebrities and go to fancy parties for work." Jade smiled.

"Not really. Too many long hours and crappy accommodations. This place is nice, but they put the nobodies in campers that we have to share with someone they assigned to us. It's not as glamorous as people imagine."

"But you know the actors. There's a ton of paparazzi and fans out there itching to get close to the stars," Jade added.

"And just like Hollywood, not everything that glitters is gold." The production assistant waved her hand dismissively.

Jade lowered her voice. "I'm curious. Do you have any idea how that reporter got into Raphael's room?"

Paige shrugged her shoulder and glanced around the room. "Who knows? Raphael could have picked him up somewhere, or the reporter could have snuck in when he saw his opportunity when no one was watching. Not a lucky break for him, though. He became the story. And now we have to work longer this week to make up for the time we missed because Olivia can't be off schedule." She cut her eyes and stifled a yawn.

A crash in the next room sent Jade and Paige scurrying for the doorway.

"Hey, it's not a party until something gets broken," Raphael said, laughing.

Ezra, the producer, said something to him that Jade didn't catch, and Raphael's jovial countenance clouded for a brief instant. Then the actor looked down his nose and smirked. "What? I tripped. Sorry," Raphael said as Ruby and a server rushed in to clean up the broken glasses and mop up the champagne that had started to soak into the area rug.

"He did it on purpose. He can't stand when someone gets more attention or lines than he does," Elle said, waving her arm at the bystanders. Her sparkling white and blue dress looked like something out of *Cinderella*. "He's impossible."

"I didn't do it on purpose. And it's in my contract. You and I get the same number of scenes," Raphael smiled a Cheshire Cat grin. "You're the one who runs to Olivia every time you don't get your way. At least I'm not the... brat."

Elle's pale link lips became a straight line, and a flush inched up her neck to her cheeks. "At least I didn't get caught with a dead guy in my room. You better be careful because it looks like you're a suspect. I can see the headlines now, 'Famous Love Channel Star Arrested for Boy Toy's Murder.'"

"He's not my boy toy. But would it matter if he was? You're just jealous. Go off and have all the flings you want. You know you still want me."

The actor turned and stomped out in her crystal-covered ankle strap pumps.

"You better watch your mouth, or somebody will get you, too," Raphael yelled behind her.

"Enough," Ezra bellowed. His face was as red as Ruby's blouse, and a vein in his temple bulged. "That will be enough."

"As you wish." Raphael turned and stormed up the steps to the second floor.

Jade scanned the room, where a handful of people recorded the event discreetly. With the two major stars gone and most of the champagne on the floor, guests started to say goodnight and ease out the door, leaving heaping trays of hors d'oeuvre on the buffet.

Nick rested his hand on her shoulder. "About ready to head out? It looks like the party's wrapping up."

Jade nodded, and he led her out to the foyer, where they said their goodbyes to their friends and Love Channel folks who remained.

Nick fired up his truck and blasted the heat to knock off the autumn evening chill.

"Well, that was fun for a little while. Poor Ruby. She wanted everything to be memorable," Jade said.

"It was dramatic," he said, putting the truck in gear and slowly pulling out, trying to avoid the photographers and reporters who lined both sides of the street in front of the bed and breakfast.

"Is Raphael really a suspect in that reporter's death?" Jade asked.

"Keep this to yourself, but no. He had an alibi. He took a phone call while he was out jogging, and he stopped at the Busy Bean for coffee. Plenty of people saw him. I'm still waiting on the full autopsy report, but we have texts from the reporter that help establish the timeline. He snuck into the room. We suspect that he was looking for dirt on the actor. And it wasn't the first time he tried to worm his way inside the B and B."

"Those gossip stories must pay well," she mused, staring out the window. *There had to be a bigger connection between the dead reporter and Raphael. Why did Elle look so surprised to see Raphael after the dead man was discovered?*

When Jade realized that Nick was staring at her, she said, "Sorry. Got lost in thought for a moment there. Thanks for the invitation tonight. It was more entertaining than anything on TV."

Chapter Seven

After a long workday that dragged on with not much foot traffic through the store, Jade practically jogged home. Chloe had to double-time it to keep up.

Once inside the bright kitchen, Jade filled Chloe's bowls and poured herself some tea. After finding the dinner choices on the sparse side, she settled for a granola bar and spent an hour transferring what she knew about the Love Channel folks onto sticky notes. Arranging the colorful squares on her dining room wall, she grouped similar facts and stepped back to look at the clusters and relationships. She stared at her handiwork for several minutes. *There had to be a connection somewhere. Lots of colorful squares, but no a-ha moments.*

Elle Valentine, born Ellen Mason in Savannah, Georgia, had starred in over forty shows for the Love Channel. Her following on social media was massive, and she had a jewelry line, a clothing line, and two books to her name. Through the years, the actor had been linked romantically to four soap opera stars and a former boy band member from the nineties, and she'd also had an on-again, off-again relationship with Raphael. *I guess that explains the onscreen chemistry.*

"Well, now," she said aloud when she read Raphael's biography. "Mr. Allard, your whole persona was created in TV land. You're not even French, but it doesn't seem like your fans really care." Chloe looked up from her fuzzy blanket. When she didn't notice any snacks, she returned to her nap.

Jade jotted notes about Raphael, born Jamie Cox in Ft. Lauderdale, Florida. *Not even close to France, though he did live in Germany when his Air Force dad was stationed there.* She flicked her right hand several times to make the cramp go away from listing all his flings. He had been linked to models, pop stars, soap opera actresses, and a string of skinny social media influencers. *Well, at least his piercing blue eyes are real.*

Jade spent time looking at the producer, director, and crew members she had met. No one seemed to have any glaring connections to the dead reporter.

After another romp across the internet, the only thing she knew about reporter Seth Davis was that he worked for a string of notorious gossip magazines and websites. He was famous for getting the juicy, embarrassing stories, and he had no obvious connection to Raphael.

After digging a Dr. Pepper from the back of the fridge, Jade pulled up the Love Channel's page for *My Coastal Valentine* and listed as many names of the crew and staff as she could find.

Light streamed in from the dining room windows, and Jade opened one eye. Her back and shoulder hurt. She had fallen asleep across her laptop at the dining room table. She stood and got a glimpse of herself in the living room mirror. *Wow, girl. You look like you partied hard with none of the fun.* Starting the coffee maker, she headed to the bathroom for a quick shower to ward off the groggies and improve her mood.

The pulsating shower helped loosen her muscles. After finding a green golf shirt with the store's logo and a pair of jeans, she packed up her laptop and filled her to-go cup. Taking one long look at her sticky notes, she tried to remember who was at the Pearl the morning of the reporter's death. Could one of the crew have killed a coworker? Or did a stranger sneak in, do the deed, and disappear into the ether? Either way, the murder was forever linked to Ruby's B and B.

Jade shook off the melancholic feeling from not finding any leads and the lack of sleep. She leashed up Chloe for the walk to work. The Frenchie pranced down the crushed oyster shell path to the street, already filled with photographers and fans. Chloe was ready for her close-up.

Jade stepped through her opening routine and started filling orders like an automaton. Work kept her busy, and the activity pushed thoughts of the murder to the dark corners of her mind.

The bells on the front door jangled, and Patti breezed in with a plate of cookies. "You doing okay? You look tired? Want some coffee?" She pulled the dividing door behind her.

"I'm good, thanks. What'd you bake?"

"I made some of those chocolate-dipped hearts." She offered the plate.

"These look festive," Jade said, taking two.

"Let me put this stuff away, and I'll help you with the orders. Morning, Chloe."

The white dog's tail wiggled like a stubby propeller.

Jade's phone dinged with a text from Amy. **I'm starving already. Thinking about lunch later. Wanna grab something?**

Perfect, Jade replied. **When and Where?**

12 @ Hot Diggity Dogs?

See ya then, Jade tapped into her phone.

"I'm done gathering the ornaments," Patti sang out. "It's kinda like an Easter Egg hunt, but with Christmas decorations." She set a basket on the counter. "We're low on the dog ornaments and the ballerina ones."

Jade nodded and printed labels as Patti boxed the remaining items.

"That's it," Jade said, pulling the backing off the label. "All ready for Simon?"

Patti's eyes sparkled. "My favorite part of the day. Though I have been stargazing in town. That's been fun. I met Raphael and saw Elle Valentine getting into a car in front of Ruby's. And I saw Carlos Alvarez." She grinned and wiggled both eyebrows.

"I'm meeting Amy for lunch. Do you want me to bring you anything?"

"Nope. I brought my leftover chicken enchiladas. I had a cooking class, and we took home what we made. Yumminess."

"I'll be back in a bit. Holler if you need me," Jade said.

"Will do. And I'll let you know if that Raphael strolls in here." Patti winked.

The camper city next door looked like a ghost town. Jade power-walked down to where the plastic fencing blocked the entrance from the street. She looked both ways and jaywalked across the asphalt.

The line for Hot Diggity Dogs was about fifteen deep. While she waited, Jade's thoughts flashed to the summer when someone tried to force Todd to sell his oceanfront property. *I'm so glad business has improved for him.*

The line moved fast, and Jade was at the counter in no time. "What can I get for you?" a teen with green hair asked.

"Hi, I'll have a Coney dog with mustard and an iced tea." Jade handed her a ten. She dropped the change in the tip jar that had held relish in a former life.

When the lanky guy behind the counter called her number, Jade made her way out the back door to look for a picnic table on the deck. Scoring a wooden table near the edge of the deck, Jade watched the waves crash onto the sand.

I'm out on the deck, she texted Amy.

Her phone dinged with, **Be there in a few. In line at the counter now**.

Jade watched a trawler cross the horizon. Sandpipers zipped up and down the beach and skirted the breaking surf. From this angle, life at Mermaid Bay looked normal.

"Hey, there you are," Amy said, sitting down on the bench across from her. Todd, who followed behind her, slid in next to her and handed Amy her lunch.

"Hey, Jade. How's life? Been hanging out with the stars?" Todd asked, slipping a straw into his cup.

"It's been interesting. I've met a couple of them. They're not quite the same as their characters," she said, wiping mustard off her chin.

"Britt Mason came in for a hot dog yesterday. I didn't know who she was, but my staff did. They informed me that I need to be more plugged in. They spent a long time taking selfies and chatting about the Loooooove Channel." He rolled his eyes and made a scrunched-up face.

"Carlos Alverez came in the bookstore, followed by a gaggle of Gen X women. I had to google to see who he was, but I got my photo taken with him. I think I may make an 'I love me' wall somewhere in the store with my photos of famous people. I'm even thinking of creating a wall where the authors and celebs can sign. Wouldn't that be cool?" Amy winked.

"So, what's the deal with the dead guy?" Todd said. "Mermaid Bay is now known for another murder."

"Seth Davis was a gossip reporter known for titillating stories in *Gawk* and *Inuendo*," Jade said, fluttering her eyelashes.

"Someone did her homework. Did he know Raphael, you know like more than just a professional relationship?" Amy asked.

"I'm not sure. I read some of his stuff online, and he liked to tease about his juicy stories. He told all kinds of embarrassing things, and he was sued a couple of times for making things up. And on Instagram, there were a ton of negative comments on his posts. Nick and his team have their hands full with a long list of suspects."

"Ruby's in a tizzy about the murder being at her place," Todd said. "She called me the other day to ask the name of my friend who helped me with my bad publicity. She remembered that Lakeisha was able to use her magical computer skills to assist."

Amy patted his arm.

Todd stared at her and smiled.

After a long pause that made Jade wonder if she was missing something, Amy cleared her throat and said, "I don't think Ruby should worry too much. People will move on to the next bright, shiny, juicy story in a day or two. I know it feels icky, but by the summer, it'll be a distant memory. Don't get me wrong, I'm still bummed about the reporter's murder, but his death lasted only a brief blip in the swirl of all the news coverage. Sadly, not that many people noticed."

"One of my part-timers said she heard from one of Ruby's cleaners that Raphael Allard was clueless about the dead guy. He blamed it on lax security, and he was more concerned for his safety at Ruby's than having a dead reporter in his room." Todd looked over his shoulder and lowered his voice. "Then the cleaning lady said Raphael snuck out that night and called an Uber to go to some club in Seaport."

"The Hollywood folks have a different way of life," Jade said. "The crew in the campers are friendly and keep to themselves. I think Ruby has the high-maintenance ones."

Todd laughed and balled up his wrapper. "I need to get back." He kissed Amy on the top of her head and stepped into the restaurant.

Jade's eyes widened. "I knew something was up. Spill it," she said after the door closed behind Todd.

"What? We have a lot in common. We've been hanging out recently, and we're casually dating to see how things go. There's no ring yet, but it's only been a couple of weeks." Amy's dimples showed when she smiled.

Jade opened and closed her mouth.

"I'm kidding. There were some sparks, and we decided to take it slow. Hey, maybe we can double date sometime. That would be fun."

"And I thought the Hollywood folks were full of surprises," Jade said.

Chapter Eight

The trill from Jade's phone jarred her from her daydream about the Love Channel actors, free publicity, and the dead reporter. Jade shuddered as she reached for her phone. "Hey, Ruby. What's going on?"

"I don't know what to do. Sebastian and a state trooper picked up Josie for questioning. What if they arrest her? She didn't kill that reporter. She was downstairs on her phone, as usual, when it happened. I'm stuck here until I get breakfast served. Can you run over to the sheriff's office and see what's going on? I'm a bundle of nerves, and I can't even think straight. I know she's in her twenties, but she's still my baby. And I know you'll be able to figure out what's going on."

When Ruby took a breath, Jade said, "Don't worry. If they didn't arrest her, they want to ask her some questions. I'll let you know what I find out."

"I'll be waiting by my phone. It's so hard to focus today." Ruby sighed and disconnected.

"Lorelei, can you watch the store while I run out? They took Josie in for questioning, and Ruby wants me to see what I can find out about it."

"They can't possibly think Josie did it. We've known her all her life." She made a shooing motion with her hands. "Go. Go. I've got the store covered."

"Thanks." Jade slipped on her jacket and headed for the Jeep. A caravan of large trucks and vans blocked most of the area near Amy's store, so Jade did a U-turn on Neptune Road and ducked down a side street. Throngs of people gathered around the pier for today's filming that blocked even the side streets. The ride to the government center took forever. Jade smiled. Mermaid Bay's administrative hub's name was bigger than the actual collection of buildings which included the library, government offices, and the sheriff's office.

Finding parking near the library, Jade walked briskly to the sheriff's office, which shared a building with the emergency communications center and the jail.

"Hi, Delia," Jade said to the deputy behind the window in the waiting area.

"I haven't seen you in ages. What brings you over here early this morning?" The dark-headed deputy closed a manila folder and set it on top of the pile on her desk.

"Ruby said that a deputy picked up Josie this morning for questioning. I wanted to check on her since Ruby's tied up at the Pearl."

Cradling the phone under her chin, Delia made a call.

Jade shifted the weight from one leg to the other.

"She's in with the task force. The Sheriff said he'd be out in a few minutes to chat. Make yourself at home over there. Can I get you some coffee?"

"I'm good. Thanks." Jade walked toward the molded plastic orange chairs that looked like they were trendy when pet rocks and disco balls were the rage.

Jade scrolled through her emails and checked her social sites. She jumped when Delia popped her head out the thick oak door. "Jade, he can talk for a bit now." She held the door and pointed down the hall. "You know where it is."

"Thanks." Jade's boot heels echoed on the industrial floor. At the end of the hallway, Nick's door stood ajar. She tapped lightly and poked her head in the gap.

After a "Come on in," she closed the door behind her. A smile lit up Nick's face. "Hey, can I get you some coffee?"

Jade shook her head. "I know you're busy, but Ruby called me in a panic this morning. Is Josie okay?"

"She's fine. We had some questions we needed her to answer. Sebastian will have her back at the Pearl before lunch."

"So…" Jade's eyebrows shot up under her bangs.

"No, she's not a suspect." Jade let out a breath. Her shoulders relaxed, and

43

she felt some of the tension melt away.

"We had some questions," Nick repeated.

"Is there anything I can do for you?" she asked.

He shook his head. "We've been logging some serious hours since the TV crew came to town. I haven't made it home before ten in a while. I promise we'll have dinner as soon as I catch up on some sleep."

"Let me know if you need anything."

"Stay out of trouble, but keep your ears open." Nick winked.

Jade rose. "You got it. I'll tell Ruby not to fret. See ya soon." Nick was on the phone before she closed the door behind her.

Jade waved to Delia and slipped out the door. Instead of calling Ruby, Jade pointed the Jeep toward the bed and breakfast and zipped through the neighborhood streets that were quiet until she got to the Pearl. It looked like a legion of reporters had camped out around the former Victorian mansion. Jade cruised through the neighborhood, crowded with cars parked on both sides. Finding a spot down the street, she texted Ruby on her hike to the B and B, and by the time she rounded the corner to the back of the Pearl, Ruby held the door open for her. "What'd you find out?" she asked, almost pulling Jade inside.

"She's fine. Definitely not a suspect. Nick said they had some questions, and she'll be home by lunch."

"Wheeeeew," Ruby said, sounding like a balloon that had lost all its helium. "I knew there was no way she could have been involved. When the police arrived this morning, I think I lost two or three years off my life. And I heard they were questioning some of my cleaning contractors and a food distributor. I mean, what's next?"

A rat-a-tat-tat that didn't stop interrupted them. Ruby paused and opened the interior door.

Elle stood behind a huge bouquet of fall flowers. "Could I get these put in a vase for my room? I've got to get ready to catch my ride to the set. I appreciate it." She shoved the bunch into Ruby's hands. "I picked these on my walk this morning. What fun."

"Sure," Ruby said with a slight twitch. "I'll bring them right up. Why don't you post about them before you leave?"

"Good idea," the petite actor said over her shoulder.

Ruby found a large vase and filled it with water. Muttering under her breath, she arranged the oleander sprigs and mums. "Looks like she found the last of the roses and a hunk of my mums. Gotta take these up to the princess and ensure she washes her hands after touching some of these."

Jade left her to her task and waved over her shoulder. "Call me if you need me. I'm headed back to the store."

Two large buses blocked the entrance to 'Tis the Season. Jade hopped the curb and parked on the grass near the back door. "I was about to text you. Looks like we have company," Lorelei said as Jade hustled inside and slid out of her jacket.

A few minutes later, footsteps ascended the porch steps. "Okay, people, we're here for an hour and a half. Then we go to the set and watch the filming. Lunch will follow that, so stay with the group and keep to the schedule." The door opened, and a woman with a bullhorn and clipboard stepped inside. "Hi, I'm Tracey, and I have some folks who want to see your store."

"Welcome," Jade said. "Wander through our showrooms and look at all the decorations. If you like a decoration, you can find it in the bins under each tree. We have baskets to help make your shopping easier. Please let Lorelei or me know if you have any questions. Oh, and be on the lookout for Neville. He's our store cat who makes an appearance from time to time."

Lorelei and Jade spent the next hour answering questions, mostly about how cute Raphael Allard was in person and how talented Elle Valentine is in all her roles.

When the final group of fans left, Lorelei plunked down on the stool behind the counter. "I'm pooped. That's more action than I've seen in a while. My face hurts from smiling."

"Can I get you something to drink? Or maybe it's time for a lunch break?"

"That sounds good. I need a quick walk. You want anything if I stop at the Busy Bean?" her aunt asked.

Jade shook her head. "Have fun. I brought some soup. I'll heat it up in a minute."

"I'll be back in a bit," Lorelei said, pulling the back door behind her.

After a long and profitable day, Jade settled in at her dining room table to pour over her notes with some warmed-up mac and cheese and a glass of peach tea. There had to be something she was missing. Taping five sheets of paper together, she spread it out on the table. After listing all the players, she drew lines to show connections. Elle, Raphael, and Olivia's names looked like a spider web when she was done. Raphael and Elle had a love-hate relationship. Olivia was friends with Elle. Raphael had lots of friends, and Elle had a thing with her security guard. The only tie to the dead reporter was that he was looking for dirt on the actors. *There had to be something else.*

Jade put on some background music for company and refilled her tea. "Chloe, what am I missing? The guards caught that reporter trying to sneak in. And then they found him in Raphael's room. Was he a friend?"

Chloe raised one eyebrow and then jumped into full security mode when she heard steps echo on the bungalow's small porch. She rolled over in pet-me mode when Jade let Nick inside. He handed her a gallon of ice cream and picked up the chubby Chloe.

"I clocked out and went to the gym. I brought dessert," he said with a slight grin.

"Thanks. Mmm. Moosetracks. Do you want whipped cream on yours?"

"Why not? I went to the gym." Nick settled on the couch with Chloe, who had found her new best friend.

Jade plopped down next to them with two sundaes. "So, how are things going?"

Nick stared at her wall, and she wondered if he was planning to lecture her about her fascination with all the suspects. After a long pause, he said, "I could ask you that. Looks like you got a pretty decent murder wall going over there. Find anything?"

Jade shook her head and licked her spoon. "No. I have lots of random facts. Anything new on your end."

"Not much. It's frustrating. The letter opener wasn't what killed him. The coroner said that happened after he was already dead. Several blows to the back of his head did him in."

"With what?" Jade asked.

"We have no idea. Something heavy by the looks of the wounds. The murderer must have taken the weapon with him or her. There was nothing in the room that might have been used. My guys even searched the house and the yard with no luck."

Jade picked up the remote and scanned through the channels. By the time she found something on Netflix, Nick's head was lolled back on the couch, and he and Chloe snored in unison. Jade covered them with a lap blanket and snuggled in to watch the movie. *Another interesting date.*

Chapter Nine

The next morning, Jade woke up on the couch when Nick kissed her on the head. The TV had slipped into sleep mode hours ago. "Gotta run. I need to meet the task force at seven." Sunlight streamed in through the windows. "I promise we'll have a real date soon."

"Thanks for the ice cream." Jade padded to her room for a shower after she saw him out.

As the warm water pulsed over her, Jade's thoughts centered on the dead reporter. Someone konked him on the head hard enough to kill him. And then stabbed him later. Was it to ensure that he was dead? Was it to make someone else look guilty? It was Raphael's room and Elle's letter opener. Time to find out about the pair's enemy lists.

Jade heated oatmeal in the microwave, and she ate breakfast while staring at her diagram. *I know very little about Paige, Ezra, Lexi, Britt, and Brian. And what about the guards and the scads of crew who do the sound, filming, sets, and costumes?* Jade let out a sigh and rinsed her dishes.

"Come on, Chloe, let's take a walk and see what today brings. Maybe more tour buses. Yesterday was a great day."

The crisp autumn breeze greeted them when they stepped outside and added some pep to their steps. "It's almost pumpkin time, puppy. And you know what that means."

Chloe turned her head and then trotted off in the opposite direction.

"Chloe, aren't you even a little excited? It's time to gear up for Christmas. It's our time of year." The Frenchie looked at Jade with her best puppy eyes, sniffed, and trekked down the driveway.

With no part-timers scheduled today, Jade opened the store and did a walk-through inventory check of all the display rooms. In the toy room, she stood and watched the animated ornaments on the carousel and another of Santa's sleigh with the reindeer. The lights and the peppermint scents in the room brought back a flood of memories of Christmases past.

Jade shook off the bittersweet memories that reminded her of the loss of her parents and grandmother. Time to get busy and stock up on the popular ornaments. After filling the online orders and submitting an order to restock, Jade sent emails to some of the local artisans to see if they wanted to participate in an open house event after Thanksgiving. She tried to showcase local artists whenever she could.

After downing a water and a granola bar for lunch, she spent hours scouring ornament catalogs for new items, but her thoughts kept bouncing back to the murder at Ruby's.

Around four-thirty, she said, "Okay, Chloe. That's enough work. Let's go see what the crew's doing next door."

Chloe yipped and ran to the back door. After a quick check on the store, Jade set the alarm and followed her dog down the back steps. Chloe sniffed the air and followed the grilled meat smells wafting from the craft tent next door.

The remaining fall flowers, the cool tangy breeze, and the smell of grilling reminded Jade of autumn at the beach. She followed the pudgy dog around the hurricane fence and down the path between the rows of campers.

"Jaaaaaaaaaaaaaade," rang out near a brown trailer. Dante jumped up and wrapped her in a bear hug as Lexi watched from the sidelines. "How are you? And you, Miss Girl." He picked up Chloe and danced around under the canvas awning with her.

"Hey, Dante," Jade said, recovering from the squeeze. "Hi, Lexi. We were on our way home, and we thought we'd stop by and say hello."

"We're hanging out here for drinks before the chow line opens. You know Lexi. This is Britt Mason. She's on a fast track to becoming one of the next Love Channel's stars. That's Bruce, our gaffer extraordinaire, and that's Marius. He works his magic with the booms, and last but not least, we have

Matilda, who is our costume wizard."

The fifty-something woman bundled in a military jacket and scarf blushed and raised her glass. "And Dante and Lexi make everyone beautiful."

"Dante, where are your manners?" Lexi asked. "Jade, wanna beer?"

"I'm good for now. How is everyone doing? I thought I worked a ton of hours as a small business owner, but y'all have some crazy schedules."

"Yep, they kinda own us when we're on set," Bruce said. We film at all hours."

"It's tiring, but I wouldn't want any other job," Marius added. "And we get to see new places. I like filming at the beach. Too bad it's not warm enough to enjoy the summer fun."

"The waves aren't what we're used to on the Left Coast," Britt said.

Jade smiled. "They surf a little here, usually when there are nor'easters coming up the coast. Most of the kids boogie board or skim board." When Jade noticed the puzzled looks, she added, "It's like skateboarding on wet sand. They get their slide on and have to balance until they run out of speed."

Several nodded, and Lexi passed fresh cans to those in need of a drink. When no one said anything, Jade asked, "Any news on the guy they found in Raphael's room?"

Britt ran a hand through her razor-cut hair. "He was one of those pond scum-sucking reporters who hound us constantly. It's kinda scary to think that they can sneak into your room, too. Nobody observes boundaries anymore."

"Now, beautiful Britt, you know that we have a symbiotic relationship with the reporters. They want the next hot story, and we depend on them to keep us front and center in the public's consciousness," Dante said.

"They are always looking for dirt on Raphael and Elle. If I were them, I'd lock myself on an estate somewhere and not answer my phone." Britt rolled her eyes and took another sip.

"Elle is nice to them. They like her," Lexi said. "And they respect her privacy to an extent. Raphael makes it too easy for them with all his hookups and 'friends.'" She made exaggerated air quotes that caused snickers among the group.

"And you didn't hear this from me," Dante said. "But he's kanoodled with everyone from Elle to Paige."

"Paige?" Britt said a little too loudly. "Olivia, I could see, but mousy Paige?" Her overly stylized eyebrows disappeared behind her dark bangs.

"That's before your time with us," Marius said. "Yep. She followed him around like a puppy for weeks. The fling lasted about the time it takes for sushi to spoil. Rumor has it that Olivia broke them up by reminding them both of their contracts and that Paige worked for her. I heard it was quite the shouting match." Marius waggled his eyebrows.

"And Olivia wouldn't give Raphael the time of day. He's too wild and childish for her," Matilda added. "That boy needs to grow up before he gets in trouble, if you ask me."

A bell sounded, and the gang jumped up.

"Chow time," Bruce said, crushing his can with his motorcycle boot.

"Just leave it here. I'll clean the remnants of happy hour later," Dante said. "Jade, you want to join us?"

"Thanks, but I need to head home and get moving on stuff like laundry that I've put off for too long. Plus, Chloe knows it's time for her dinner. See y'all around." The little dog turned her head ninety degrees and stared at Jade.

"Bye," Lexi waved and followed her coworkers to the large white tent.

Paige and Raphael. Elle and Raphael. Raphael and almost everyone. That opens up a lot of possibilities on the suspect list.

Chapter Ten

The front doorbells chimed, and Chloe made a beeline for the open door. Jade gently scooted her back and slipped out to the entryway. "Hi, Olivia. What can I do for you?"

"Ezra and Brian thought your store would be perfect for our latest production, and I'm here to talk to you about the possibilities. They'd like to do a scene here with Elle shopping. So that would mean indoor filming for an afternoon and shots around the front of the store. We'd prep it one evening and film the next day. And, of course, you and some of your staff could be extras."

Patti will be over the moon. "Oh, wow. Thanks for considering us. We'd love to be included. What do I need to do?"

"Not much. We'll take care of the heavy lifting." Olivia whipped out a folder from her messenger bag. "Here's the contract. Look it over and sign it. This page talks about the rental fees we pay since your store will be shut down for a couple of days. The terms are similar to the contract you had for the use of your lot. And this section talks about the extras and what they can and can't do. Any questions?"

Jade shook her head as she skimmed through the contract. She signed one copy and kept the other for her files.

"Very good," Olivia said, taking the folder. "We'd like to put it on the schedule for three days from now. We'd do the setup, test clips, and rehearsal on the first day. Then filming would begin the next morning around nine. The main office will send you a check for the rental. Any issues?"

Jade shook her head, and Olivia continued. "It's a pleasure doing business with you. The guys will do the lighting and test shots, and we'll move what we need to adjust for the scenes." Olivia glanced around the lobby. "We love the Valentine trees. Just leave everything the way it is. For now." She turned and headed for the porch.

Jade texted Patti, Lorelei, and Bernie to see if they wanted to be extras. Her team replied instantaneously that they'd be there with bells on and couldn't wait.

Butterflies in her stomach stirred every time she thought about filming at her store. This was a chance to get on the national scene in front of millions of Love Channel viewers. Maybe this would put her store on the map of must-see places to visit. Her thoughts quickly flashed to ways she could market the store's appearance once the show aired. She flipped over her contract and started jotting down ideas.

Jade's phone alerted and distracted her from her planning.

I'm leaving on time tonight. Wanna go out for dinner? Nick asked.

Sounds like fun. What do you have in mind?

Seafood? He replied.

She fired back with smiley, fish, and heart emojis.

Pick you up around six?

Perfect, she tapped into her phone and leaned back in her chair.

"It's date night, Chloe." The dog looked up from her napping spot. With no treats in sight, she turned her head and rolled over.

A little after five, Jade finished her closing routine and picked up her stuff. "Come on. I need to go find something to wear." Chloe had other ideas, trotting toward the campers next door. The little dog picked up speed when she heard voices. Jade waved to Lexi. Before either could speak, Paige slammed the door and stomped down the metal steps of the camper next door.

"Hi, Paige," Jade said.

The tall production assistant looked at her and took off running in the opposite direction.

That was odd. Jade opened her mouth to say something but stifled her comment.

"Don't mind her," Lexi said. "She's always annoyed at something. And it's not you. Ezra and Olivia have been riding her hard over some recent mishaps. I don't know what her issue is, but she's been a walking disaster."

Jade shrugged, and Lexi laughed. "We've gotten used to her, uh, eccentricities."

"Everything else going okay?" Jade asked.

"Yup. As soon as I repack some equipment, I'm headed to dinner. I heard we're filming at your place soon. That will be fun. See you around."

"I'm excited to be part of the show. Bye," Jade said, guiding Chloe toward the street and home.

Back at the bungalow, Jade spent too much time in her closet trying to find the perfect date night outfit. Finally settling on an oversized, cream-colored sweater and black leggings, Jade plopped down on her bed and pulled on her black leather boots.

After a round with the curling iron and the makeup brush, she was ready for an evening out. A knock on the door engaged her French bulldog alarm system. Jade flipped off the lights and found her purse.

"Hey," Jade said, opening the door. Nick stepped in, kissed her, and patted Chloe, who rolled over for tummy rubs.

"Seafood still okay with you?" he asked.

"Sure. I missed lunch." Jade followed him outside and locked the deadbolt. A slight smile crossed his lips. Always the cop.

After a short drive to the restaurant, he pulled into the parking lot of the Red Herring, a family-owned fixture in Mermaid Bay. Its dark paneled walls harkened back to the seventies, but the décor was all dime store, pulp detective novels from a bygone era.

The hostess seated them at a cozy wooden booth under a wooden ship's wheel next to framed posters of Sam Spade and Philip Marlowe. A tiny candle flickered and cast a warm glow on the dark corner. "Here are your menus. Our catch of the day is on the front, and your server will be with you shortly."

After flipping through the menu, Nick set his down and reached for her hand as a waiter strolled to the table. He set a basket of hush puppies and two glasses of water on the table. "Hi, I'm Pete. What can I start you off with tonight?"

"I'll have the grilled shrimp, a side salad with Italian, and an unsweetened iced tea," Jade said.

The waiter with nickel-sized gauges in each ear nodded. "It comes with rice pilaf and seasonal vegetables. Is that okay?"

Jade nodded, and Nick said, "I'll have the tuna steak with rice and vegetables and the salad with ranch. And water's fine for me."

"I'll put this in for you." The waiter headed for the doorway behind the bar.

"So, what's new in Christmas land?" Nick asked.

"*My Coastal Valentine* wants to film a scene in the shop. And Patti, Bernie, Lorelei, and I get to be extras. I'm excited about the opportunity, and maybe this will introduce my store to a worldwide audience." Jade refrained from doing a fist pump.

"Sounds like fun. I hope it doesn't cause too much disruption," he said.

"These will be some downtime for a couple of days, but there's a rental fee involved, so it's a win-win."

Nick smiled and rubbed his temple.

"You okay?" she asked.

He nodded sluggishly. "It's been a long day. A long week," he corrected. "And we don't know that much more than we did before. The reporter was killed by a blow to the head. The coroner said that was enough force to kill him, but the injury was exacerbated when he fell and hit the floor. And all the major players have alibis." He let out an extended breath through his nose.

"So, there's some strange killer running loose?" she asked, picking up a hush puppy from the wicker basket.

Nick shook his head and grabbed one for himself. "I don't think so. I think it's connected to the filming somehow. We need to figure out the missing pieces. The process takes a while. We have hundreds of leads and tips that we need to weed through and vet or discard. And we're still waiting on the final tox screens and autopsy report from Richmond."

"It looks faster on TV." Jade loved TV thrillers, but she had learned long ago that if she watched them with Nick, she would get a running commentary of what was and wasn't realistic from a cop's perspective.

The waiter returned with her tea and a refill of the water. As he turned to leave, he paused. "Hey, you're the sheriff, aren't you? You came to my apartment complex once when my roommate's car was stolen."

Nick nodded.

"I guess you get a bunch of calls. It's been crazy around here since that film crew arrived. But it's all good. Tips have been great. Can't believe there was another murder...."

"The task force is working on it," Nick said.

"That's comforting, if you all catch the guy." The waiter paused, and when Nick didn't add anything, he hustled back to the kitchen.

Pete returned a few minutes later and covered their table with plates. In that time, the restaurant had filled with diners, and the noise level had risen several decibels. The pair ate in silence as Jade watched through the wall of windows as the seagulls dove into the water and resurfaced seconds later. They looked peaceful, gliding on the breeze and dipping into the waves for their dinner.

"You look lost in thought," Nick said.

"I've talked to most of the actors and crew. They're an interesting bunch, but no one stands out as malicious. That reporter had tried previously to sneak in at Ruby's. She said they added additional security. And fans have descended on Mermaid Bay. It's like tourist season without the warm weather." Jade pulled the remaining grilled shrimp from the skewer and popped it in her mouth.

"And reporters. My team has been inundated with requests for information and interviews. I feel like I'm waging a two-front war. I'm glad the state police are helping with the investigation. We've all been working a boatload of OT. It's been a wild ride."

Jade pushed her plate toward the center of the table and set her napkin beside it.

"What? No dessert?" Nick winked. "Their key lime pie is the best."

"I'll nibble on yours. How's that?"

Nick waved the waiter over. "Hi, could we get a slice of key lime pie and some water?" He pointed to his half-empty glass.

"Be back in a flash." The waiter picked up Jade's plate and hesitated.

Nick and Jade stared at him. "Mermaid Bay is buzzing all over the internet about that murder. It'll be cool for your team when you solve it. We've had a boatload of reporters and photographers in here. And true crime podcasters. They seem to be flocking to see what's going on. You'll get to be in some interviews when you find the killer. Make us famous. Everyone will know where Mermaid Bay is."

Nick nodded. When he didn't say anything, the waiter retreated to another table.

"Great. I'll be famous," Nick muttered. Suddenly, he looked ten years older in the soft light and shadows of the candle's flickering flame.

The waiter approached noiselessly and dropped off the dessert.

Jade took a bite of the pie and put her fork down.

"That's all you want?" he asked, taking a large bite that included some of the graham cracker crust.

"I just wanted a taste. I'm glad you're my dessert buddy."

"Never let good pie go to waste," he said, shoveling in another bite.

By the time Nick paid the check and left a tip, the restaurant had filled to capacity, and a line formed at the door. Jade and Nick walked around those waiting for a table and wandered to his truck. The parking lot had expanded to the sandy lot next door. A blue Tesla zipped in Nick's spot as soon as he had vacated it.

"You want to watch some TV?" Jade asked as Nick flew by 'Tis the Season on the way to her bungalow.

"I want to, but I know if I sit down for more than five minutes, I'll fall asleep on your couch again. I'll take a rain check, and we'll do something fun as soon as I've caught up on some sleep." His phone sounded like a buzz-saw. "Driscoll, here. Yep. Got it. I'll be there in a minute." He set his phone in the cup holder. "Just got a call of a break-in at the Pirate's Chest. I'll drop you off and see what's going on. So much for an early night."

"I don't mind if you go there first, if it'll save time."

Nick nodded and sped to the building that housed the antique store, the realtor's office, and an empty spot where the CPA had an office until he was arrested.

"Stay in the truck. I'll be right back." Nick pulled into the spot next to Sebastian's SUV. Not seeing his deputy, Nick unholstered his gun and crept around the brick building. Jade hunched down but made sure that she still had a clear view of the strip mall.

After what seemed like hours and way too much waiting for nothing to happen, an older white Volvo pulled in next to Nick's truck. Kelly Jamison hopped out and waved at Jade.

Before either of the women could speak, Sebastian opened the front door and shooed Kelly inside.

More waiting. Jade started to fidget when no one else appeared. About the time she decided to leave Nick a note and walk home, he stepped outside, followed by Kelly and Sebastian. She locked her front door and hopped in her car as Sebastian said something Jade didn't catch.

Nick climbed in the truck. "Hey, I left you the keys. You could have kept the heat on. It's chilly out here tonight."

"I'm okay. I didn't know how long you'd be gone," Jade said, rubbing her hands together. "What happened?"

"We got a call from the alarm company. Someone broke in the back of Kelly's store. Nothing was taken, and no one was inside. I'm hoping it's just kids, but you never know around here. The only damage was to the lock on the back door."

"I checked my outdoor cameras, and they didn't catch anything. The back of this building is out of range," Jade said, looking at her phone.

Nick waited for Sebastian to exit the lot, and he turned in the opposite direction, headed for Jade's bungalow. "Sebastian will check in with Tish. Maybe she has cameras at her place. Claude's office is still empty. If it was a burglary, it makes sense to break into the antique store, but they didn't take anything. Or hang around. If they were looking for a place to hang out, I would have picked the empty office. It's probably kids goofing off." Nick pulled into her driveway behind her Wrangler.

Nick walked her to the door. "Thanks for dinner. Sorry about the diversion on the way home." He lightly grazed her cheek with his palm. Their good night kiss turned into several. Jade wrapped her arms around him and enjoyed the warmth of his hug and the spicy smell of his cologne.

"Night," he said as she locked the door behind him.

At least our dates were always noteworthy. Who else got a burglary call with dinner and key lime pie?

Chapter Eleven

Jade and Chloe arrived early and checked to see every tree was lit and twinkling for the crew's walk-through and rehearsal today. By the time she brewed her second cup of coffee, Patti breezed in the front door with a tray of vanilla peppermint fudge and some chocolate-dipped heart cookies.

"How's everything in Hollywood land? I am so excited. I made these in case anyone wants a nibble." She set the plates down on the counter and wiggled out of her jacket.

Lorelei walked in right behind her. "Hey, hope I'm not late."

"Nope. We're getting settled before the crew gets here," Jade said.

"There's already a crowd outside. I thought filming wasn't until tomorrow," Lorelei said.

"It's not. I guess word travels fast. Everybody wants a glimpse of what's going on," Jade said.

"I saw a post on Facebook about Elle doing a scene here and then another one about them doing shots in Williamsburg." Patti put her mug under the coffee maker's nozzle. "I hope she brings Raphael and Carlos today."

The bells on the front door jangled. Bernie Nash, Jade's jovial handyman and part-time Santa, wandered in in his full Santa outfit.

"Morning, Bernie," Lorelei said. "What brings you by so early in full regalia?" Jade's aunt had a mischievous twinkle in her eye.

"Heard Elle and the Love Channel were coming by today." He adjusted his hat and fluffed his snowy beard.

"You look perfect," Lorelei added, retrieving a mug from the cabinet. "Want some coffee?"

Bernie shook his head. Before he could comment further, the front door banged open, and they all hustled to the front to see what was happening.

"Morning," Olivia yelled. "Everyone ready for us to invade?"

"Good morning," Jade said to the production manager, Paige, and five guys in all black who looked like muscular backup singers. "I'm Jade Hicks. And my team, Patti, Lorelei, and Bernie, want to welcome you to 'Tis the Season."

"And Chloe," Lorelei added, holding up the white Frenchie and waving her tiny paw.

"How cute. Yes, we need her to be an extra, too," Olivia cooed. "Paige, go over the extra contracts with them and get all the paperwork signed."

When the tall woman stared blankly, Olivia squared her jaw. "Now. We've got a ton of things to get through this morning before rehearsal."

Paige rummaged through her messenger bag and pulled out a folder.

"You can use the office back here," Jade said. Paige lumbered after Jade's team as the burly men started moving boxes and bins into the store's lobby.

"Here's the contract," Paige said, dropping a stack of papers on the worktable. You'll get paid fifty dollars a day. You'll wear your own clothes unless we decide to outfit you for wardrobe. If you end up with a speaking part, you'll get paid an additional fifty dollars. Any questions? And you have to sign a non-disclosure amendment stating that you won't talk about the production before it airs. And if you do, you'll be sued."

Patti's lips formed a small "o" as she stared at Paige.

Changing the subject, Bernie asked, "Is this okay? Or should I wear something that shows off our beachiness?"

"Who am I to tell Santa how to dress?" Paige said. "You look fine to me, but I don't make any decisions. Wait until the director and producer get here. You'll have to sign the dog's contract," Paige added. Her stare felt like it was boring a hole in Jade.

"Your own contract, Chloe," Lorelei said, hugging the butterball of a dog.

When Paige collected all the signed documents, she stuffed them back in the folder and scurried out to the lobby.

"What do we do now?" Lorelei asked. "So far, this movie-making thing has been a whole bunch of waiting and watching."

"We can peek out the door and see what they're up to. I can't wait to see the store on TV. Jade, you'll be famous. We'll have fans from all over coming to see where they filmed *My Coastal Valentine*. This is so exciting," Patti said.

Fanning himself with his beefy hand, Bernie said, "It's getting a little warm in here for me. I need to catch up with the guys on all the Hollywood encounters. Plus, it's lunchtime. Call me if they need me to rehearse anything. If not, I'll be back bright and early tomorrow."

When Bernie stepped out the back door, a roar and cheers echoed across the parking lot. Bernie waved and made his way through the crowd.

"He's in his element," Lorelei said, taking a bite of one of the heart-shaped cookies.

The trio sat for hours watching the crew move lights, cameras, and microphones all over the store. Marius and another guy used a light meter in the lobby and in the display rooms. Two men brought in a large camera and took measurements of the space.

"As much fun as this is, I have a lunch date. I'll be back tomorrow. Call me if you need me." When she stepped out back, cheers went up from the crowd. Lorelei waved and made her way to her Lexus.

"This really is so exciting. I've never been part of anything like this before. Thanks for including me," Patti said. "And we get to meet the actors tomorrow. I know I won't sleep a wink tonight." She pulled out her phone and snapped pictures of the crew.

"I should get some, too, for the newsletter. But first, let's do a selfie with them in the background." Jade held up her camera and took a series of shots.

"What are you wearing tomorrow? I may bring multiple outfits to see which one they like best. I have Valentine's sweatshirts, sweaters, and leggings. We're going to be on TV," Patti squealed.

"I hadn't thought about it. Maybe a red or white sweater. I guess we're playing ourselves. I wonder if I should wear something with the store's logo on it?"

"I'd go with the sexy store owner look. And don't forget a fancy collar for Chloe."

A knock at the back door interrupted their conversation. Jade opened it, and Todd stood on the steps with a to-go bag from Hot Diggity Dogs and a drink tray with four cups. "Hey, y'all. Thought you could use lunch, And I really wanted to see what was going on over here."

"Come on in. We're watching them get set up for tomorrow's filming," Jade said.

"Yes, come sit here. We can watch them move equipment as we eat. I brought goodies if you want something sweet," Patti said.

The three turned their chairs so they could see the activity in the lobby as they ate hot dogs and chips. Chloe, more interested in the smells coming from the bag than the activity from the TV crew, plopped down where she was in range to scarf down anything that hit the floor. The humans chewed and stared at the activity in the front room while Chloe waited in anticipation for a snack.

"A lot of movement, but not much movie making." Todd balled up his tin foil wrapper.

"Thanks so much for the hot dog," Patti said as Todd rose.

"No problem. It's good to see y'all. I've got to get back. We've had a steady flow of customers all week. And if it keeps up, I'll be in the black, even with all the bad stuff that went on." He slipped Chloe a bite of his hot dog.

"I'm glad your sales are back on track," Jade said, opening the door for him.

"Me too. Business was a bit hairy during tourist season." He saluted with two fingers and jogged toward the street. Jade's thoughts flicked to the online harassment and Todd's abduction. Shaking off the dark memories, she straightened the items on the kitchenette's cabinets. Jade and Patti spent the rest of the day fielding texts and emails from friends, all vying for a spot as an extra or a chance to get near the stars.

"If you don't need me, I need to get my stuff together for tomorrow. I am so excited." Patti grinned from ear to ear, and her blond curls bounced as she danced around the office. "I love working here."

"You'll be fabulous. You always have the best wardrobe," Jade said. "See you tomorrow. I'm leaving, too, as soon as these guys are done."

Then, like the sudden retreat of the tide, the crew packed up and started to leave. Olivia popped her dark head in the doorway. "Hey, Jade. How's it going? I hope your folks had fun watching some behind-the-scenes action today. We'll be ready to start at nine, so have them here by eight for hair and makeup."

"Will do. Do you have recommendations on what to wear?"

"What you'd normally wear. You all will be playing yourselves. Well, except the Santa. He'll greet Elle when she comes to shop. Are you planning to lock up?"

Jade nodded, and Olivia continued, "The guys left tomorrow's setup in place. Be careful if you have to walk around all the wires and equipment. See you all bright and early." She wagged her finger.

Olivia left through the front door, and Jade locked it behind her. "Okay, Chloe, let's shut everything down." When the little dog started sniffing around the equipment, Jade picked her up and tucked her under her arm like a football. "Let's not get into their stuff. I don't want us getting fired before we even get to be on the show."

After double-checking all the doors and windows, Jade fired off a quick text to Patti, Lorelei, and Bernie with Olivia's update for tomorrow. She glanced at her phone. All three had responded quickly with smiley faces and thumbs-ups.

"Okay, let's hotfoot it home and figure out what we should wear tomorrow. Everybody else seems to have a plan."

Chloe pranced out the back door. The crowd had moved from her parking lot to the sandy area near the temporary fencing. People strained to see anyone related to the show. From Jade's vantage point, it looked like most of the crew headed to the craft tent and the chow line.

Jade and Chloe stepped out to some ooos, and a gaggle of reporters scurried closer to them. "Are you part of the filming," one of the guys in a canvas jacket with two cameras around his neck yelled.

Jade shook her head. "I'm the owner of 'Tis the Season Christmas store. You guys should stop in sometime. I have some novelty ornaments for photographers." She winked and kept walking down the sidewalk. Chloe pranced like a star with her head held high for the paparazzi.

Chapter Twelve

J ade's eyes popped open at four-thirty in anticipation of the day's filming. After coffee and four outfit changes, she was ready to see what was in the fridge for breakfast.

I really need to get some groceries. She found some leftover cheesecake, an orange, and a yogurt.

Grabbing the yogurt, Jade dipped her spoon in and stared at her murder wall while she ate. Not having any epiphanies, Jade downed the last sip of her coffee and offered Chloe a lick of the yogurt on her spoon. "You ready, girl? Oh, wait, you need a fancy collar for today." Jade opened the door to the laundry room and rummaged through the bins that held the dog's holiday wardrobe. "Here. This one with hearts is made for today." Jade snapped it in place, and Chloe strutted to the door. "Looks like you're ready for your scenes."

The pair hurried to the store to get everything ready before the crew arrived. Throngs of people already lined the streets, trying to get a glimpse of anything Love Channel-related. Three tour buses sat in front of The Pirate's Chest. Some from the crowd waved and called to her as she climbed the steps to the store's porch. Jade returned the salute and let herself inside. *A girl could get used to all this adulation and attention.* By the time all the trees twinkled and the coffee maker chugged, Lorelei and Patti bustled in.

"Did you get a look at that crowd? You'd think the King of England was visiting," Lorelei said, plunking her things down on the workspace.

Patti balanced a suit bag, an oversized purse, and a tray of red and white heart-shaped cookies that she set on the counter. "How do I look?" she asked, trying to contain her excitement. "I think I'll go with this outfit. But I have several others if the TV people don't like this one. I want everything to look just right."

"Fabulous. I wore red and cream." Lorelei smoothed the hem of her sweater over her slacks.

"You always look like you stepped out of a fashion magazine," Patti said. "I'm going for the Valentine vibe, but I brought three tops in case this was too busy for the cameras." She spread her arms wide and modeled the black sweater with red, sequined hearts. Her red leggings were covered in white, pink, and yellow candy hearts.

The bells on the front door jangled, and a "Whoooo hoooo" echoed through the lobby. "Good morning, Mermaid Bay people. Who's ready to make a movie." Dante's voice boomed.

Lexi poked her head in the back. "We're setting up hair and makeup back here. Do you mind if we commandeer this table and chairs?"

"Help yourself," Jade said. "And I have coffee and drinks on the counter."

"And I made cookies," Patti added.

"Homemade cookies. I do miss those being on the road so much," Dante zeroed in on the platter and took two.

Jade helped the stylists rearrange the table for their make-shift salon.

"That'll do," Lexi said. "Who's first?"

Lorelei nodded at Patti, who hopped in the chair in front of Lexi.

"I'm ready, too, "Dante said, pointing to Lorelei and his empty chair.

The pair curled, brushed, and created a blush storm in the back of the store. Chloe hid under the desk to avoid getting fluffed or exfoliated.

As the crew started to wander in and set up, they heard a roar and cheering outside. Jade, now camera-ready, thanks to Dante, poked her head out the back door.

Bernie, in full Santa garb, waved and high-fived the line of spectators along the sidewalk. He finished greeting his fans and trotted inside with his velvet sack. "Morning, ladies. And gentleman. And Chloe. I hope everyone's been good. But I already know you all have." Bernie laughed, and his belly jiggled.

"You're next, Mr. Claus," Lexi said, pointing to the chair. "Gotta get you ready for the cameras."

Bernie dropped into the chair. "Jade, you got any coffee?"

"I'll get it," Lorelei said. "And since you're our star, I'll bring you some of Patti's gourmet cookies."

"What's the matter?" Bernie asked, looking at Jade.

"Oh, nothing. I'm not used to wearing this much makeup. My face feels like it's about to crack."

"You'll get used to it. I've been playing the big guy for years, and it's a part of looking fabulous for the camera."

Lexi combed his puffy eyebrows and fluffed his cottony beard. She rosied up his cheeks and lips. "There. You're about done."

Olivia rolled in like a hurricane, barking orders at Paige and the crew. She looked in the back and paused. "Looks like it's all under control in here. Britt and Elle will be here in a minute." She pivoted and returned to the lobby.

Lorelei raised one eyebrow but refrained from her usual comments.

A constant roar from the crowd outside caused Patti to stretch to see out the front windows. "There's a car. It's Britt and Elle. And oh my stars, Carlos Alvarez, too…. Oooooh, okay, now my life is complete. Raphael Allard is walking through your front door, Jade." Her voice went up three octaves.

Olivia led the actors to the back for hair and makeup while Patti buzzed around taking coffee and tea orders and selfies.

The director and producer arrived, and the actors hungrily looked over last-minute script reviews to see what had changed. Jade and Chloe wandered around, trying not to disturb anyone or trip over any wires.

"Places," someone yelled from the lobby, and that caused a flurry of activity.

Paige walked into the back and yelled, "When they get the scene set, Olivia will direct the extras to their marks. Stay where she puts you and do whatever they tell you. Santa, you'll come in to greet Elle in the second or third scene. And one of you will have to hold the dog so it can be seen. You can stay back here until we call for you. Any questions?"

"I'm sure I'll have oodles when we get ready to start, but I'm good for now,"

Patti said.

"Try not to. You and her are the store workers. Act like you normally would. Stand there and smile." Paige pointed to Jade and Patti. "And you're a shopper," she said to Lorelei. "Take any breaks now or get anything you need. You'll be standing and smiling for a long time. And turn off your phones. You don't want to face the wrath of Ezra if a phone goes off during filming. Got it?"

"Got it," Lorelei said, wrinkling her nose and stifling a sharp retort.

A guy in all black wearing a headset ushered the three into the lobby and showed them the tape marks on the floor. "Stand here and face that way," he pointed. Everyone found a spot and verified that the phones were silenced.

Showbiz wasn't exactly as glamorous or fun as it seemed on TV. They spent hours shooting and re-shooting the same scene. Jade's face ached from all the fake smiling. The real drama occurred when they had to stop a couple of times because someone from the crowd rushed the porch or tried to bang on the front door. Ezra and Brian fumed. Olivia fretted, and Paige stormed out when she had to deliver a warning to the guards outside for the third time.

Chloe had the most fun of all the Mermaid Bay extras. She had scenes where Raphael and Elle each picked her up for on-camera cuddles. *She'll need her own publicist after this.*

When the director yelled, "Cut. That's a wrap," Jade let out a sigh of relief. She could mark off actress from her bucket list. It was time to wash off the layers of makeup.

Organized chaos ensued as the stars were whisked away in dark SUVs, and the crew zoomed in like ants to disassemble the equipment. Lorelei and Bernie waved goodbye and headed out for the evening.

As Dante and Lexi repacked their bins, he said, "Hey, Jade. If you don't have any big plans tonight, a bunch of us are planning to have our own beach party near the pier. Come and hang out with us. Unless you've had enough of us today."

"Sounds like fun," Jade said. "Thanks for inviting me."

"Bring a chair at sundown and anyone else you want," Lexi added.

Then, as quickly as they arrived and took over her store, the TV crew evaporated like the mist over the bay at sunrise. The quiet echoed in her ears. Jade and Patti did a walk-through and cleaned up the trash in the kitchenette.

"I've got this," Jade said, picking up the two trash bags. Enjoy the rest of your evening. And thanks for the sweets."

"Thanks for including me today. I was a total fangirl, and it was amazing. See you tomorrow," Patti said. "Today was a dream day. Can't wait to post all my pictures."

When the door shut behind her part-timer, Jade asked the dog, "Did she literally waltz out of here? Where does she get her energy? Let's go see what we have for dinner, and maybe we'll take a walk later to see what's shakin' on the beach."

Chloe's ears shot straight up at the mention of the "W" word.

The first things Jade did at home was to change into jeans and a soft, baggy sweater and scrub her face until it was slightly pink.

After feeding Chloe, she searched through the refrigerator and the cabinets for dinner for herself. "This is called scrounging. I really need to go to the grocery store. Let's see. We can do a bacon grilled cheese and some tomato soup."

Chloe agreed and plopped down underfoot to ensure she didn't miss anything important like bacon or cheese.

Jade spent dinner staring at her wall of suspects. *That sounded better than having a murder wall in one's dining room.* Again, no a-ha moments. This had to be someone involved with the show or some random killer. Either way, she was no further along in her ideas about suspects than she was last week. Shaking off the feeling of dread, Jade put on her boots and found Chloe's leash. "Maybe a change of scenery will clear our heads." She pocketed her keys and phone, and they trotted off toward the path to the beach.

The cool, autumn breeze ruffled Jade's hair. Pulling her sweater closer around her, she picked up her pace to keep up with her jogging dog. On the back side of the dune, Chloe decided to chase a gang of seagulls vying for the remains of a crab in the sand. Her barking and sudden advance scattered the flock like a bowling ball connecting with pins. Tugging on the leash, Jade headed toward the pier, where a small group sat around a firepit dug into the sand.

"Jaaaaaaaade," Dante yelled, waving both hands. "You and your little dog made it. So, how was your first day of being a professional actor? Your little Chloe is a natural. She'll have her own fan club soon."

"Long, but fun. I can't wait to see Mermaid Bay and all our friends on TV," she replied.

"You all will have to have a watch party when it airs. We should come back and do a premiere. That would be fun. Come on over and pull up a seat. You know Matilda, Marius, Britt, Bruce, Carlos, Eddie, and, of course, Lexi."

Jade waved and plopped down in the sand next to Matilda, who was wrapped in a blanket. Chloe greeted everyone nearby.

"I haven't been to a beach party in years," Matilda said, sipping from a can of beer. "I'm having flashbacks to my high school days."

"Do tell, Tilde," Dante said. "I want to hear about all those wild sixties and seventies shindigs."

She smiled. "The music was epic, even if it was a crazy time. Lots of political upheaval. But you all read about it in your history books."

When the conversation drifted off, Jade looked at the faces illuminated by the flickering campfire. Jade decided to shake things up a bit. "Any word of why that reporter was in Raphael's room? Or who would want him dead?"

"Who wouldn't," Carlos added. "Seth was notorious for ruining careers and stirring up stuff in his stories. We all have morality clauses in our contracts. A big scandal could end our job."

Matilda nodded. "Corporate is concerned about its brand."

Jade hesitated.

Britt laughed. "I know what you're thinking. Corporate doesn't want to know if there are foibles. They want stuff kept hush-hush, and they certainly don't want any of us to make the rag mags. If someone has a skeleton in the closet, he better keep it locked up."

"Or she," Marius added. "Some of the females around here are just as catty as their gentleman counterparts. And we all can guess who I'm talking about."

The others laughed but didn't comment further.

"I'm kinda hoping it's some crazed lunatic or someone from here and not our team," Lexi added. "I'm stressing just thinking it could be one of our coworkers. You know someone we practically live with every day."

"So, you'd rather have some crazed psychotic killer?" Carlos asked.

"It's better than it being one of us. What if it's your roommate?" Lexi looked around and took a swig of her drink.

"I'm up for getting a new roommate, if there are any volunteers." Matilda raised her beer and laughed.

"I don't think Marius wants me to trade him for Paige," Dante said, punching Marius in the arm.

"You can always bunk on our couch if it gets too weird or you need a break," Britt said.

"Thanks. I think I can stick it out for a few more weeks. Filming will be over soon. She comes and goes at all hours, and she is on the blasted phone so much that I think it's another appendage. But enough about that. Anybody got any happy news?" Matilda leaned over and scratched Chloe behind the years.

The group chatted and told funny stories about the shows they've been a part of until the wind picked up.

"I feel like I'm getting sandblasted here," Dante said, pulling his hood up and tying it snuggly under his chin. "I'm ready to head back. Who's the Smokey Bear in charge of this fire? One of you crazies needs to be the adult tonight."

"I'll take care of it," Bruce said. "I'll hang out for a bit longer. I'm enjoying the view. I like watching the ships inch across the horizon. And the sound of the waves is peaceful if the wind'll die down."

Several in the crowd rose and folded towels and blankets for the hike over the dunes.

"Thanks for including us tonight. This was fun. Chloe and I need to be going, too," Jade said, dusting the sand off of her jeans.

On the walk back, Jade did a mental inventory of everyone around the fire. What if the killer really was someone not affiliated with the show? What if it were a random stranger or a person from town, just like the murder and kidnappings that happened before?

Chapter Thirteen

P atti announced her arrival with a "Whooo Hooo. Good morning everybodeeeee. How are you on this bright, sunshiny fall day?"

"Hi," Jade said from the rainbow room, where she gathered decorations for an online order that was pink-themed. Each tree in the display area had a dedicated color, and the mixture and all the twinkles made it a visual explosion of hues. The room reminded Jade of a kaleidoscope.

"I had so much fun yesterday, and my pictures of the filming went viral. I've never had so much attention on Instagram before. I got likes and comments from people from all over. And a bunch wanted to know the storyline. Can you believe they wanted spoilers?"

Jade set the orders on the back counter and glanced at her.

Patti waved her hand in front of her face. "Don't worry. I'd never give up any information like that. Plus, how would I even know? I saw them film a scene of Elle and Raphael shopping over and over again. But I will say that the scene had some fabulous extras in it."

"I didn't realize that movies weren't filmed in the order that they appear on the screen. I guess I never really thought about it, but when you're watching them create it, it doesn't seem like a story. There. I'm done with the orders." Jade wiped her hands together. "Want anything from the Busy Bean?"

"That sounds great. Could you get James to make a Peppermint Patti? He made me one last week. It's peppermint-flavored hot chocolate with an itty-bitty kick of cayenne. Whooo hooo, what a zing."

"First a role in the show, and now you have a drink named after you. You're a celebrity. Way to go," Jade said. "Be back in a minute."

Jade slipped on her puffy parka and zipped out the door. The crowds from yesterday had disappeared or moved on to today's filming location.

As Jade cut through Amy's parking lot on her way to the Busy Bean, a figure in shorts and a gray hoodie stumbled around. Hurtling forward, the man struggled to regain his balance. Then he stood there for a moment, swaying from side to side. He put both hands on his head and grimaced.

"Raphael? Is that you? Are you okay?" Jade asked.

He pushed the hood off of his head. "I dunno. I felt fine earlier. A few minutes ago, I started sweating and feeling dizzy. I think I'm about to be sick."

"Why don't you sit down for a minute? Do you want me to call anyone for you?" Jade asked, stepping closer to the actor.

"Just give me a minute. I'll feel better after a ressht." Raphael stumbled, and Jade helped lower him to the bookstore steps. "I don't freel so good."

Amy rushed out. "What's going on?"

"I don't know. Can you get him some water and a cold towel?" Jade asked, pulling out her phone and dialing 911.

"Of course. Stay right there." Amy dashed back into the store.

"This is Jade Hicks. I'm in front of Mermaid Books with a jogger. He's dizzy and disoriented. And he's sweating a lot."

"Have him stay calm and stay seated. We'll send an ambulance. Okay. One is en route. You should hear it in a couple of minutes. Can you have someone direct them to where you are?"

"We're on the store's front steps," Jade said.

"I've let them know. Is he breathing okay? Talking?" the dispatcher asked.

"He is. We've got him seated because he was stumbling around. He's talking, but he's slurring his words. I hear the siren. Thank you for your help."

"Yes, thank you for all, all. Well, you know," Raphael said. "And thanks for introducing me to Cassidy. But Olivia will be mad at me if I leave with the ambulance. It'll messsh up her schedule, and she'll be hot. Not that she isn't hot. But she's too bossy for me. I think I'll stick with Cassidy for now. I don't have time to play with the ambulance. I have to get back to work.

74

Olivia will be mad."

Jade looked at Raphael and disconnected the call. "Just wait right here. It'll be okay," she said, not sure what he was telling her.

The ambulance arrived as Amy returned, and two medics took charge of the scene. They checked his vitals and his eyes and collected information about him from Jade and Amy. Within minutes, Raphael was loaded into the ambulance, and Jade and Amy watched from the porch. Amy still held the compress and a glass of water.

"I'll let the people at the studio know he's going to the hospital. Which one?" Jade asked.

"Riverside Hospital," the second EMT yelled over his shoulder.

Jade punched in Olivia's number and gave her a quick play-by-play of what happened to Raphael.

After a string of obscenities, Olivia said, "Thanks. We'll figure out how long he'll be away from the set. I guess we can shoot around him." Olivia disconnected, and Jade stared at her phone.

"That sounded pleasant. So, she's more worried about the schedule than she is about Raphael. Nice," Amy said.

Jade nodded and texted Nick a quick summary of what transpired in the parking lot. "There. I sent Nick a note. I don't know what Raphael was on, but he didn't look right."

Amy nodded. "That sweaty look wasn't becoming, and he was slurring. It's kinda early to be celebrating."

"He got worse as time went by. I hope they can figure out what's wrong with him."

"I hope it's not a stroke or something." Amy squeezed the damp washcloth in her hand.

"I'm headed to the Busy Bean. Want anything?" Jade asked.

"Nope, I have a Zoom with some authors. We're planning a romance conference for Valentine's Day. Let me know if you hear anything about Raphael." Amy disappeared into the store.

It's too early for Bloody Marys and mimosas. These Hollywood folks lived in a different world. Jade shrugged off the melancholic feeling that tickled the back of her brain as she pushed open the glass door to the Busy Bean. The décor's bright aquas and silvers welcomed her into the cozy coffee shop, packed with round tables, baked goods, and coffee-themed gifts. The smell of ground beans and the promise of a delicious shot of caffeine and sugar improved her mood.

"Hey, Jade. What can I get for you?" James Fornier called from behind the counter.

"Patti wants one of your Peppermint Patti hot chocolates, and I'll have a pumpkin spice latte."

"Ha. Her signature drink. I need to get it added to the menu the next time the artist stops in." James pointed to the chalkboard above the counter.

"She'll be thrilled to have her namesake on your menu."

James smiled as he processed her debit card. "Your drinks will be up in a few."

She glanced at her screen when the text alert sounded.

Dinner tonight? Not sure when just yet, Nick texted.

How about tacos at my house? Jade responded.

Nick sent back a heart and some taco emojis. **I'll let you know later about what time.**

Jade picked up the drinks James put on the counter. "I saw the ambulance this morning. Do you know if Amy is okay? I had a crowd of folks in here at the time and couldn't get away," he said, brushing his longish hair off his forehead.

"She's fine." Jade leaned forward and whispered, "It was Raphael, the actor. He was jogging and suddenly became dizzy. They took him to the hospital."

"I hope he's okay. It's not the right season for heat stroke. I heard they filmed at your place yesterday. Exciting. They're doing a coffee shop scene here next week. Tell Patti I'll have her drink on the menu by then so everyone can see it." James winked and moved on to the next person's order.

Jade waved and balanced the drinks as she opened the glass door.

Later that evening, Jade buzzed around the house before Nick arrived. She set the table and picked up a ton of dog toys. When he knocked on the door, she threw the remaining toys in Chloe's basket and raced the dog to the door.

"Hello, how are you?" she asked as Nick stepped in with a fresh-from-the-shower look, wearing a wine-colored sweater and jeans. The ends of his military-style haircut were still damp.

He kissed her and handed her a container of cannoli. "Sorry. It doesn't go with tacos, but they're still dessert."

"Dessert is always good. Come on in. How's it going?" She pointed to the dining room, and Nick paused to stare at her wall. He took a seat, facing the brightly colored sticky notes. "I spent a big chunk of my day at the hospital with Raphael and his minders."

Jade loaded up the lazy Susan in the middle of the table with taco fixings. *I'm glad I finally went to the grocery store.*

"Mmm. This looks wonderful. Thanks for making dinner. How's life at the shop?" he asked, reaching for a couple of taco shells and changing the subject.

"The filming was fun. Chloe's got a fan club now. I think she was on camera more than the rest of us extras." Jade loaded a taco shell with ground turkey, lettuce, and cheese. "It was a little weird today. When I saw Raphael earlier, he wasn't that steady of his feet. At first, I thought he was having a heart attack or a stroke. Then it looked like he was on something. He was acting odd and slurring his words. Thankfully, they rushed him off before the crowds started gathering. I don't think the paparazzi knew it was him."

"I'm waiting on the tox screens to come back," Nick said, loading his two tacos with sour cream and salsa.

Jade paused in mid-bite. "Illegal substances or poisons?"

"Both," he said, taking a huge bite that cracked the corn shell.

"Hmmm." She picked at the cheese and meat that had fallen on her plate. "Their normal screens cover certain drugs and poisons. Since he presented a little loopy, the doctors ran some additional ones on him for things that don't show up in the standard tests. Hopefully, we'll have the results back soon."

"He didn't make much sense. He was wobbly, and he kept ranting that he didn't want to cause scheduling problems with the day's filming. He talked about some girl like I knew who she was," Jade said.

"We'll find out what's going on. The investigation continues."

"You think this is related to the murder?"

Nick nodded and took another bite of his taco.

Jade hoped she didn't look too elated that Nick's theory matched hers. If the two events were related, the killer was somehow linked to the Love Channel people. This will send Ruby into apoplexy if something else happened at her place. Drugs or poisoning? Either way, she won't be pleased.

Chapter Fourteen

Jade gently nudged the bungalow's front door shut with her hip, while balancing the leash, her messenger bag, and a to-go cup when her phone rang. "Hello, Ruby. What's up this morning?"

"Jade, I don't know what to do. Sebastian and that state trooper are back here, and they're going through my kitchen and pantry. When they showed up with a warrant, the TV folks decided they didn't want to finish breakfast. And they made a big deal about not eating food at my place. Can you come over here? This is all too much. And now Elle's back to posting snarky comments on her instawhatever."

"It'll be okay. I'll be there as soon as I can." She disconnected and looked down at Chloe. "Change of plans. Sorry. I need you to guard the house." Jade unleashed the Frenchie and watched her settle in her bed. "I promise. I'll make it up to you. I need to go check on Ruby."

After a quick ride through a warren of side streets, Jade parked in front of Mrs. Vanderbeek's three-story Victorian across the street from the Pearl. Multiple police vehicles and a forensic van blocked the driveway to the bed and breakfast. The heavy front door flew open before Jade could duck down the path to the kitchen. Ruby tore down the steps and pulled Jade toward the porch.

"I'm so glad you're here," Ruby said, almost dragging her inside the foyer. The police have been all over the downstairs. I can't imagine what they're looking for. What did these Hollywood people bring with them?"

"Didn't the police say?" Jade asked, following Ruby to her office.

"They're interested in the food and drink items and the menus I've served for the past week." Ruby plopped down in the office chair behind the antique desk and put her head in her hands. "This is too much. I don't know how we'll survive this."

Ruby continued as Jade patted her shoulder. "That Raphael told the police he had coffee and breakfast here this week before his incident. No one will want to stay or eat here if patrons were poisoned." Ruby dissolved into sobs.

Jade found a box of tissues and handed one to Ruby. As the B and B owner composed herself, movement in the hallway caught Jade's attention. A flash of bright pink zipped by the doorway and returned.

Elle paced back and forth and waved her arms. "First the breakfast fiasco, and now no ride. I'm stranded here in this house of horrors." The actress stamped her ballet slipper on the floor. "Well, tell him to hurry up. I'll be at the front door, and I don't like waiting."

Elle's voice drifted into the office. "I'm fine. Thoughts of that dead reporter have been keeping me awake. I'm not getting any sleep in this creepy old house."

Ruby's face looked like she had been slapped. Jade put her hand on her friend's shoulders and blocked her path to the foyer. Ruby's defensive stance relaxed a couple of centimeters, and Jade mimed a shushing librarian.

After a pause, Elle whispered, "He said he had photos of me that I would be interested in. And then the idiot went and got himself murdered. I'm beside myself. What if someone else gets a hold of them? I have no idea now how to get those pictures back."

After what seemed like forever, Elle replied, "Thanks for taking care of this. I feel better." She disconnected and was startled when she spotted Jade and Ruby in the office doorway.

"Good morning," Jade said.

"Oh, hi," Elle's features softened. "I'll be right out here waiting for my ride."

"Do you need anything?" Jade asked.

Elle's smile dimmed when Ruby approached her tentatively.

"I'm fine. I'll wait over here." She stepped closer to the door and peeked out the small window at the side of the massive oak door. "It should only be a couple of minutes in this tiny town, right?" Not waiting for an answer,

Elle pulled out her phone and scrolled.

"I need to scoot, too." Jade turned toward Ruby. "Call me if you need me or if you hear anything. Everything will be okay. Things will calm down. Don't worry."

Elle looked up from her phone. "I'm sure it will be. It's just been one thing after another for me today."

Ruby's brow furrowed, and Jade stifled her comment to the actor.

"Hey, you have a car. Can you take me to the set?" Elle said, pointing at Jade.

"Uh, okay," Jade replied. "Where is the filming today?"

"Back over there near the pier on the beach. I could have walked in the time I've waited for that driver. But I don't know how safe that would be. I need to go find Lexi and go over my lines. I'm kinda in a big hurry."

"My Jeep is across the street. Let me go get it, and I'll pull up as close to the driveway as I can get. Ruby, call me later with the details."

"You're a dear." Elle cut her eyes at Ruby, who nodded. Then, the actor made a production of turning her focus back to her phone.

The crowds of fans had thinned, but the sidewalks were still packed with photographers and news crews. Some shouted questions at her as Jade emerged from the Pearl. She waved and power walked to her Wrangler. Dodging questions and reporters seemed to be the thing to do. She pulled up to the mailbox, and the reporters nearby stepped back for a second until the oak door opened. When they realized it was Elle, the whole area flooded with people and camera flashes.

Jade moved slowly over the curb. The photographers stepped back as Elle tiptoed down the driveway and waved for the cameras. She rushed toward the passenger side and hoisted herself in the shotgun seat. "Go, go, go. Before they surround the car, and we can't get out."

Jade threw the car in reverse and inched back out into the street. Photographers ran after them until she accelerated.

"That was fun," Elle said. "You can drive for me anytime."

Jade glanced in the rearview mirror. Three cars followed closely behind them. "Looks like we have company."

"They're always around. I ignore them most of the time," Elle said, smoothing her oversized sweater across her lap. "You get used to having people follow you. It comes with the territory. It's when they're not around that you have to worry."

"What about the reporter they found inside the B and B? Did he follow you often?"

Elle rolled her eyes. "He was one of the worst. Most are okay humans if you give them a statement or a photo op once in a while. Seth was pure nasty. He'd do anything, including doctoring photos to fit his story. I had nothing to do with his demise, but I'm not sorry he's out of the picture. I don't think anyone misses him."

"You seemed surprised that morning that he was in Raphael's room."

"Not really. Raphael has lots of friends. I was curious, that's all." Elle picked at a spot on her sleeve. "I wanted to see what all the hubbub was about."

"About their relationship?" Jade's brows furrowed as she glanced sideways at the actor.

"Let's say business relationship. Seth had some personal photos that he approached me about..." Her voice trailed off as she stared out the window.

"And you were wondering if he was shopping them around..." Jade added.

"Something like that. I think he was working all available avenues. Everything he did was to benefit Seth. He was always out to make as much money as he could. It was always about working a deal."

"Did you pay him?" Jade asked.

"Here's my stop. I'm heading over to those tents. Thanks for the ride." As she hopped out, she added, "No, I didn't pay him. That's why he threatened to sell them to someone else." The petite actress slammed the door.

After swinging by the bungalow to pick up Chloe, Jade opened the store and got to work on the pile of overnight orders. She replayed her conversation about Seth over and over in her head. Could his shady business dealings be the reason for his murder?

Before her second mug of coffee finished brewing, she heard a loud noise out front that sent Chloe yipping and zipping to the front door. Jade peeked out the window and gasped. A black hearse sat in front of her store. When she opened the door, a horn rendition of Bon Jovi's "Wanted Dead or Alive" greeted her.

Amy rolled down the passenger side window and waved. "Isn't this great? Todd's been taking me on a tour of the town. Come check it out."

Jade leaned in through the open window. "Wow. Hi, Todd. Where did you get this?"

A grin crossed Todd's face. "It was too good to pass up. I can haul surfboards to competitions in it. It's better than my roof racks. The perfect vehicle. Look at all that room back there. And Amy's come up with a ton of ideas for this beast. Hop in."

Jade wrinkled her nose but added a quick smile when the pair stared at her.

"Next week, we'll park it in front of the bookstore and do a Fill the Hearse book drive for Halloween. Oh, and we might do a pub crawl in it. Wouldn't that be a hoot," Amy said.

"Definitely interesting," Jade said.

"I may even have a wrap put on it and park it out front of the store. Rolling advertisement. Hot Diggity Dogs, Hot Dogs to Die For. Speaking of that, we need to make one final stop before heading to work. Gotta run."

"Wow." Jade stepped back, and Todd serenaded the neighborhood again with his musical horn.

That's something. Not sure if that's the right message for a marketing campaign, but I'll give him points for originality.

Chapter Fifteen

After the second tour bus of the morning pulled out, Jade sunk down in her office chair. "Whew. That was a workout. But I am loving all the shoppers from these tour stops."

Patti smiled and leaned over the top of the Dutch door. "They kept me hopping with all the questions about the filming. In that final group, Lillian and her friend Nancy said they're planning to watch the filming after a stop for lunch. They are sooooo excited to see all the action of a real TV set. And, of course, Raphael."

"You became an instant sensation with your Raphael stories." Jade winked and pulled gift basket materials from the cabinet.

"Whatcha doing?" Patti asked.

"Since we can't go visit Raphael in the hospital, I was thinking about leaving him a gift basket at Ruby's for when he returns."

"Ooh, good idea. Want me to go find the perfect ornaments to put in it?"

Jade nodded and pulled out ribbons and a wicker basket. She added two mugs, hot chocolate, and some postcards of Mermaid Bay. Scrounging through the marketing cabinet, she pulled out some tea, specialty coffee, and gourmet snacks.

Patti returned in a flurried rush. "What about these? I found a beachy mermaid with sunglasses and one of those little movie clapper board thingies."

"Perfect additions. Here, let me borrow a hand as I try to get those ribbons around the cellophane." Jade bunched the plastic into a topnotch.

"There. That looks nice. He'll love it," Patti said. "I hope he's doing much better. He gave us all a scare. Speaking of that. Did you see what was in front of Todd's? I hope everything's okay," she whispered.

"It's his new toy. He bought it to carry his surfboards."

Patti squinted and closed one eye. "Wow! Is that the best thing to park out in front of his business? But I guess it'll work to haul his boards around."

"Amy said she wanted to plan some kind of Halloween tour."

"Oooo, maybe he could do a ghost tour for us," Patti said as she turned to greet the customers at the door. Once the pair of women wandered toward the display rooms with their baskets, Patti continued, "Or one of those true crimes of Mermaid Bay tours. She may already have enough material to do one of those."

"I need to drop this off at Ruby's. You okay here by yourself for a bit?" Jade asked.

"No problem. I'll text you if any tour groups show up."

The ride to Ruby's didn't take long. In front of the B and B, Jade had to slow down to avoid the paparazzi that lined both sides of the street near the Pearl. Jade dodged what looked like hundreds of photographers and tripods. "They're worse than the summer tourists who stand in the streets staring at the bay," she muttered to herself.

Grabbing the basket and her purse, she trotted around to the kitchen door as the flashbulbs went off around her, and the photographers yelled at her to get her attention. After knocking repeatedly with no answer, she texted Ruby.

By the time she hiked around to the front door and had her picture snapped again by the gaggle of reporters, Ruby opened the door, a smudge of flour stretched across her forehead. "Sorry, Jade. I was up to my neck in alligators in the pantry. I just saw your text. I'm having to throw out anything that had been opened. It kills me to waste so much food, but I can't take any chances."

Jade chewed on her bottom lip. "You have to throw out all of it?"

"Everything that's not factory sealed. Word got out, and it's making its way across social media as we speak that Raphael was poisoned here. I have to be on the safe side and take a loss on all this stuff. I want to ensure all those reporters see me cleaning out the food stock." Ruby wiped her hands on her black slacks, leaving streaks of white. "That's a nice basket. What's it for?"

"Raphael's release from the hospital. I'm sorry about your pantry. It's probably for the best, and that way, they'll know that you all are being cautious."

"The Pearl is still a hot topic on social media. Right now, half the fandom thinks he was poisoned from what I served at breakfast."

The front door opened, and a crowd roar erupted outside. Jade followed Ruby to the foyer, where Olivia and a petite woman with a razor-cut black bob stood. The woman's shiny, ruby lips stood out like neon against her pale skin.

"Hi. This is Wren Pierce. She's the executive publicist for the Love Channel. She'll need a room for a couple of weeks. She's coming in to help us tamp down the noise from Raphael's unfortunate situation," Olivia said.

"That's not a problem. We can get a room made up for her on the third floor next to Elle. It'll take a minute or two." Ruby wiped a stray lock that had escaped from her bun.

Wren nodded. "I'd like some sparkling water and a couple of aspirin if you have them. Which room is it? I'm sure it's fine?" She climbed the steps and left her aluminum suitcase at the foot of the stairs.

"Room three to the right. I'll get you a key." Ruby retreated to the kitchen as another whoop rang out from outside. The door opened, and the bald security guard escorted a pale Raphael inside. He waved to the photographers until the guard slammed the door.

"Let's get you to your room," Olivia said. "I have to get back to the set. If you need anything, call Paige."

Raphael's lips curled into a slight sneer. "I'll be fine. Tell her not to bother. I need to sleep off all of this. It's been a nightmare."

"This is for you," Jade said, offering the basket. "We're glad that you're feeling better. You have so many fans at my store."

"Cool, thanks," he said, grabbing it with one hand and tossing the bow on the floor. His mood changed in a flash. "Oh wow. Classy chocolate candy from Seattle and hot chocolate. And snacks. Thanks. Can someone bring this to my room? Like now?" he asked, thrusting it at Olivia. "Glad to be back from my near-death experience." He climbed the steps to the second floor.

Olivia trotted behind him, grumbling under her breath as Jade followed the guard out the front door.

Why would someone want to kill Raphael? And he seemed awfully calm for someone who survived a poisoning attempt.

Chapter Sixteen

During her walk through the store to restock some of the display rooms, Jade's phone binged with a text from Amy. **Whatcha doing tonight? Can you and Nick do dinner with us?**
I'll check. I don't know what his schedule is, Jade replied.
Please, please, please. We'll have so much fun.
Jade tapped in a text to Nick. **Any chance you can get away for dinner tonight with Amy and Todd?**
After six. Long day ahead.
Have fun, she replied.
See you at your place tonight. Gotta run to a meeting. He ended his text with a string of heart emojis.
Jade smiled and responded to Amy. **We'll be there.**
Our first double date. Pick you up after 6. Dress for fun, Amy replied.
"I wonder what she has up her sleeve," Jade said to Chloe, who trailed along behind her, sniffing around the peach baskets full of ornaments. "Sorry. No Neville today. You'll see your buddy later this week."
Jade printed the nightly order sheet. "Four pages," Chloe. You want half?" The chubby dog raised one eyebrow and trotted off toward her puffy bed.
After boxing all the orders and greeting a steady stream of walk-ins, Jade settled in at her desk with a cup of hot tea to update her newsletter and website. Looking through her pictures of the Love Channel's folks, she decided to feature a behind-the-scenes section with notes on all the activities so far. She put the pictures of the filming inside 'Tis the Season front and center.

Jade spent most of the day greeting walk-ins, answering questions about what the stars were really like, and working on her website.

A little after four-thirty, Jade stood and stretched. "Come on, Chloe. Let's wrap up things here and see what Amy has in store for us tonight." She and the little dog walked through each showroom, following her closing routine.

When the Frenchie toddled into the back office, Jade said, "Okay, that's enough fun for today. What do you think?"

The dog yawned and lifted her head.

"Let me put this in the safe, and we'll head home. I need to find something to wear tonight."

Chloe decided to stretch the walk out as long as possible. She sniffed every blade of grass on the way home.

"Okay. I know it was a boring day for you. Let's go see what's happening on the beach."

The white dog's ears perked up, and she darted down the shell path toward the sand. The breeze ruffled Jade's curls, and she tasted the salty tang of the sea spray on her lips. Chloe greeted the lone jogger and his black lab and sniffed around for crabs.

When Chloe plopped down in the sand, Jade said, "Okay. Time to go home. I've got to get a move on, and you're getting tired."

After feeding her Frenchie, Jade changed outfits twice before she settled on jeans and a grey cardigan with a wine-colored T-shirt. Slipping on her thigh-high brown boots, she switched out her purse to a matching one.

A noise on the porch caused both their heads to turn, and Chloe trotted off to do her security dog duties.

When Jade opened the door, Nick folded her into a long embrace. She kicked the door closed with her boot, and he kissed her.

"Missed you," he finally said. "I will be so glad when we get a break in these cases."

"Plural?" she asked, looking up into his green eyes.

"Right now, the task force is treating them as two separate incidents, but it's the same team working on it. They're not convinced that they're truly related yet," he said, wrinkling his forehead.

Before he could continue, a horn rendition of Bon Jovi's "Wanted Dead or Alive" blasted from her driveway. Nick stared out from behind the curtain and raised one eyebrow when he looked at Jade. She tried not to roll her eyes.

"He bought it for his surfboards." She grinned and grabbed her coat and purse. "Chloe, be good while we're gone."

Nick held the door for Jade as he scrutinized the black behemoth parked behind his oversized truck.

"Don't ya just love it?" Amy turned around in the passenger seat. "This is too much fun. How are ya doing? Sheriff, it's nice to see you out of uniform." She giggled. "You know what I mean. I'm not used to seeing you in civvies. Are ya ready for an adventure and some wicked fun?"

Nick nodded. "Jade is always up for an adventure."

"And not like your job isn't one every single day. It must be exciting. You never know what's headed your way, Mr. Sheriff," Amy added.

"What, not all police chases and shootouts?" Todd asked.

"It's more like lost kids, barking dogs, and fighting neighbors," Nick said.

"Well, we're glad you could get away and go out with us. Are ya good with Tex Mex for dinner?"

"Sounds fine," Jade said as Nick nodded.

The hearse drew quite a few gawks from people on the sidewalks and the nearby drivers at the stoplights. Todd rolled down the window and waved at the passersby.

"Todd's planning to decorate this fabulous vehicle for Vivian's Trunk or Treat event. I'm trying to talk him into doing a ghost tour of the area in it. With Yorktown and the other nearby battlefields, we could find all kinds of places with spooky stories. I have some books at the store on area haunts. Oh, maybe that would solve Ruby's problems. She could come up with some kind of story and end up on the true crime or ghostly circuits." She turned around in her seat as Todd pulled into the lot of the Tex-Mex restaurant, Tequila Mockingbird. For good measure, he blew the horn as they all climbed out. All heads within a twenty-foot radius turned to stare at them.

Inside the restaurant that had been a family steakhouse chain in the eighties, the hostess seated them in a booth in the back corner. "Your waiter will be here shortly." She doled out menus like she was dealing a poker hand.

"What are you getting?" Amy said. "This is a new place for me."

"I like everything here, especially the extra spicy stuff," Todd added.

A stocky waiter stood at the edge of the table, waiting for Todd to finish. "I'm Sean, and I'll be serving you tonight. What can I get you all to drink?"

"Iced tea," Jade said. "And I'll have the Tex Mex Nachos with no jalapenos."

"Iced tea, too," Nick replied. "And I'll have the surf and turf fajitas."

"I want one of those big, pink margaritas with the flamingo in it," Amy said. "And I'll have the Tex tacos with extra guac."

"And you, sir," Sean said to Todd.

"Let's go with a Coke, and I'll have the shrimp fajitas, extra spicy."

"Very good. I'll be back shortly with your drinks and chips and queso." Sean moved on to the next table.

"So, what's new in Hollywoodland?" Nick asked. "I haven't seen anything except the four walls of my office. No time to catch any of the filming."

"They were at Jade's store, and they filmed next door at the coffee shop. They've been on my porch and front lot twice. I wish they'd do a scene or two inside," Amy said. "The closest I got was when Olivia stopped by and bought some books. For those with inquiring minds, she bought four romance novels, a book on poisoned plants in your garden, and two true crime novels."

Nick didn't say anything, but Jade could tell he was processing what Amy said. One of his eyebrows shot up as he listened intently.

"They've been at the pier a lot and near my deck. I'm hoping folks will be able to identify Hot Diggity Dogs when the show airs. I'm thinking about hanging a big banner with my logo on the deck," Todd said.

Sean sidled up to the table and delivered drinks and a basket of chips and queso. "Your dinners should be out soon."

Nick's head bobbed slowly, and he reached for the chips.

"Any news on the murder front?" Amy asked, taking a sip of her Barbie pink drink.

"Just waiting and digging through leads. Not as exciting as it is on TV. I'm still expecting the final autopsy report on the reporter and the tox screens on that actor," Nick said, dragging several chips through the bowl of white cheese.

"Now, that was an interesting day. When Raphael came near the bookstore all wobbly and slurring his speech, I thought he was on something. It never occurred to me that he'd been poisoned," Amy said.

"Do you really think it was from Ruby's?" Todd asked.

"It's hard to tell. It could have been ingested in food or drink. He said he had dinner at the tent the night before. We took samples there, too. He had coffee and juice early that morning and some kind of egg casserole. We'll know more when the test results come back."

Before anyone could pepper Nick with any additional questions, Sean and another waiter appeared with sizzling platters. "Be careful. Those plates are hot. Does anyone need anything else right now?" When the four around the table shook their heads, he continued, "Then I'll check back on you all in a little bit."

"Any obvious connections between the actor and the reporter?" Amy asked, taking a bite of her taco and wiping the green goo that oozed out off of her chin.

"Nothing other than they all are in town for the filming," Nick said, loading tortillas with sizzling steak and shrimp.

The two couples dug into their dinners, and the conversation drifted off.

"The shrimp's good," Nick said. "Wanna try it?" he asked Jade.

She reached over and speared two of the grilled bits with her fork. "Thanks. You want the rest of my nachos? I can't eat all this. And I'm not sure if it would taste the same tomorrow if I get a box."

"I'll eat it," Nick said.

"Isn't that cute? They're at the share food stage in their relationship," Amy said. "We're not there yet," she smiled at Todd.

"Nope," said Todd, shoveling another bite of fajita in his mouth. "I'm an only child. I don't share my food."

Amy rolled her eyes and snagged a shrimp off of his plate.

When Sean finally returned, he handed Todd and Nick the checks. They finished their drinks and took care of the bills.

Once outside, Jade shivered and pulled her jacket closer. "Brrrr. We're getting close to a frost. I think the chance for any surprise, warm days is almost over this season. That's always bittersweet. I'm happy that we survived another summer season, but I know winter's around the corner."

"So, let's play tourist tonight," Amy said. "What's there to do around here?"

"Most of the seasonal places are closed until spring," Todd said. "No bumper boats, paintball, or bungee jumping."

"The go-cart place is open." Nick grinned, stepping out onto the sidewalk.

"You game?" Todd said.

Nick nodded, and Amy said, "Always."

Within fifteen minutes, they were strapped in four carts that sounded like souped-up lawn mowers.

"Are we playing for pinks?" Amy yelled. "What's on the line here?"

"Bragging rights," Todd yelled, revving his engine.

The teen in the emergency vest and headphones, yelled instructions and stepped off the asphalt track. The lights on the pole changed from red to yellow to green, and Nick and Todd were off like bullets out of a gun. Jade tailed the pair, and Amy putted along, bringing up the rear.

After a minute or two, the three leaders lapped Amy and raced around the serpentine-shaped track. Jade floored her gas pedal and passed Todd on the inside of a curve.

She and Nick were neck and neck as the teen waved a white flag. *One more lap to go.*

Jade stood on the gas pedal and skidded around the next turn. Nick looked over his shoulder and cut in front of her. *You're going to play it that way, huh?*

She sped up and drafted off of his bumper on the straightaway. At the next turn, she turned the wheel sharply and zipped parallel to Nick's cart. He grinned and stomped on his gas pedal. His cart lurched forward, and he scooted across the finish line as the teen waved the checkered flag.

"Impressive," Nick said as Jade climbed out of her vehicle. "You gave me a run for my money." He hugged her.

"And y'all are still speaking? Two competitive streaks," Todd said, waiting for Amy to finish her final lap and pull into the pit area.

"That was fun. Who's up for another run? Or dessert?" She bent over and fluffed her dark hair and then flipped it backwards.

The other three glanced at each other. "I need to check on some work stuff before I call it a night," Nick said.

"Then we'll do this again when everything is open for the season." Amy slapped Todd lightly on the back and said, "I'll race you to the hearse." She took off running before her friends realized what she was doing. Nick and Jade strolled behind Amy and Todd, who ran through the parking lot and hurdled over curbs like ten-year-olds.

"That was fun. Thanks," Jade said.

"You can drive getaway for me anytime." Nick smiled and kissed her on the head.

A group of teens took selfies in front of the hearse. Amy and Todd smiled and photobombed. After the kids wandered off, Todd smacked the hood with his hand and yelled, "Winner." He jumped inside the car and locked the doors, all while doing the happy dance in the driver's seat.

"Unlock the door," Amy whined.

"It wasn't a fair start," Todd yelled out the crack where he lowered the passenger window. "I want a rematch."

"Okay. Back at the bookstore," she said as the door locks clicked open.

Nick held the door for Jade, and she slid across the bench seat to make room for him. His phone's jarring ringtone broke the silence.

"Driscoll here. Yep. Got it. I'll be there in about twenty minutes." He disconnected. "Sorry to be the wet blanket, but I got a call. I need to swing by a crime scene."

Amy turned around, and her eyes lit up.

"Sorry. I need to be dropped off at Jade's so I can get my truck. I think if I rolled up in this, it would freak people out."

Amy snapped her finger. "I had hoped that we'd hang a uey and haul butt to a crime scene." She pinched Todd in the arm as he signaled to get back to Neptune Road.

Todd idled in front of Jade's mailbox as Nick hopped out. "I'll call you later or maybe tomorrow," he said, kissing Jade on the forehead.

As Nick slammed his truck door and backed out of her driveway, she waved to Amy and Todd. "Thanks for a fun evening. We'll do it again soon."

"Todd owes me one more race, and then we'll pop by his apartment to listen to his police scanner. Can't wait." Amy waved as they watched Nick zoom toward town." But be sure to let me know if you hear anything juicy."

Todd mashed his musical horn and drove off as Jade noticed two or three curtains move in the windows across the street.

Chapter Seventeen

Chloe noticed the lone figure in one of the white rockers on the store's porch before Jade did.

"What are you doing up so early?" Jade asked Raphael, who pushed the hood off of his head.

"I went out for a run. This was my first one since, well, you know."

Chloe climbed the steps and sniffed around his sneakers. Then she jumped in his lap.

"Thanks for the basket. It was nice." Raphael stroked the smooth fur behind the little dog's ears. "I heard through the grapevine that you're dating the sheriff, and I was hoping you could help me."

"How?" she asked, resting one foot on the bottom wooden step.

"The studio execs have added extra security, but I feel like I've got a target on my back. I also feel like I'm under a microscope," Raphael said. "You know cops, reporters, and true-crime podcasters."

Jade chewed on her bottom lip and listened. "Uh-huh."

Raphael made a face. "Besides the obvious. There are a lot of haters out there. Just look at all the blogs and comments. I ignore it most of the time, but I encounter hundreds of people a day. I feel I need to be hypervigilant all the time. It would be nice to know the police are close to solving the cases. And that I'm not one of their suspects."

"Do you think it was some fan or stranger?" Jade asked, watching his face for any tics or twitches that might give her a clue to what he was thinking.

"I guess it could be a stranger. There are tons of trolls and sleazy reporters out there, but they've always been around, and I've never had issues before."

He lowered his voice and nuzzled the dog under his chin, "It could be someone on the inside."

"What makes you think that?" Jade asked.

"This shoot feels different."

Before she could ask for any details, he said, "On other sets, we laughed and joked a lot. It was always fun to hang out with the gang. Now, everyone seems to be so uptight and at everyone's throats. Paige is okay. Well, she was until we messed around after a night of drinking, and then she got all clingy. She didn't like it when I said I wasn't into relationships, but I think we're okay now. Olivia watches me like a hawk. Her constant helicoptering makes me want to sneak out just to tick her off. And Ezra is all business these days. All he does is yell. It's not the same. Elle got all serious about her career, and now she's no fun. And Lexi used to be my party girl, but she's been giving me the cold shoulder."

"What about Seth Davis?"

Raphael's smile vanished. "We used to be friendly. But he turned into a Judas and sold me out for cash. We haven't talked much recently. Well, before you know."

"How friendly?" Jade arched an eyebrow.

"Not like that. We used to hang out. He was cool when he started in the Hollywood scene. We'd talk. I'd give him pictures and exclusives, and he always kept me on the front page...in a good way. Then, he changed jobs and became one of the parasites. He'd spend his final breath looking for dirt and threatening to post it if you didn't give him something better."

"What did he have on you?"

Raphael let out a long puff of air. "Elle and I have had a thing going for a long time. Nothing serious. No commitments. It's all casual. I think part of it is that we're thrown together so much and all that on-screen electricity. Anyway, he got his hands on some racy hot tub photographs that the network execs wouldn't like. He wanted money to sit on them."

"Did you pay him?"

"No. I decided to take my chances. It wouldn't be my first rodeo that hit the front pages of the scandal sheets. My agent said to ignore him. My stock at the Love Channel is soaring now. My agent didn't think they'd pull out the morality clause and risk losing a star over photos that would generate a buzz about me and the show."

"Do you know if anyone else paid him?" Jade asked.

Raphael shrugged. "Doubt it. Elle, maybe. She has to keep her sweet image front and center. She's always worried about what everyone thinks."

"What was he doing in your room?" Jade asked, feeling like a reporter.

"I have no idea. We really hadn't talked in weeks. The Wonder Twin security guards caught him climbing up the trellis that one time. And then he was found in my room when I was out jogging. So much for security. But it happens. People fake deliveries and try to weasel their way close to us all the time." He paused and kissed Chloe on the head. "I was hoping you could poke around and work your connections to see if his, uh, demise was related to my poisoning. Food poisoning feels like a coincidence. I heard you were a whiz at finding stuff out. They said you helped solve a murder here before."

Jade nodded. "I can try. But the sheriff is playing his cards close to his vest. I'll see what I can find out."

"Here, type in your contact in case we need to chat," Raphael said, handing her his phone.

Jade tapped in her cell number and returned his phone. Her phone dinged with a text with his number. *Raphael Allard is now in my address book. Patti would pay big money for that number. And so would the paparazzi.*

"Look into all of them," he said. "Olivia has a soft spot for Elle. She can do no wrong, and Ezra agrees with whatever Olivia says, which doesn't always work in my favor. And even Lexi and Dante take sides. I think they're spying for Olivia. We're here for a couple more weeks. I'll have to make the best of it and try to be boring like regular people, but I will be looking over my shoulder constantly." He stood and put Chloe on the porch.

"I'll see what I can find out."

"And it could even be someone from town like the owner of the B and B or her family. I just want to feel normal and safe again." Raphael strode down the steps and stretched. Then he continued on his jog toward the beach.

Jade didn't have a chance to defend Ruby or Josie. It couldn't be them. That makes no sense. Then, memories from last summer and Emory Jessup's murder flashed across her thoughts. *Okay, that murderer was a townie, but this situation feels different. That was because a business deal soured.*

Shaking off the gloomy feelings, Jade led Chloe inside and whizzed through her morning routine. After packing all the internet orders and filling the bin for pickup, she settled in her desk with a mug of hot tea. She kept playing the conversations in her head. *I need to focus on the "My Coastal Valentine" folks. They have the most to lose.* She scrolled through dozens of articles about Raphael online, and the comments were split about fifty-fifty in his favor. Adoring adulation or snarky critiques. Not much middle ground with that one. Jade typed in Elle's name and scrolled through the feedback. Her comments were all positive. *Either her fans are rabidly devoted, or she's got a better publicist.*

Jade spent the next hours searching for anything related to the cast or crew. Besides creating a list of sixty-three names of women Raphael was purported to be linked to, she didn't have any eureka moments. Ezra had been divorced twice, and his second wife was the family's nanny. Compared to the volume of Raphael's escapades, that didn't even cause her to raise an eyebrow.

"I'm tired of searching for dirt on these people, Chloe. I don't know how these reporters can do this all day, every day." The dog looked up from her nap with one eye open. "It's time to check the inventory." Jade picked up a legal pad and pen. As she strolled through the rooms, watching the twinkle lights flash, she looked at all the stock on hand. The pet ornaments were running low, and the flamingos, motorcycles, and mermaids had been selling like hotcakes. She paused in front of the large glass display case full of collectibles. Some of the European glass ones by Christopher Radko caught her eye. The bright colors, along with the twinkle lights on the nearby trees, created a festive holiday moment that brought back a flood of fun memories.

Jotting down notes for her next order, Jade jumped when the bells on the front door jangled. She made her way through the forest of Christmas trees to the lobby. "Good afternoon, may I help you?" she asked the pair of seniors in velour jogging suits.

"We heard about this place on the Love Channel fan page. Did they really film here?" the woman in the magenta suit with purply hair asked.

"They did. They're currently filming *My Coastal Valentine*, and some of my staff got to be extras. It's been fun. I've never seen a movie or show filmed before, and I can't wait for this one to come out."

Both women oohed and aahed, and the one in the tangerine outfit said, "What can you tell us about what happened? I'm dying to get the scoop on the latest show. I love that Elle and Raphael. They were made for each other like Cinderella and her prince."

"Like I said, I've never seen filming before. They do the scenes out of order, and they do multiple takes. My team got to be part of the segment they did with Elle here in the store. It took most of the day to film one scene."

"What did she buy?" The geriatric visitor in green asked. "I want to get the same thing."

Jade smiled. "She shopped through the store with some of the actors. I think she picked up some of the ornaments in different colors from the rainbow room."

"I've got to get me some. Come on, Janice. Take my picture for my blog," the woman said, picking up the shopping basket Jade offered. "Which way?"

"Go through the toy room, and you'll see it. It's the next room over, and you can miss all the color."

"Awesome." The pair bustled off to look at the displays.

Jade glanced at her phone. **I'm leaving on time tonight. Wanna grab a quick dinner?** Nick texted. **I've got to drop something off for the movie folks. Feel like hot dogs?**

That works, she tapped into her phone.

I'll stop by the store to get you.

Jade smiled when the pair of shoppers returned to the cash register to check out.

"We love your store," Janice said. "Peg and I found so many cute things. I'll take these and any other spicy tidbits you care to share with us about the filming. I'll mention your store in my post."

"Thanks so much. Don't forget to tag us. I'll be glad to share it." Jade handed her a business card with all her contacts.

"Is Raphael as handsome in person as he is on the screen?" Peg asked, putting her basket on the counter.

Jade rang up their purchases and scanned their credit cards. "He is. He has piercing blue eyes, and he's taller than he looks on TV."

"Come on. You've got to know some scuttlebutt. We heard about the murder in town. What are the locals talking about? You must have heard something," Janice said.

Everyone's looking for a scoop. "I don't know all that much. I see the crew that's staying over there in the campers every once in a while. There are quite a few reporters in town. They're everywhere." Jade gave a slight smile.

"Hmm. That's an idea. Come on, Peg. Let's take a walk. Thanks." The women picked up their bags and scooted out the front door.

Jade glanced at the time on her phone. Nick would be here soon. She double-timed her closing routine and packed up her notes. This snooping for clues business was harder than she thought. Maybe she should leave it to Nick's team. She didn't seem to be getting anywhere fast.

A little after five-forty, Chloe and Jade heard heavy footsteps on the porch, and Jade unlocked the front door for Nick.

"Well, howdy, Sheriff." Jade stood on her tiptoes and kissed him on the cheek. "Wearing jeans today. Casual day in law enforcement?"

He laughed. "I changed at work before heading over. I had to drop off some permits to Olivia. They're all over at the craft tent. It's lasagna night."

"Mmmm. Maybe we should sneak over there for dinner." Jade winked. "Let me get my stuff, and we'll be ready to go." Jade slung her messenger bag over her shoulder and clicked Chloe's leash in place.

"Hot dogs, okay? Or would you rather go somewhere else?" he asked, pointing to Todd's place across the street.

"Chloe loves hot dogs. Todd always gives her free samples."

They walked across the street and stood in line behind a group of teenagers who stared at them when they walked inside. Jade suddenly felt older than her mid-thirties. Chloe walked over and greeted them, and she became an instant sensation when she posed for pictures with them.

Jade ordered and settled in a booth near the kitchen and glanced over her shoulder at the large windows in the front of the store. Her thoughts flashed back to a memory. She had avoided sitting in front of them since someone had thrown a weight through it, shattering the glass all over Todd's restaurant.

"You okay?" Nick asked, sliding in the booth across from her. "You look like you've seen a ghost."

"I'm fine. I was thinking about something." She nodded her head toward the window.

Nick rose and returned to the counter to pick up their order when the skinny teen called out their number.

"So, what's new with the TV crew?" she asked when he returned.

"Catching up on permits. They want some road closures for filming next week. According to the schedule I saw, we've got about two weeks until they wrap things up, and you get your empty lot back."

Jade smiled. "They've been pretty good neighbors. At least, they're quiet." She unwrapped her straw and jammed it in her drink lid.

"No scuttlebutt that I need to know about?" He asked, taking a bite of his fully loaded foot-long.

"I was going to ask you the same question. Any news on either of your investigations?"

"Not really. The preliminary tox screen came back on that actor. The usual suspects didn't show up on it. I think we can pretty much rule out him being on something. The attending physician noticed some symptoms and ordered additional screens for things they don't routinely check for. It's a waiting game until they come back."

"Sounds intentional," Jade whispered.

"Looks that way. And if so, it may be related to the murder. We've stepped up patrols, and the execs are beefing up their security around the actors," he said under his breath.

"I've had a steady stream of foot traffic and sales since the filming began. I'm hoping I can use the shoot at the store in some of my marketing stuff.

I haven't heard any complaints from our business owners, except for, well, Ruby, but that's a different story."

"I've got my guys on OT and called in some backup from neighboring jurisdictions. You'll see more police presence, and we're extending our outer perimeter by blocking off additional areas. We're pushing the fans and reporters back. Ruby's neighbors have been pitching a fit with all the crowds and noise."

"I haven't had any issues around the store. There have been gawkers and people hanging around the temporary fencing, but I haven't noticed any problems. It's like mid-July in a beach town, only chillier." She slipped Chloe a bit of hot dog and balled up her wrapper. "So, what's on the agenda tonight?"

"A nice, quiet walk back to get my truck with my girlfriend. I dunno. I don't have any plans." Nick gathered their trash and dropped it in the receptacle near the door.

"There's always Netflix," Jade winked, following him out the door.

The fall chill put a spring in Chloe's step. She pranced down the sidewalk and sniffed everything in sight. With some coaxing, she followed them around the sawhorse barriers and across the street.

A scream and shouting caused them to pause for a moment to find the source.

Two security guards were half-carrying, half-dragging Peg and Janice out of one of the campers.

"I'll be back," Nick said, hustling across the street.

"Come on, Chloe. Let's see how close we can get." They crossed the street and stood behind the plastic fencing. It was too far away to hear the conversation, but Jade watched as Nick talked to the guards and the two women, who were waving their arms around. Nick nodded a lot and pulled out his phone.

Peg and Janice continued to whirl their arms and talk at the same time.

By the time Jade's legs started to tingle, a squad car from Seaport made a whooping noise and drove around the barricade. The officer parked on the street and left his lights flashing as he jogged over to where the trespassers stood.

About twenty minutes later, the officer handcuffed the women and escorted them to the patrol car. Nick jogged over to Jade and Chloe. "Sorry about this. I need to go with him to book them."

Jade stared at him and the two women in the back of the patrol car.

"The TV folks want to make an example of them. They'll make bail tonight. Don't worry about them. They won't be in custody long, and they shouldn't have snuck in the trailer. The guards have strict orders to insist on having violators charged, especially after what's happened recently."

Jade pursed her lips. A twinge of guilt jolted through her when she remembered that she had mentioned the campers to the two shoppers. "Both of those ladies came in the store earlier today and talked about being big fans of the show. They seemed harmless." She hugged her parka closer to her.

"They still entered someone's temporary residence without permission. I'll call you tomorrow. I don't know how long I'll be, and the press has already got wind of us arresting two granny fans." Nick tilted his head toward a gaggle of reporters snapping pictures and filming the incident. "Not good optics for us. Gotta go. We'll get lots of calls about arresting helpless grandmothers when there's a murderer running loose."

"Talk to you soon." Jade wiggled her fingers at him. "Come on, Chloe." The pair skirted the edge of the growing crowd, trying to avoid the photographers.

Chapter Eighteen

As Jade stepped through her closing routine, her phone echoed in the empty display rooms and distracted her from her thoughts. "Hello, Amy." No reply. Then it rang again. "Hey, what's up?"

"Hi, sorry to bother you. Can you come over here? I have a situation, and I'm not sure what to do." It sounded like Amy was at a rock concert.

"You're at your store?"

"Yep, come to the back door. It'll take forever if you try to come around the front. I don't know how this happened."

"Okay, be there in a sec." She disconnected and gathered her things. "Come on, girl. Let's go see what's going on at the bookstore."

Jade could see and hear the crowd before she got to Hot Diggity Dogs. A sea of people, mostly women and paparazzi, surrounded Mermaid Books, the parking lot, and the street. She picked up Chloe and hustled around the side of the building and up the weather worn, wooden stairs to Amy's apartment.

Before she could knock, the door flew open, and Amy grabbed her arm. "Thanks for coming. I am so stressed."

Amy slammed the door when Jade stepped inside with the little dog.

"What's going on out there?"

"Come with me. I'll show you." She pulled on her arm to lead her through the apartment and down the inside staircase into the store. Jade's eyes took a moment to adjust to the dimness. Raphael sat in one of the cozy reading nooks with his feet on a low table, looking through a magazine. "Hi, Jade. And there's my friend."

Jade set Chloe down. Getting her second wind, the little dog trotted over toward the actor, who picked her up for cuddles.

"What's going on?" Jade asked.

"I stopped by after my scenes to pick up my next read, and a crowd appeared out of nowhere. They've swarmed the place, and I can't get out. But if you have to be trapped somewhere, a bookstore is a perfect spot." He settled down in the chair with Chloe in his lap.

"The crowd is growing by the minute," Amy said, her voice going up an octave. She peeked out the large front display window where her cat, Mr. Darcy, had taken up residence on a stack of Love Channel books. "Oh my stars, they're rushing the porch."

The thick, wooden door shook as a group of women pressed against it and tried to force it open.

"This has gotten out of hand." Amy pulled out her phone and called the sheriff's office. Jade tapped in a quick text to Nick to give him a heads-up.

When Amy disconnected, she glanced around the store for Raphael. "I think he's back far enough that they can't see him. If this gets worse, we may want to sneak him upstairs." An impish grin crossed Amy's face. "Sneaking Raphael Allard into my apartment. I may have to take a selfie to record the event." Amy winked.

Raphael grinned and continued to flip through the magazine.

"Did you tell people you were coming over here?" Jade asked.

"Nah. Olivia has us on lockdown. I can't breathe without asking for her permission. I needed a walk and a break, so I scooted out when no one was looking. Who knew it would turn into a mob so quickly? Maybe I should go out and talk to them?"

"No," Amy and Jade yelled in unison.

Jade took a quick breath. "I think it's best if we keep you out of sight. And if they figure out a way in, be prepared to hightail it up the stairs and lock yourself in the apartment. We may be able to sneak you out the back exit before too many of them notice."

"Has this happened before?" Amy said. "I've never seen anything like it. Who knew there were so many fans in our little town? Or that you were so popular?"

Raphael cut his eyes at her. "We were mobbed at a mall once in Rhode Island, and they had to sneak us out through the loading dock. And it happened at a fan signing in Ohio when the convention center staff shut down the autograph lines. So, it's not anything new. I didn't expect it to happen here. Those other events had advance publicity. I wonder if someone posted something on social media?"

Women and photographers pounded on the door and the front window. Flashes from cameras looked like strobe lights.

"I think you better head upstairs," Amy said. "If they break my door or that window, it's over. It'll be a surge of bodies in the store. We can't fend them off."

As Raphael rose and put Chloe on the floor, sirens approached. The three stared out the front as four police vehicles pushed their way through the crowd.

"Step back," an officer announced through the PA system in his SUV's grill. "Step back and move out of the way of the emergency vehicles. For public safety, this crowd needs to disperse."

The police vehicles inched forward, scattering the women. Seconds later, they pulled into Amy's lot, and the crowd started to move back. More police and two black SUVs arrived. The police, with helmets and nightstick, ordered the people out of the parking lot. The women seemed to comply, while the male photographers continued to capture photos and video.

After what seemed like constant yelling, the noise dissipated, and the crowd disbanded. Jade let out a breath that seemed to take her energy with it. "Wow. You created a mob scene," she said to Raphael.

He grinned. "I'm not sure who leaked it, but it spread quickly. It must be my boy-next-door looks and magnetic personality." He pulled out his phone. "Come on, let's take some selfies to commemorate the bookstore riot. I didn't expect this today."

Amy pulled Jade and Chloe reluctantly into the picture, and they snapped multiple shots until the police banged on the door. Amy undid the locks and held the heavy door for them.

Sebastian and two officers from a nearby town stepped inside and looked around. "Everything okay?" he asked.

Jade nodded. "It was a little frightening for a moment there."

"The crowd is pretty much gone," Sebastian said. "We'll do one final loop of your building to check on things and head out."

"Don't worry. I won't hesitate to call if anything flares up," Amy said as the officers returned to the parking lot.

"Gotta get my books," Raphael said, turning toward the interior of the store.

Footsteps on the wooden porch caused everyone to turn toward the door. Olivia and Wren rushed in with Paige tagging along behind them, her arms loaded with a clipboard, files, and a cardboard box.

"There you are. See what you caused," Olivia planted one hand on her hip and glared at Raphael. "I thought we had an understanding that you would lay low after what's happened." If her stare had been a laser, it would have bored a hole right through Raphael.

"We called the police as soon as the crowd started pounding on the door," Amy said. "They took care of it."

Olivia's countenance softened as she faced the bookstore owner. "Thank you for helping Raphael. This could have turned out much differently without your fast thinking and the police's quick response." Turning to Raphael, "Let's get you back to the B and B and decide what to do next. It might be time to sequester you. We need the rest of the filming to stay on schedule."

Raphael's smile faded, and he looked like he was about to say something but didn't.

"Paige, let Ezra know we're headed back to the Pearl. Wren, do your magic and turn this into some kind of fan extravaganza. Raphael, let's go." Olivia pointed her manicured hand at the door and tapped her boot. "Paige, go now. If you don't get a move on, you may get left behind again," she ordered.

Paige looked around and lumbered down the stairs toward the black SUVs.

"Thanks for letting me hang out here. It was fun." Raphael leaned down and patted Chloe. "I've got to go now. Mom says so." He winked at Amy.

"Text me the titles of the books you wanted, and I'll get them to you," Amy said with a grin, handing him a business card. "I'll be glad to bring them over to Ruby's."

Raphael nodded as Wren stepped toward him. The look on her face sobered, and her lips almost curled in a sneer. "No sneaking off. Or I'll leak another story about where you're going. You can't win this game. I've got you beat, and you won't fly under the radar as long as I'm around."

A look of surprise crossed his face, and he masked it with a charming smile. "Thanks for getting my fans together so quickly. It's nice to be loved. Glad to see you doing your job."

"Don't test me," Wren said, turning on her stilettos and marching toward the waiting vehicles.

Chapter Nineteen

Patti zoomed into the store's office and dropped her purse on the counter. "Did you hear about the stir Raphael caused yesterday? I wish I had been there. A mob right here in Mermaid Bay!"

Jade looked up from her spreadsheet and held up her phone.

Patti's eyes widened, and she reached for the phone. Scrolling through the pictures, she said, "You were trapped with Raphael Allard. How exciting! And romantic, if you weren't already in love with our handsome sheriff. Speaking of which, Nick looks cute in this one with Chloe."

"The thing at the bookstore was mostly scary. Fans kept storming the porch and banging on Amy's front door and her windows. And the reporters were everywhere. Thankfully, Sebastian and his backup arrived in time to move them off the property."

"I told you the Love Channel was popular with lots of different age groups. There are fan groups, chatrooms, and blogs. And, of course, Raphael is their most popular heartthrob, so he's always at the center of everything. This is sooooo exciting."

"He was kinda subdued yesterday. He was reading a magazine in Amy's store. Oh, and he and Chloe have bonded."

"Girl, you've got exceptional taste." Patti leaned over and scratched the pudgy dog behind the ears.

The bells on the front door rang, and Patti sprang into action.

Jade zoned out, staring at her laptop screen. Wren's comment to Raphael yesterday kept popping up in her thoughts. She had caused the mob by releasing Raphael's whereabouts on social media. *Reckless and vindictive. And how did she know where he was. Obviously, he wasn't adept at sneaking out.*

Before Jade could ponder the reasoning behind the leak further, her phone rang. "Hey, Ruby. What's up?" *I wonder what the TV folks have done now?*

"Sorry to call you again about these Love Channel guests, but I need to talk to you. They've moved Raphael to another location for his own protection, and I overheard Ezra and Olivia talking about moving everyone out to a larger, safer hotel. Jade, this will ruin the Pearl. I don't need this right now."

"I'll be there in a sec." Jade disconnected and stuck her head through the doorway.

"Hey, I'm headed over to see Ruby. Be back in a bit."

"No problem. Say hi to Raphael and Elle for me," Patti gushed.

The ride over felt like an eternity. Jade had to navigate through a sea of bodies, all trying to get a glimpse of something at the Pearl. She parked next to Mrs. Vanderbeek's yard again and jogged over to Ruby's place. As she crossed in front of the former Victorian home, reporters called out to her, and cameras flashed.

Jade hustled around to the side, and Ruby met her at the door. "Thanks for coming over again, Jade. This has gone from bad to worse." After closing the kitchen door, Ruby continued, "They moved him to an undisclosed location for his safety, and now they're talking about pulling out the rest of them. I heard the guards talking. They're taking them to a big hotel in Williamsburg."

"Ruby, that crowd was scary yesterday. We were afraid they were going to break Amy's windows and door. Maybe moving them is for the best. At least for a little while. They aren't canceling their reservations, are they?"

"No, but we didn't talk about money. Actually, we didn't talk about anything. They just moved him out. I can't afford the damage to my reputation right now or a refund on his room, for that matter. The bad press will damage my business forever. Having a TV crew in town was supposed to be a boon. It's been nothing but a boondoggle." Ruby let out a long puff of air.

Jade patted her shoulder, but before she could reply, something in black zipped across the kitchen window. The figure was hunched over and too big to be some kind of animal. "Wait a sec. I'll be right back. You may want to get security."

Concern flashed across Ruby's face as she dashed out to the foyer.

Jade ran out the door and across the yard after someone in a black hoodie heading for the trellis. She gritted her teeth and launched herself forward. She tackled the tall figure before he could start his climb.

The guy landed partially in the flowerbed with a loud umph and Jade on his back.

The guy bucked like a bronco and rolled over. Jade tried to pin him down again by planting her knees on his legs and putting her hands on his torso as she tried to keep him on the ground. He grabbed both of her wrists in one hand and put his other hand on her waist like he was about to chuck her off.

"What are you doing?" he sputtered, trying to wriggle out of her grasp. "Let me up before the reporters show up. Or worse, Olivia or one of her evil minions."

A spark of recognition. Jade hesitated. "Raphael?"

Flashes blinded her as the paparazzi snapped closeups of her on top of the actor in the grass.

"Hey, hey. Off the property," one of the TV crew's security guards yelled. "Now. Before I call the cops." He thundered toward a gaggle of photographers, and they hightailed it through Ruby's rosebushes and around the house.

The guard lifted Jade off of the actor's back. Raphael rose slowly and dusted himself off.

"What were you doing back here?" Jade asked. She brushed dirt and grass off her clothes.

The guard pulled a twig out of her hair and handed it to her. *Wow. Those pictures will look lovely. Christmas card material, not.*

Raphael interrupted her thoughts. "I didn't like being in the hotel all by myself, so I checked out and took an Uber over here. I figured if the reporter could climb up the trellis, so could I. Nobody would be the wiser." The actor turned toward Jade, "Did you play rugby or something in high school?"

Jade shook her head. "No. Sorry about that. I thought it was another intruder trying to sneak in Ruby's place."

"Well, you've got a mean wallop. You knocked the air out of me." Raphael smiled his dazzling, megawatt smile, and for a moment, a flutter of excitement zapped Jade.

"Come on." The guard grabbed Raphael's elbow. "We need to go talk to Wren, so she can counteract this. I'm sure you're persona non grata this afternoon."

Raphael waggled his head and rolled his eyes. "Wren and Olivia are rarely happy. They both need to lighten up a bit. They'll get over it when the next crisis comes along."

The guard guided him toward the back door. "You know they don't like a stink. And you have a way of keeping things stirred up."

Raphael smiled. "The photos are hitting social media right about now." He winked at Jade and followed the guard inside.

Panic shot through her body like a bolt of lightning. *How am I going to explain those photographs?* What would Nick say? Would it affect her shop? Maybe, she needed to talk to Wren, too. She wiped some additional stray blades of grass off her clothes and tried to pat down her unruly hair.

Jade opened the kitchen door and spotted Ruby listening through a crack in the other door to a conversation in the foyer. Before Jade could speak, Ruby turned and gave her the universal five-year-old's sign to be quiet. Jade leaned forward to hear her better.

The women scooted closer, so they could both get a glimpse of Raphael and the backs of Wren and one of the guards through the small opening.

"It's for your own good. You need to be away from the crowds for a while. The guards will take you back to the hotel until you have to be on set," Wren said, stepping closer to Raphael.

"No. I don't like being isolated. I like it here. I'm staying." Raphael's lips formed a straight line, and he crossed his arms.

"Ezra's is blowing a gasket right about now," Wren said.

"I don't care. It's only for a couple of weeks." Raphael turned and headed toward the stairs. "And have someone get my bags. They're out back near the flowerbed."

"Now, if I could get him to post that he likes the Pearl better than that fancy hotel to his kajillion fans," Ruby whispered. "I better go get his bags before someone walks off with them."

Jade whispered as Ruby closed the door to the common area. "Are you really going to ask him to post something?"

"Use this to my advantage. Raphael is my new ally. When I take his bags upstairs, I'll try to convince him to tell the world how great it is here. Wish me luck."

Jade flashed two thumbs up. *I hope nothing comes of those photos of me with him.* Jade chewed her bottom lip.

"Nick will understand. It wasn't what it looked like. You weren't rolling around in the grass with Raphael. For fun," Ruby said.

Jade closed her eyes for a moment, trying to will away the incident. She took a deep breath and headed back to the store. *How bad could it be? Would it alienate Raphael's fans? I'm holding my breath, waiting for the blowback.*

No sooner had Jade stepped foot in 'Tis the Season, Patti and Chloe rushed her. "Is this really you? What happened? And why were you on top of Raphael?" Patti asked.

Jade felt the blood rush to her cheeks. She grabbed Patti's phone and stared. She opened her mouth, but nothing but a squeak came out.

Then her phone started alerting, staccato style. "It's not what it looks like," Jade said softly.

"I know. I was giving you a hard time. There's got to be a reasonable explanation. Hey, it's already gotten thousands of views and shares. Everyone wants to know the identity of Raphael's new mystery woman."

"Ruby said they had moved Raphael out to a hotel, and she was worried that the rest of her guests were planning to leave, too. And that it would affect future reservations. When we were talking in the kitchen, I saw someone sneak across the backyard."

"And being Nancy Drew, you went after him. Did you tackle Raphael Allard?" Patti's eyes sparkled like one of those Saturday morning cartoon characters with stars in her eyes.

"Yes," Jade whispered. "I guess the photographers got the shots when I was wrestling with him on the ground."

"My boss. The new Love Channel mystery woman and secret ninja. You've got to figure out how to capitalize on this. Maybe you need a press conference. Or a publicist."

Jade tried not to roll her eyes. "I'm hoping it'll be a blip."

"Hope is not a strategy. You need to get in front of this."

"I've got too much going on around here to worry about it." She glanced at her phone. Forty-five unanswered texts and thirty new emails. *Will this day ever end?*

Chapter Twenty

Lorelei and Neville the Devil cat waltzed in as Jade poured her second cup of coffee of the morning and stifled a yawn.

"Howling all night again?" her aunt asked.

"Hardly," Jade replied. She had spent most of her free time fielding calls and texts from friends who had seen her escapade with Raphael and wanted all the details.

"Well, hello," her aunt said, heading for the coffee machine. "So, how's it feel to be the envy of all the Love Channel fans?"

Jade stuck her tongue out.

"That's fabulous. Can I get a selfie with the mystery woman? You know I'm teasing. It was fun to see you all over the internet. I heard your romp in Ruby's grass even got a quick mention on *Entertainment Tonight.* And they knew your name. Too bad we couldn't see your 'Tis the Season' logo on your shirt. All I could see was your puffy parka."

"Thanks. I had grass and a stick in my hair. And it's not what you think."

"Tsk. Tsk. What did Nick have to say about it?"

"We haven't had a chance to talk. He's been kinda busy. Someone was sneaking around Ruby's backyard, and I stopped him. Unfortunately, it turned out to be Raphael, and the paparazzi captured it for all the world to see."

Her aunt let a giggle slip. "Don't worry about Nick. He'll think it's funny."

"Doubtful. I think his patience with the TV crew is wearing thin. But the good news is the store's online comments and orders have almost doubled."

"See, something positive did come out of it. Let me get settled, and I'll

116

help you with those."

Midway through packing the orders, Jade's phone rang.

Before she got out a greeting, Patti blurted, "Cheese and crackers, Jade. They outed you as the mystery woman. Your face is everywhere. And they're calling you the Christmas Lady. You're famous!"

"What?" Jade sputtered.

"Here, I'll text you some links. I am soooooo excited for you. I've got to tell everyone that I work for the mystery woman." Patti clicked off before Jade could protest.

"What?" Jade repeated, clicking on the gossip page links Patti sent.

"Jade, what is going on?" Lorelei said, setting a basket of ornaments on the counter.

"Patti just called." Jade sighed. "And one of these sites is promising more scintillating photos at a big reveal tomorrow."

"What else did you do?" Lorelei asked.

"Nothing," Jade said, a little too loudly.

Her phone started alerting, and both of the store lines lit up.

"I'll take care of the store phones." Lorelei headed to the lobby.

Her aunt finished packing the online orders as Jade plowed through questions from friends and acquaintances. *This is out of my comfort zone.*

She took a break and flipped her phone over. *Time to concentrate on work stuff. Stuff that matters.*

After updating her newsletter with some recent photos that didn't include Raphael, she checked on the store's website. Eighty-two comments since yesterday on her post about the filming in town. Scanning to the bottom, one submitted by "Broken Hearted" caught her eye. "Leave him alone, you floozy. You'll be sorry. I'm coming after you."

Resisting the urge to delete it, she took a screenshot and checked to see if she could find out any information about the account. Not having any luck, she reached for her phone. *It's probably nothing, but maybe she should call Nick.*

Jade hesitated, closing her eyes to concentrate on both sides of the argument going on in her head. Delete it and forget about it. Just a troll. Or was it? Could it be more ominous? She picked up her cell again.

After listening to his professional sheriff voicemail, she said, "Hey, there. Sorry to bother you. Some weirdness is going on. I'm getting some comments online, and one feels like a threat. I wanted to talk to you about it. Call me when you can. I'm sure it's nothing..." Jade disconnected. She let out a breath that puffed out both of her cheeks.

"What's up?" Lorelei asked, bringing another load of filled orders to be packed. "This pile came in while we were filling the others."

"I'm hoping it's nothing. I got a ton of comments on the website. One was from some troll, but it felt weird. I left Nick a message. I'm a big girl. I should have deleted it and moved on."

"No, not necessarily. Let's see what he recommends," her aunt said, handing her the basket and the order forms. "I put the store phone on the auto-attendant. Most of the calls were to talk to you about Raphael. It'll be easier to delete the junk from voicemail later. I'll go round up the rest of the items for this set of orders and be back in a bit to box these."

Jade nodded. "I've had negative feedback before. I don't know why this comment bothers me so much. It makes me feel like I should be looking over my shoulder."

"And why have you been avoiding Nick?" Her aunt raised one stylized eyebrow. Before her niece could protest, Lorelei continued, "If he gets upset over anything, it'll be you chasing down and tackling a trespasser. Not the silly rumors about you and Raaaaa-phael."

"I just called him," Jade muttered under her breath.

"If the threat bothered you, it may be worth looking into. Remember the notes and the voodoo dolls last summer?"

Jade shivered at the memories of Emory Jessup's murder. "You're right. I'll let you know what Nick says. In the meantime, it looks like we'll need another couple of bins for today's delivery driver."

Lorelei winked and disappeared to hunt down the remaining ornaments.

Jade hauled the final bin to the lobby for the afternoon pickup, heavy footsteps pounded on the porch. Nick pushed the door open, and Jade smiled at her beau in his sheriff's uniform. His frame filled almost the entire doorway. Taking off his Smokey Bear hat, he said, "Hey, Jade. What's going on? Any other threatening communications?"

"No," she shook her head. "Just the one."

"I sent it to our computer forensic guys. They'll do their best to trace it. When they're done, you can delete it. Just hang tight for now."

"Thanks." She looked up and caught his intense stare.

She stared back, and he cracked a smile first. "Nice photos. Can I get this one autographed?" He handed her a shot of her surprised face on top of Raphael.

"Not funny."

"Oh, I think it is. And what were you doing chasing someone around Ruby's?" He snickered and set the photo on the counter.

"She was concerned about the TV execs moving the actors to a hotel. While we were talking, I saw someone in a black hoodie traipse through her backyard."

"And you gave chase."

"I had to. The guards weren't around."

A grin crept across his face. "I wouldn't expect any less. You are always in the middle of things. Promise me you'll be careful and call me the minute something smells hinky."

"That a law enforcement term?" She pulled out a black marker from behind the counter and autographed the photo with her best John Hancock signature. "For your collection. And thanks for checking on me."

He cupped her face in both of his hands. "I love you, and I want you to be safe. And I know telling you to stay out of it isn't going to work." He kissed her, and her anger and embarrassment melted away.

"Get a room," Lorelei said, breezing through the lobby. "And by all means, don't let me interrupt." She hustled to the back office. "Good to see you, Nick."

"Nice to see you too, Lorelei." Nick kissed Jade again and sent a spark through her all the way to her toes. "Call me if anything, and I mean, anything looks or smells fishy. Got it?"

"Ten-four," Jade replied with a two-fingered salute.

"And stop chasing those TV stars," he said with a wink, picking up his autographed photo.

"See, I told you he wouldn't be upset," rang out from the back after the front door closed.

"Now, to figure out what to do with all these calls and posts," Jade said, returning to her desk.

"Hey, as long as the orders keep coming, don't sweat it. Maybe you could auction off some of those mystery woman and Raphael photos for charity," her aunt added.

"That's an idea. I should be getting the cast to autograph stuff. I should have thought of that earlier." Jade's enthusiasm dimmed slightly when thoughts of the Facebook post crept back into her thoughts.

"What's the matter?" her aunt asked.

"I'm hoping the comment by that creepy person was a one-off. I don't want to egg on any copycats. I took a 'how to handle trolls on social media' class once, and the expert said to respond professionally if it wasn't something illegal or immoral."

Jade pulled out her phone and typed, "He's all yours. My calendar is full, and there's no time for any new romances. I'm busy with all the orders from my great customers." Jade smiled and pressed save.

Chapter Twenty-One

Jade and Chloe stopped in mid-step as they rounded the corner and noticed the crowd around 'Tis the Season. Throngs of people encircled her store's porch, and some of them spilled out onto Neptune Road and around the lot filled with campers. It looked like the bookstore all over again, except no one was advancing on her front door.

She picked up Chloe and jogged around to the back as text alerts sounded from the phone in her purse. Jade flipped on the lights, but left the front door locked. Remembering her phone, she pulled it out and scrolled through the texts and emails. It seems that gossip website was teasing again to release some more must-see pictures. *Please let them not be of me. I'm not ready for fame's spotlight.*

Jade dashed off some quick responses to friends who were concerned about her and her new-found celebrity and to those who asked her to introduce them to Raphael.

Red and blue lights from outside bounced around her lobby. She and Chloe peeked out the front window. Two Mermaid Bay Sheriff's SUVs moved slowly into her parking lot. The crowd parted ahead of them like the Red Sea, giving Nosy Nell clear access to the store's porch, where she staked out a spot next to a flowerbed. The local reporter marched toward the front like she was on a red carpet in Hollywood.

A deputy slammed the driver's side door of his vehicle while Nick reached in his and pulled out the radio's microphone. "May I have your attention? You all are blocking traffic, and some of the residents aren't able to exit their driveways. You cannot impede traffic."

Mumbles rose, and the crowd slowly moved toward the sidewalk. A woman in a pink parka and matching furry hat made her way through the crowd toward Nick. She said something, and he nodded and handed her the mic. When she turned, Jade spotted the signature blood-red lips and nails of the show's publicist. *Wren was out and about early this morning.*

"Hello, Love Channel fans. It's so great to see you all out here. Like the Sheriff said, some of the residents can't get to work, and even worse, you're blocking the crew in. Filming is scheduled today outside the pier, and we've got to get there and set up. We need to move our trucks and equipment out of the lot next door. If we can't, it could delay the debut of *My Coastal Valentine*. And nobody wants that, right?"

A steady stream of rumbles emanated from the crowd, and groups of people started walking down the street.

"Filming's over there, and it's outside, so you can watch. If you head over there now, you should be able to stake out a primo viewing spot behind the yellow tape." Wren waved her arms, and most of the people headed toward the pier.

Nick climbed the steps as Jade opened the door and scooted Chloe back with one hand.

"Thanks, Nick. That was quite the surprise when I opened this morning."

"Not a problem. Some of your neighbors weren't too happy. We got quite a bunch of calls this morning, and then Olivia sent Wren over when the crew couldn't get out. You're always in the middle of stuff, aren't you? It's kinda fun to be linked to all these celebrities."

Jade stared at him, and before she could zap back with a smart retort, Nick grinned. "And I wouldn't have it any other way. Just be careful and try not to stir up any crazy excitement. All my guys are on OT as it is." He winked and held out his hand.

"A handshake?"

"I'm on official business this trip, and hey, I don't want to be the one that comes between you and Raphael. There are way too many photographers out there. That's all I need is to be the subject of the next town council meeting or, worse, to show up in the tabloids as the other man. We try to fly under the radar at the Sheriff's Office. I'll call you later." Nick saluted and returned to his vehicle. Jade made a face at his back.

When the crowd had finally retreated like seagulls running from an approaching wave, Jade unlocked the door and took the phone off auto-attendant. She blew out a puff of air that fluttered her bangs and listened to the voicemails.

After deleting most of the messages from people who wanted to know about her fling with Raphael, she headed to her desk. Trying not to be distracted by all the gossip sites and social media, she paused to print the overnight orders while her mocha surprise brewed.

A little before nine, the bells on the door jingled, and Chloe ran to the dividing door.

"Hey, there, famous lady," Patti sang. "You are all over the internet. This is exciting. And to think, I knew you when. I wonder if I can put all those birthday cards with your autographs on eBay?" Patti tee-hee-heed all the way to the back of the store.

"It's been exciting, all right. Nick and a deputy had to disperse a crowd out front this morning. The neighbors, including the TV crew who couldn't get their trucks out, weren't all that pleased at our newfound fame. But if this is a byproduct, I'll take it." Jade handed her six pages of overnight orders. "Can you start on these? I'll be done with this and payroll in a bit, and I can start boxing and labeling."

"Wow. I think you've hit a record with this one. They always say that any publicity is good." Patti winked and picked up two baskets for the orders.

After packing and labeling for hours, Jade returned to her computer. The gossip posts about her and Raphael seemed to have multiplied by the hour. Growing tired of reading the comments, she stopped. This whole thing was like a tsunami, and she felt overwhelmed. She switched to watching puppy videos.

Patti interrupted her moment of dog Zen when she rushed in. "Did you see the tweet? Do you think this is just the first of many?" She let out a squeak that sounded like a toy whistle.

Jade felt a sharp pain behind her eyes. She rubbed her temples and closed her eyes for a moment. "More of what?"

Patti's eyes widened. "That one site that the dead reporter worked for is teasing that more scintillating pictures are coming tonight. Everybody is jabbering about what they could be. Odds are on you and Raphael. They think he's having a whirlwind affair while he's filming in Mermaid Bay. And they want to know if you're planning to move to LA with him."

"He may be, but it's not with me. And no to California. I'm a Mermaid Bay girl." Jade wracked her brain to remember any other photos she'd taken with the actor that might have been misrepresented. "I took some photos with him when I met him, and we took selfies at Amy's the day the mob appeared. I can't imagine what that gossip site has. I hope it's not my middle school braceface picture."

"This is exciting. How much would all this publicity cost if you paid for it? Sales are spiking, so bonus." Patti patted her arm.

Jade made a face. "You always see the glass half-full. Right now, I'm wishing they'd forget about me for a while."

"I'm doing a wine and paint class tonight. Wanna go to get your mind off of things? It'll be fun."

Jade smiled. "Thanks for the invitation. But I think Chloe and I need a quiet evening at home."

"If you change your mind, we'd love to have you join us. Plus, all the girls want to hear about your fling with you-know-who," Patti said as the jingle bells on the front door sounded. She bustled off, and snippets of her conversation with the guests about the Love Channel drifted back into the office.

Jade finished all the tasks she could think of. Staying busy helped her not think of Raphael, the crazy fans, and all those gossipy websites.

She paused from her busy work when Patti yelled, "You can't go back there. No, really, that's for staff." Nell huffed into the back room.

"Jade, gotta minute?" the reporter yelled.

The throbbing behind Jade's eyes started again. "Sure, Nell."

"Need a favor," the woman in jeans and a gray sweatshirt with her signature yellow Crocs with fuzzy pink socks said, plopping down in the captain's

124

chair across from Jade's desk.

"What can I do for you?" Jade closed her laptop's lid and glanced around her desk to ensure that any document that the local reporter could use in a story was out of sight.

"Everyone is trying to get an interview with you. And I was hoping you'd give me a couple of minutes and a head start on the competition. You know, a professional courtesy. We've known each other for a long time." The plump woman raised one eyebrow and stared across the desk.

Jade hoped Nell didn't hear her sigh. "What do you want to know?"

"Oh great," Nell said. Her eyes sparkled as she pulled out her phone and set it on the edge of the desk near Jade. "Tell me how you and Raphael met."

"I met him at Ruby's when I took welcome baskets to her guests from my store, 'Tis the Season. And then I met him again at the reception at the B and B."

"The same B and B where the reporter was found murdered?" Nell sounded like she was revealing some big state secret.

"Yes. That one. But the murder didn't happen that night."

"Everyone in town knows you've been dating our sheriff. Sheriff Nicholas Driscoll. Is he aware of this fling with the actor Raphael Allard?"

"Nell," Jade huffed. "There is no fling with Raphael Allard. And you know I'm dating Sheriff Driscoll and that we've known each other since middle school. The Raphael thing is all a big misunderstanding that's been blown out of proportion. It's a big nothing burger."

"Your history with the sheriff sounds like a high school sweetheart tale. Are you willing to risk that for a fleeting moment with a Love Channel star?"

"Nell, for the last time. There is no fling and no romance with Raphael Allard. You want a scoop. Here's the behind-the-scenes story of those photos."

Nell leaned forward in her seat. "Go on." She looked at Jade like Chloe looked at bacon.

"I was at the B and B one day talking with Ruby Ellis, the proprietor of the Pearl, and someone was sneaking around the backyard." Jade paused and took a deep breath. "We ran outside, and I chased after the figure and tackled him while Ruby called the security guards. I thought it was another intruder. I guess the paparazzi got the pictures while all this was going on. There was no romance. And really, no story. It was all a big misunderstanding."

"Why was Raphael sneaking around in the backyard?" Nell asked, settling back in the chair.

"He was locked out of his room, and he was trying to climb the trellis to get back in." *Well, that could be stretched to be true.*

Nell laughed, and Jade quickly added, "But please let your readers know that Raphael and some of the really nosy reporters have tried it. The trellis wasn't meant for climbing, and Ruby's roses are getting trampled in all this. People should be respectful of private property."

"What else would you like to tell the readers out there?" Nell asked.

"We're excited to have the Love Channel in town and to share Mermaid Bay with all of its fans. If you come by, please visit our local merchants and make plans to come back next summer."

"Jade, I owe you one," Nell said, retrieving her phone. "You're helping me get noticed. Just do me a favor, and don't talk to any of the reporters until I can get this out there. Can I go out your back door? I don't want to deal with that crowd right now."

Jade held the door for her. When the door shut behind the reporter, Chloe looked up from her bed.

"Thanks for all the help. You left me hanging. You could have come over and been totally adorable to distract her." Chloe looked around and returned to her nap.

"Sorry about that, Jade," Patti said, zooming in from the lobby. "She waited until I had a line of customers, and she slipped back here."

"Not a problem. She wanted a favor, and I gave her a little scoop. She seemed okay with it. She doesn't have me packing to run off with Raphael when the story comes out. I wonder if I should warn Nick."

Patti laughed. "Everyone who knows you knows that Nick is the one. We've known for a long time. But isn't it nice to think for a minute that you're the 'It' girl that all the fans are talking about?"

"It's flattering, but I prefer my life here. I can live without all the paparazzi and gossip." I'm a beach girl who owns a Christmas store." Jade's voice trailed off.

"I've straightened up out there and jotted down some of the areas that need restocking. Here's the list."

"Thanks. I'm about ready to pack up. I'm hoping the reporters will get tired of me and move on to something else."

Jade's phone dinged with a text from Nick. **Nell wants a statement from me on your lurid affair.**

Which one? Just kidding, she replied.

Don't worry. I said no comment. I won't spill your secrets.

Thanks. I hope she doesn't take that as a confirmation, she typed. She rolled her eyes, and that made her head hurt worse.

Chapter Twenty-Two

The next morning, Jade and Chloe drove the short distance to the office and parked around back. After tossing and turning all night, she was in no mood to talk to reporters. The pair slipped in the back and opened the store quietly.

After coffee and an instant oatmeal, Jade started to feel better. Having caught up on all the administrative work, she busied herself with watching French bulldog videos on the internet.

Jade walked to the lobby when the bells on the front door sounded.

"Morning, y'all," Patti said, juggling an oversized purse and a half-empty platter of cookies.

"Good morning." Jade stared at the picked-over platter.

"Oh, I tried out some new heart cookie recipes, including that jam one you did. I thought I'd share them with the reporters out there. Jax and Stevie ate most of them."

Jade frowned slightly, and Patti continued, "They're freelance photographers. They've been following the Love Channel actors around every time there's a filming. Stevie said that Elle and Raphael are always fodder for stories."

"Nell had the same thought about me."

Patti let out a belly laugh. "You are too funny. Did you see what she published?"

"No. I haven't checked the local stuff today. Jade and Patti pulled out their phones.

"I don't see anything on the *Beach Comber*'s website, but they usually

128

publish once a week during the off-season," Patti said.

"I wonder if she sold it to a bigger outlet?" Jade asked.

"This could be her big break," Patti said. "She's been trying for years to have a story picked up by somebody outside of Mermaid Bay. Just think, you could have been her first giant news story."

"Yay," Jade said, straightening the stack of plastic shopping baskets by the counter. "Glad I could help." She scrunched her face.

"Hey, do you hear that?" Patti asked.

Jade shook her head. "No. Just the quiet."

"That's what I mean. It seems weird, huh," Patti said.

They stole a look out the front window. The gaggle of reporters and fans had thinned out.

"Interesting," Jade said. "The next big thing must have come along."

"I'll text Stevie and see," Patti said.

Jade was about to comment on her part-timer's new paparazzi friend, but she let it pass.

"Oooh, that explains it," Patti said, reading some texts that popped up on her phone. "Stevie said new scandalous photos dropped, and everyone's trying to get a comment for a follow-up."

Jade's pulse raced like a snare drum.

"He sent me a link. Let's see." Patti tapped on her phone. "Wowzers. I can't believe it." Patti leaned on the front counter.

"What?" Jade reached for her friend's phone.

"It's Elle. Elle was who they were all talking about. I don't know if this is good or bad for her. But it's great for you. That gossip site where the dead reporter worked published a story about Elle and her security guard boyfriend. Love Channel fans will be heartbroken that she and Raphael won't reunite in real life. Folks have moved on to the latest tale. You are yesterday's news."

Jade let out a long breath that sounded like air leaking from a faulty beachball. "Wow. Raphael will be okay. He said that their thing was on again, off again. It didn't sound like any kind of commitment. Plus, he's always got someone in the wings."

"From the hundreds of comments already, the fans seem happy for Elle and thrilled that Raphael is back on the market," Patti remarked.

"Another fun day in Hollywoodland." Jade ran her hands through her curls. "I'm glad the story wasn't about me."

By the time Jade returned to her desk and pulled up the full story on Elle, she heard a tap, tap, tapping on the back door.

"Hi, Bernie. What brings you by so early this morning?" Jade held the door for him.

"I've got some videos I want to post." The Santa look-alike waved his phone in front of her.

Jade's eyes widened, and she stifled her retort.

"And I want to know how to get them on the internet thingy, so my grandkids can see them. The Twittertok stuff is the only way I get to see pictures of them." Bernie sighed.

She exhaled and smiled. "Sure. Where do you want to post them?"

"In the cloud or the sky or wherever my family will see them, I guess. I have a couple of videos with me and Elle and some pictures. My grandkids like TikTok, I think. I have no idea what that is."

"Are you on Facebook?"

The Santa double nodded. "And Instagram." He handed her his phone.

"Okay, you go to either site and create a post."

Bernie stared at her.

"Okay, we'll start with the video. Open Instagram. What do you want to say about it? And who's in it?"

"Me and Elle. She kissed me. I'm hoping to go viral," he said with a wink.

"Okay. How about if I type, 'check out who's on my nice list this year?' And we can tag Elle and the show, so they might see it." She typed and did a quick proofread. "Are you okay with that?"

He nodded. "Then click that button, and it's live. You do the same thing for each one you want to post."

"Okay, let's do the pictures next."

"Are they all related? You can do one post with a bunch or each one individually."

CHAPTER TWENTY-TWO

"They're all me and Elle," he replied. "She's a cutie pie."

After a staccato of taping on his phone, Jade said, "There. All done on Instagram. Now, let's put them on Facebook. What do you want to say about the pictures?"

"I dunno. Something like meeting with Elle to review her list this year."

Jade typed away as Bernie stared over her shoulder. "And you can put those on your Santa website, too. This one is really cute. Can I send it to myself for the store's website?" she asked.

"Of course. Just don't forget to tag me." Bernie winked and looked at his posts. "Comments are already starting to come in. I've got to go and show the guys. And call my daughter to tell the kids to check it out. Thanks, Jade. I'll figure out the TickyTocky thing later."

After an unusually quiet afternoon, Jade and Patti packed up and headed out. Patti to yoga class and Jade to see if there was anything in her refrigerator that she wanted for dinner.

Not finding anything interesting at home, she and Chloe settled on the couch with a bag of microwave popcorn to scan the gossip sites. The paparazzi and the fans had moved on.

A vehicle door slammed in the driveway, and Chloe yipped and dashed for the door.

Nick stood on her front porch with a dozen red roses and a cheesecake.

"Hey," she said, opening the door. "I thought you were working tonight."

"I needed a break and thought I'd drop by. These are for you."

"They're gorgeous. What's the occasion?" she asked.

"No occasion. Just thought I'd surprise you."

Jade threw one arm around him to hug him, and a flash distracted them.

Patti's friend Stevie waved and hustled down the street. His camera and oversized lens bounced as he jogged.

"You sad about not being the story of the day?" Nick asked with a grin as he followed her inside.

"Nah. It's kind of a relief. I'll leave the drama to Elle and her pals. Though that photo of you and me and the roses may cause a stir. We may be back in the spotlight."

"Mystery woman jilts Raphael twice," Nick said as he kissed her.

Chapter Twenty-Three

J ade and Chloe enjoyed the quiet morning walk to the store. She and
Nick ate cheesecake and watched a football game on TV until he got
an emergency call about a car accident on the outskirts of town. *I bet
dates with Raphael weren't this interesting. With Nick on call, I never know how
long my date will be or what crazy thing will pop up.*

With no reporters or fans outside the store, Jade busied herself with the
online orders.

Midway through her second cup of coffee, her phone rang. "Hi, Ruby.
What's up?"

"I seem to call you too much about this mess that never ends. Sorry. I hope
you're having a great day." Before Jade could comment, Ruby continued,
"As you probably know, that gossip site released pictures of Elle and her
bodyguard, and the reporters are swarming again outside."

Not seeing the connection, Jade asked, "The outing of Elle and her
boyfriend was the hot story they kept teasing about. We should all be off the
hook."

"Are you kidding? And if the Elle thing's not enough to bring out all the
cockroaches to surround my place, some of those photos were taken from
inside the Pearl. Olivia and Wren want to talk to me at nine. It can't be good.
They think we're snapping pictures of our guests and invading their privacy.
Jade, I'm about to lose it. I know you're busy, but this takes the cake. We
have always prided ourselves in our hospitality and professionalism." The
older woman sighed into the phone.

Jade scanned the internet for the scandalous photos. "I'll be over in a few."

133

She disconnected and thumbed through the photos of Elle and the guard. Several were of the inside of the bed and breakfast. Jade printed them and created a quick "be back in an hour" sign for the front door.

She locked the doors. "You're in charge, Chloe. I'll hurry." She folded the photos and put them in her coat pocket, and locked the back door behind her. Jade looped around the crowd in front of Ruby's B and B, where cars and news vans filled every available space on both sides of the street.

Josie answered her knock at the kitchen door. "Come on in. Mom's in the library with the TV folks." Jade followed her down the hallway toward the voices. Josie and Jade stopped in the hallway and watched Ruby and the three women through the open doorway.

"I want to know how someone got in to take those photos." Wren punctuated her words by pointing one of her red talons at Olivia, Ruby, and Paige. "You two were responsible for keeping the talent sequestered and safe here. And you, I thought you valued privacy." Wren's glare at Ruby looked nasty.

A storm crossed Olivia's face. "Paige, it was your job to watch over Elle, Raphael, and the rest of the team."

"I can't be everywhere at the same time. I checked on them all the time and answered their every beck and call. These fourteen-hour days are killing me. It's stupid for you to think you can keep piling on the tasks. Plus, I'm not even staying here. I can't be everywhere and watch everyone." Paige sputtered as she struggled to get out the few remaining words of her sentence.

"And you," Olivia said, pointing again at Ruby. "Photographers and riffraff are finding their way inside your place. I thought you said this was a safe establishment. Don't your locks work?"

Ruby pursed her lips.

"Excuse me," Jade interrupted, pulling out the folded copies of the photos from her pocket. "These were taken with a high-powered lens. I don't think the photographer was in Elle's room or even inside the Pearl."

Wren shrugged one shoulder. "It doesn't really matter." Then she turned to Paige. "You had one job. And you blew it. Now I have to spend hours cleaning up this mess. The executive producer is not happy. And he knows whose fault this is." She stared daggers at Paige, who fidgeted. "Ezra and I will do what we can to smooth this over. Thanks for another headache."

As Wren turned, Paige picked up a large leatherbound book from the side table and stared at it for a second. Then she tossed it at the shorter woman.

The publicist stepped back and let the book land on the area rug with a thud. "See that. She attacked me. Your days here are numbered, missy." Wren stomped off in her designer shoes.

"I didn't throw it at her. It slipped," Paige whimpered.

"Pick it up and make sure you didn't damage it," Olivia ordered. "And go check on Ezra. I'll take care of Elle. Move. Move it now!"

Olivia waited for Paige to exit the front door, and then she hurried up the stairs.

"Thanks," Ruby mouthed. "This has been an adventure. For a romance channel that broadcasts happy love stories, their employees are always in a kerfuffle about something."

"No problem. Can I help you with anything?" Jade asked.

"You helped tremendously with those photos. I can't thank you enough." Ruby shook her head. "I'll try not to bother you again for such meaningless stuff."

Jade smiled. "I'll let myself out."

"Thanks again," Ruby called to her back.

On her way down the stairs, a hunch wiggled its way into her thoughts. She wended her way through the crowd of reporters to Mrs. Fairchild's pale yellow, three-story Victorian across the street.

Jade climbed the cement steps and pressed the doorbell that chimed Beethoven's "Fur Elise" and looked across the street at the Pearl. *Nice view, even with the leaves that are still on the big trees.*

"What now?" Mrs. Fairchild asked, jerking open the front door. "Oh, hi, Jade. I'm sorry. I thought you were one of those infernal reporters. They won't leave me alone. What can I do for you?" The older woman's face softened as she opened the door wider.

"I'm sorry to bother you. I had a question for you. Have the paparazzi across the street been on your property recently?"

"Oh, heavens, yes. Every single day. I can't tell you how many times I've had to call Nick's office. They've been in my driveway and yard. One even wanted to use the bathroom. They've trampled my azalea bushes. I caught one up in my oak tree with a camera. Animals. Can you believe the audacity? I'll be glad when this is all over. It's been nothing but a headache."

Before Jade could speak, Mrs. Fairchild continued, "That's an odd kind of question for this early in the morning, but nothing has been normal around here, dear, since those folks invaded Ruby's place. If this continues, I may have to talk to the town council."

"I'm sorry for the imposition. Thanks for the information."

"Sure, sugar. I didn't do anything, but if it helped, I'm happy. Send my best to Lorelei." Mrs. Fairchild closed the heavy door.

That should make Ruby feel slightly better. The paparazzi always seem to be involved somehow.

She hurried back to the store and tore through her tasks so she could get back to her research on the tabloid sites. Thoughts of all the events at the Pearl bounced around in her head and slammed into each other. Jade paused a moment and squeezed the bridge of her nose.

Stopping to assist a handful of customers and down a granola bar for lunch, Jade plowed through hundreds of online gossip sites and jotted down conversation topics and key points in the comments. Wren was responsible for keeping the show and the actors front and center. She was even ruthless enough to leak stories to reporters and whip up a frenzy like the day with Raphael and that mob at the bookstore when it suited her position.

Jade rested her eyes and rubbed her temples. Not sure if any of this would lead to something, but she had pages and pages of gossip notes covering the previous three months. Needing a change, she pulled up Wikipedia and IMDb and read everything she could find on the actors, staff, and crew. *If nothing else, I have lots of new material to add to the wall in my dining room.*

"Chloe, let's head home," she said. The little dog scampered after her as she did her evening walk-through.

After staring in her refrigerator and still not finding any answers, Jade heated up a mishmash of leftovers and settled in at her dining room table with a stack of sticky notes and a felt-tipped pen. She put all of the notes from the gossip sites on green stickies and posted them on the wall. All were centered around Elle and Raphael, and the stories about him outnumbered hers four to one. What was it about him that would cause him to dominate the headlines? Not only did he have some kind of gossip-worthy story each day, some days, he had multiples. And did this constant barrage of publicity somehow relate to the murder or his room and his poisoning?

Chapter Twenty-Four

The next day, Jade straightened the front counter as Patti breezed in from the stock room. "Have you dug up anything new on Raphael yet?" Patti asked, straightening the fliers on the front counter.

"I scoured the net for the stories about him, and I made a list. He is in the news constantly. I knew he was famous, but his mentions are off the charts."

"And every day seems to be a new love, crisis, or scandal. I don't know how someone can function with all that drama in his life. It would be exhausting," Patti said.

"I was surprised. I knew they headlined a lot, but when I started grouping the stories by topic and date, the volume was impressive. A publicist or a media professional had to have something to do with all of this."

Patti's eyes widened. "I never knew about any of the behind-the-scenes stuff. Most of what you see on TV isn't like it happens on set. Who knew there was a puppet master behind the scenes?"

"It's been interesting. So, the shows try to keep their actors in the news. The actors try to keep themselves in the news. And the reporters go to any length to get the latest story. It's a vicious cycle."

"It's kinda sad," Patti said. "Can you imagine having your self-worth defined by whether or not you're in the news or whether you got a bunch of comments on a post? They already pretend to be other people for a living, and it seems that most of what surrounds them is made up or exaggerated. I don't think I'd want that job."

"It feels kinda empty. I had fun when we filmed here, but it's not something I'd want to do every day," Jade said. "I'm happy to live here by the bay." She let out a slight puff of air as her stomach rumbled. "Time for lunch. Want anything from the Busy Bean? It may be salad day for me."

Patti pulled out a ten from her wallet. "Yum. I think I want a chicken salad on a croissant and a Peppermint Patti." Her eyes twinkled when she mentioned her signature drink.

"Be back in a few," Jade said.

"I'll call you if any tour buses show up," Patti yelled behind her. "Fingers crossed."

"Yes, please. We could use a boost." Jade looked for signs of life around the campers on her stroll down the street. All's quiet. The parking lot at the Pirate's Chest and Mermaid Books were empty, too. This part of Neptune Road looked like a ghost town.

Jade opened the front door to the Busy Bean and merged into the long line at the counter where James and his part-timers buzzed around like bees in a hive. Their happy banter with customers and the frequent peals of laughter made the wait feel minimal. When it was her turn, Jade ordered Patti's lunch, a chef's salad, and two Peppermint Patti hot chocolates from the teen with aqua hair and a variety of piercings.

After scanning her debit card, Jade moved down the counter to watch James and his team flit around, filling orders.

"Here you go, Jade. Enjoy lunch," James said, handing her two bags and a drink tray.

"Thanks. Glad to see things are hopping here," she replied.

"It's been like that since the TV people landed." James smiled. "We've met Britt, Carlos, Raphael, and a bunch of the crew. It's fun having them hang out here. I'd love to have the Busy Bean in the news, but not with any of their scandals," he whispered. "Though I did have to lock the doors when Raphael was here. Word got out that the star liked caramel lattes, and we were mobbed that afternoon. Oh, hey. Can I get your autograph?"

Jade paused and furrowed her brow when he laughed. "I saw you on *Entertainment Tonight.*"

"Of course, darling," Jade winked and headed out the door.

As Jade cut through the lot next to her store, Wren leaned up against one of the campers. She puffed out tiny clouds from her e-cigarette, and Olivia waved her arms. "I know what you did, and I know it's part of your job. But this time, you went too far. The execs could fire either one of them. And you know the actors have a morality clause. Why draw attention to their foibles?"

"Yeah, you and Ezra dangle that over their heads constantly to make them do what you want them to do. Nobody's ever enforced it. Who cares? And I didn't take or pose for the photos. I just used them to create a buzz. It's their own fault," Wren said.

Olivia's face turned almost scarlet. "Your hands aren't clean. You had something to do with the timing. And Elle's upset. Like really upset. She wants her new relationship to work, and she doesn't want Raphael to spoil it. She hasn't eaten in two days."

"If she really likes him, then it will stick, not like all these made-up relationships and dates set up for photo ops," Wren replied.

"You're kinda callous." Olivia planted one hand on her hip.

"And you're way too deep into these actors' lives. Your focus is to make a quality show. Mine is to make sure it's in the news. Every. Single. Day." Wren jabbed her manicured nail in Olivia's direction to emphasize her point.

Olivia got ready to say something, and she noticed Jade standing there. "Oh, can we help you?" Her face relaxed, but Jade could still see her flushed cheeks.

"Just stopped by to say hello. It's nice to see people out here. I thought y'all were on the set."

"We're taking a break. Olivia walked over with me to talk about some things. And I had to get something from a trailer," Wren said. "'bout ready to head back. I bet Ezra's hyperventilating without you."

Olivia's mouth curled up on the ends to a slight smile. "Yep, we should be getting back."

"Let me know if I can do anything," Jade said as she hurried to the store.

Wren and Olivia weren't staying in a camper. Why were they outside Dante and Marius's place?

Jade's phone dinged, interrupting her thoughts. **It's your lucky day. Not**

one, but two tour buses just rolled up. Patti ended her text with a string of bus and surprised emojis. Jade hustled inside the back door and set their lunches in the fridge.

"Hey, thanks for the heads up," Jade said, handing Patti her hot chocolate.

"Yum. Thanks for this," Patti said between welcoming guests and handing out baskets. Jade put on her best customer service smile and jumped in to help move the line along.

Hours later, Patti plopped down on the stool. "Whew! That was a workout. Maybe I don't need my spin class this week."

"It's time to restock. That group cleaned out some of our baskets. But I'm not complaining. I'm thrilled with all the tourists. Oh, lunch is in the fridge."

"Thanks. I'm starving." Patti made a beeline to the kitchenette. When Jade caught up with her, she handed Jade her salad. The pair dug in while Chloe watched from under the table to ensure nothing hit the floor.

"With a late lunch, I'll be too full for dinner before book club tonight, but there's always wine and cheese there. And they have sweet goodies in case I need a snack. Hey, and sometimes, we even talk about the book. Do you have any big plans tonight?" Patti winked and offered a sly smile.

"Nah. Quiet night with Chloe. I need to catch up on things and do some research."

"Hey, guess what I saw?" Before Jade could comment, Patti said, "Goat yoga. There's a farm near Toano that offers it. You bring the mat. They supply the goat. You get a workout while the little guys jump around and play. Here, look at these pictures. Adorbs, right? Wanna go?"

"That's something," Jade said, looking at the pictures of people doing stretches with cute baby goats on their backs. "Not sure if I'm ready for that." Jade hoped she didn't sigh out loud.

"I'm gonna try it. They are so precious. Let me know if you change your mind." Patti slipped her phone in her back pocket.

On the walk home, Jade nudged Chloe toward the campers, and she eagerly complied with anything that extended her evening walk. Jade wanted the time to think and to see if Olivia or Wren were back. The whole discussion with the pair bothered her. Why were they at the campsite when no one else was around?

Chloe led the way around the back of the fence line and down the rows of campers. Spotting Dante outside, where Jade had stopped earlier in the day, Chloe bound off to greet her friend.

"Hey, baby," Dante said, reaching down to pick up the wiggly dog. "And hi to you, too, Jade. It's nice to see you. I love your dog's enthusiasm."

"She's my store greeter," Jade said.

"Perfect job for her. What brings you by on this lovely evening?" The stylist glanced at his phone and set it next to him in the plastic chair.

"Just out for our walk before we head home for dinner. How are things on the set? Anything juicy? I came through here at lunch and spotted Wren and Olivia almost in this exact spot."

Dante turned his head slightly. "That's interesting. We filmed right up until four o'clock. There were no breaks or dead time today. And with lots of costume changes, Lexi and I were hopping with makeup and hair. They were probably slacking. Coming over here to hide." Dante winked. "We all have secret places when we need a break or to get away." He paused and checked his phone. After tapping on the screen, he continued, "And I see you got a little taste of the tabloid life this week. You go, girl!"

"Enough to last me a lifetime."

"And don't you worry about it for more than ten seconds. Anyone who's talked to you knows you wouldn't play around with the likes of Raphael. It'll die down. And I see Elle one upped him by being the star of the latest scandal. He'll hate that." He raised one manicured eyebrow and put a finger to his lips. "It'll make him crazy jealous, and he'll have to do something to get back in the spotlight."

"Does he leak stuff to the tabloids, or does his publicist help keep him in the news?" Jade asked, glancing around to see if anyone else was within earshot.

"Sometimes it's the actors when they feel nobody's talking about them. Poor babies, they always have to be in the center of things with their fragile, little egos." He looked over his shoulder and lowered his voice, "But I think someone else sicced the paparazzi on Elle and her boy toy." He looked round

142

and whispered, "Wren. The top brass usually send her in when there's a problem to fix. And we all know how buddy-buddy our Olivia is with Elle. She's the favorite child. So, we know she didn't do it. Wren, on the other hand, doesn't care about anything except the story of the moment. She takes pride in the number of things that go viral."

Jade leaned forward. "You think Wren leaked the boyfriend pictures?"

"Who knows, but I wouldn't put it past her to slip a tip to whomever her favorite reporter is at the moment. And she's been known to do that to punish the bad actor children if they get out of hand and don't do what Ezra or the execs want. She's vindictive and capricious." Dante's phone blared, "Dancing in the Dark." "Sorry. I've got to take this. I'll let you know if I hear any more dirt. Ciao, baby."

Jade waved and guided Chloe down the row of campers. It was time to update her notes and stare at her wall of suspects that just got a little bigger.

Chapter Twenty-Five

Jade stood and rubbed her neck. She stayed up until the wee hours, pouring over her notes on all the players from the Love Channel. Lots of people with possible motives. No clear suspect. *What am I missing? Arrrgh!* "Chloe, it's time for a change of scenery. Let's get busy with our real job."

She picked up a clipboard and did a tour of the store's display rooms. Not wanting to miss anything, the chubby dog trotted behind her. Between the final batch of tourists and the online orders, supplies were low in the toy and rainbow rooms. She also added college and hobby-themed ornaments to the list. Before she could place her restocking order, her phone buzzed. The ringtone echoed through the quiet store. "Hi, Ruby. What's up?"

"Hey. Have you seen Olivia this morning? Everyone's looking for her, and her room doesn't look like it was slept in. It's always neat as a pin, so it's kinda hard to tell when she was last here."

"Most of the crew were gone by the time Chloe and I got here this morning. I saw Olivia and Wren talking outside one of the campers yesterday afternoon."

"Okay. If you see her, tell her to check in. Ezra has called me at least four times and insinuated that it was my job to find her. These Hollywood folks. Who has time for all this?"

Maybe she decided to hang out with someone or take a break from work?

Jade jogged to the lobby and locked the door behind her. Time for a quick tour of the campsite. No crew. No fans and no paparazzi. The only sounds were the birds and the occasional passing car.

A camper door closed somewhere nearby, and Jade picked up her pace. Paige flew around the corner of a brown and white trailer and almost plowed into her. "Uh, sorry," the production assistant muttered as she kept walking.

"Hi, Paige."

Paige, dressed in jeans and what looked like a brown poncho, stopped suddenly. "What?"

"Ezra's looking for Olivia. Have you seen her?"

"What? He called you, too? Everyone's checking up on me. Geez. Let me do my job. Ezra and his tantrums." She threw her arms in the air. "I have no idea where she is. And I flippin' don't care. If she wants to run off with some guy, that's her business." She made a face like she had licked a pickle and disappeared between a row of campers.

That was an odd response. Did Olivia leave with someone? Before Jade could ponder what Paige said, Lexi zipped around the corner.

"Have you seen Olivia?" Jade asked.

Lexi cracked a smile. "They've got you looking, too? I see Ezra's been busy reaching out to everyone. He thinks he needs Olivia to function."

"Is it usual for her to disappear? She doesn't seem like the type to go AWOL."

"She's not. Everything is in order, on time, and color-coded in Olivia's world," Lexi said. "Most of us would have run away screaming years ago from all the pressure. She always seemed to be able to juggle a million things. Maybe she finally had enough."

"Is she seeing someone?" Jade asked.

"Not right now. She was living with this guy in Los Angeles, but he didn't like that she was always working. I don't think she's even dated anyone since then. She really is always working. That's what she does."

"What are the odds she met someone and decided to have a sleepover?" Jade watched Lexi's expression.

"Doubtful." Lexi shrugged. "Like I said, her work is her life. She's at Brian and Ezra's beck and call twenty-four seven. There's not much room for a life outside of that. And she has high standards that she holds all of us to." Lexi snickered. "Paige'll get her fill of what Olivia really does around here.

She's been mooning over wanting to have better assignments. She should be careful what she asks for. She may not like the reality. Gotta run. I can't leave Dante too long by himself. He'll break out the pink hair dye and the flatiron. See ya."

Jade hurried back to the store. Where did Olivia go so suddenly? And shouldn't her coworkers be more concerned about the person than whose job it is to keep the show on track?

Settling in at her desk with a hot cup of tea, Jade updated the store's event calendar and added information to her newsletter. Thoughts of Olivia kept popping up in her head. What would cause the workaholic production manager to not show up for work? Dark thoughts wormed their way front and center.

Brushing them aside, she flipped through her notes again. Olivia was the model employee and embodiment of everything in the Love Channel brand. After an afternoon with not many customers visiting the store, Jade packed the internet orders and did some online shopping to restock the inventory. When the sunlight started to fade, she dusted her hands on her jeans and looked at the little dog. "Let's go out for dinner. Good idea?" Chloe yipped and waddled to the back door as Jade blew through her closing routine.

The pair crossed the street and headed for Hot Diggity Dogs. After a short wait, Jade and Chloe approached the counter. "Hi, I'll have a Coney dog with mustard and an unsweet iced tea. Is Todd working tonight?"

The teen behind the counter with the green hair smiled. "Nah, Todd's got a date tonight. We could tell. He wore pants instead of board shorts."

"Even if they were jeans. They count as pants," the second teen at the grill snickered.

Jade laughed. "Good for him." She tried to remember if she had ever seen him in anything other than swim trunks and a T-shirt. And when it was cold, he'd add a hoodie. She paid for her meal and took the bag and cup from the cashier.

Chloe and Jade made their way to the empty deck out back. She ate her dinner in silence while the Frenchie waited patiently under the wooden bench for her cut. Seagulls inhabited the pier. No sign of the TV people.

CHAPTER TWENTY-FIVE

And the only beachgoers were dog walkers or joggers.

"Come on. It's getting nippy out here. Let's head home."

Chloe hustled down the wooden stairs and romped in the sand. She chased four gulls and barked at a jogger and then at Wren, who was seated in the sand, watching the waves.

"Hey," Jade said. "How are you?"

"Just getting some me time after today's craziness," Wren said. The normally steamrolling dynamo looked subdued in jeans and an oversized sweatshirt. "Sometimes, it's nice to find a quiet spot."

"The beach is my happy place, too. Did Olivia ever turn up?" Jade asked as Chloe sniffed around the publicist.

"Nope. Her absence caused chaos and too much screaming. I swear you'd think a group of adults could function without one person." A slight smile crossed her lips. "And Paige got a workout with Ezra and Brian pelting her with requests. She didn't appreciate being in the hot seat. I think they got through filming today, but everyone was in a foul mood when they finally broke for dinner. I hope Olivia shows up tomorrow. They'll be at each other's throats if this goes on for too long." *So much for peace, love, and happiness.*

"Any indication of where she went or who she left with? Would it have something to do with Elle?"

"Doubtful. Olivia gets too wrapped up in the actors' worlds. All she babbled on about was Elle. She needs to realize it's just a job. She's there to keep things on track. Not to cater to their whiney whims. She has no life." Wren stared out at a ship crossing the horizon. "I'll be glad to get back to the corporate offices. I hate these clean up assignments. She'll turn up sooner or later. And if she doesn't, I hope she found what she was looking for."

"What would she be looking for?"

"Who knows? Whatever floats her boat. I'm sure she had enough of catering to the crazy around here. If you want to know what happened to her, talk to Ezra. He is the one who knew her best, besides Elle. I really don't care that much. It's better that way. I try not to get too involved."

Jade nodded. Not knowing how to reply, she chewed on her bottom lip.

And why did she reference the producer in the past tense?

"Okay, enough Zen for now. I need to get back and check on things." Wren rose and walked off toward the pier.

Chapter Twenty-Six

When Jade and Chloe stepped outside the store into the cool afternoon, voices from the nearby campers caught the dog's attention, and she led Jade over to see who she could visit. The white Frenchie waddled around a camper and down a path to where Dante and Marius stood.

"Look who it is," Dante said, stooping to pick up the jiggly dog. "Hey, baby. And hi, Jade. What's shaking?"

"Not much. How are things with y'all?"

"Another day in paradise," Marius said, leaning against the camper.

"Not," Dante added. He rolled his eyes. "Olivia is missing in action, and everything is crumbling around us. I don't know how many more days like this I can take. Scenes changed on us, and we were backed up for hours. I can't function in chaaaaaaa-os."

"If you thought it was bad in your tent, try prepping the set only to have everything change twice," Marius said, rolling his eyes.

Dante spread his arms wide and swirled them around for emphasis. "All the changes gave me whiplash. And a headache. Even Lexi was snappy because of all the stress. And that is so not like her. She's usually my rock, Miss Sweetness and Light. It's all Paige's fault. You'd think she'd have learned a thing or two from her boss, but she is a total incompetent. We may have to have drinks after dinner to unwind from all this. What I really need is a spa day."

Marius tilted his head toward Dante and made a slight shushing signal.

Dante paused, not picking up on the sign. "I mean, today was an epic fail on Paige's part. That girl is a hot mess, and not in the cute way."

"I'm doing the best I can. At least I don't slink off like you two," Paige said, glaring at the two men. She turned and stomped off toward the craft tent.

Dante made a face and mimicked her walk.

"I tried to warn you, man, but you were on a roll," Marius said.

"When did she sneak in? Oh, well. It's the truth. And sometimes it hurts. She's got to know she stinks at this. I hope Olivia comes back soon. Please!" Dante said, scratching behind Chloe's ears.

"Any idea where Olivia went?" Jade asked.

"Nope. And it's so unlike her. My girl is all work. You never see her goofing off. She was the one who always had her hand raised first in class. I miss her ability to keep all of this running smoothly."

"No boyfriend or new guy she'd take off with?" Jade pressed.

Marius shook his head. "She never talked about her personal life. I don't think she had one."

"I don't think there was anyone after her last break up. She's totally devoted to Ezra and this show. Smells like dinner's about ready. Wanna head over?" Dante asked.

Marius nodded, and Dante set Chloe down next to his feet.

"Take care, and text me if you hear anything about Olivia," Jade said.

"Oh, I will," Dante said over his shoulder. "If Paige's still employed here tomorrow, there will be a whole new list of screw-ups to share. She dumped an entire cup of coffee on Brian's super-expensive shoes this morning. And, of course, they were pricey suede loafers. Were is the key word in that sentence. Can you say ruuuuuu-ined?"

Jade tugged on Chloe's leash. The dog wanted to follow her friends and the smell of grilled steak.

"Girl from the Bookstore" by Jack Jones blared from her phone and distracted Jade for a minute. "Hi, Amy. What's up?"

"You off yet?"

"Uh-huh. What're you thinking?" Jade asked.

"If you don't have dinner plans, I was thinking I could get takeout and wine, and we could hang out at your place. You're not off doing something exciting with Nick, are you?"

"No, I haven't seen much of him. He's up to his elbows in alligators with these two cases. What's Todd up to?"

"He's closing tonight. I thought I'd see what you were doing besides helping Nick solve murders."

"Dinner sounds perfect."

"How about if I call in an order to the Fat Dragon. My treat since I invited myself. What would you like?" Amy asked.

"Let's go with a small order of sesame chicken with fried rice and an egg roll."

"I'll be there in about an hour. Do you have anything for dessert, or should I get something?" Amy asked.

"Oreos and Pop-Tarts."

"I'll get something gooey and sweet. It is girls' night. We gotta take it up a notch. See you in a bit." Amy disconnected.

Jade hurried home and buzzed through her bungalow, picking up clutter and straightening the kitchen.

Jade plopped on the couch and turned on the TV as the doorbell rang and Chloe serenaded with a shrill bark.

"Hey, there. Mmmm. That smells delicious," Jade said, opening the door for Amy.

"Hot off the grill. Let's eat. Oh, wow. You have another one of these," Amy said, staring at the wall of rainbow stickies behind the dining room table.

"So, what does your law enforcement boyfriend think of all this? You giving him some competition?"

"He always checks it out. And he constantly tells me to be careful." Jade handed Amy a wine glass, and the pair filled their plates.

"So, what is all this? Anything new and juicy?" Amy asked, wiping orange chicken sauce off her fingers.

"Have you seen Olivia?"

"I haven't seen anybody from the show. What's up?" Amy asked.

"She left this week, and no one has heard from her."

"The tall one with long, straight hair that is a tad on the bossy side?"

Jade nodded. "She's the production manager. Ruby called yesterday looking for her. She said that her room hadn't been slept in."

"Like kidnapped vanished or just took off for some hot rendezvous?" Amy asked.

"I hope it's nothing nefarious, but no one thinks she's the type to take off with someone and not tell people where she's going."

"So, no hookups, and it's probably too early to report her missing." Amy stared at the wall. "What? I watch a lot of TV crime shows. Let's see…we've had a murdered reporter, a poisoned actor, and a missing woman since the TV show came to town. I don't really believe in coincidences."

"Me either. At first, I thought Raphael was the target, but if Olivia has disappeared, I don't see how that's related, besides working for the same production company." Jade's lips formed a straight line. "The reporter had pictures of Elle and Raphael that he was using to try to extort money from the actors. They were worried because of the morality clause in their contract. Elle has a new boyfriend who is also her bodyguard. And if that's not enough, the reporter ended up dead in Raphael's room. Oh, and he was later poisoned."

"But there's still a big stink about the leaked story. And it wasn't about Raphael."

Jade nodded. "He told me that the dead reporter's photos were of some racy rendezvous of him and Elle in a hot tub. I don't know if those ever got published or whether someone paid the reporter off. But the story of Elle and her bodyguard boyfriend's escapades broke this week. That was the latest hot thing."

"Even though the reporter was dead?" Amy pursed her lips.

"Someone from his company broke the story. And Raphael was poisoned before that."

"Do people really care that much about all this dating drama?" Amy sighed. "I don't have time to keep up with all that mess." She took a bite of her fried rice and stared at the rainbow diagram on the wall. "Hey, wait. You left out an important detail."

Jade took a bite of her egg roll and stared across the table at her friend.

"You had your fifteen seconds in the spotlight when your photos on top of Raphael went viral. I mean, you think you would have sent me copies or something. I had to find out from Todd on Facebook. That would be my Christmas card photo this year if it were me."

Jade made a face. "I was at Ruby's, and some guy dressed in black was sneaking around the back. He ran. I chased."

"And tackled Raphael, the hunk." Amy's eyes sparkled. "That part of the story is way better than you chasing after some trespasser. And trust me. I saved copies. You never know when I'll need to blow them up life-sized. When's your next milestone birthday?"

Jade tried not to roll her eyes. "No big birthdays for a while. And it wasn't my most flattering look. We don't need to see those again."

"Who gives a rip? You were on top of Raphael in the grass, and the whole world saw it."

"Don't remind me. Thankfully, the story about Elle broke, and all eyes were back on her," Jade said.

"Did it hurt your sales any?" Amy asked, licking duck sauce off her fingers.

"Nope. In fact, the online orders are off the charts. Though I did get one threatening post, but nothing came of it. I think it was a jealous Raphael fan. Now that you mention it, I forgot to go back and delete it." Jade pulled out her phone and scrolled to find the rude comment. "There. Gone."

"So, Nancy Drew, any ideas on who's behind all this?"

"No. Maybe if we thought of them as three separate incidents, then something would jump out." Jade pointed to sticky in the top right corner. "The dead reporter had dirt on Elle and Raphael, who hooked up from time to time. Elle has a new security guard boyfriend who's the size of The Rock. The dead reporter was into blackmailing. And he was found dead in Raphael's room. They had been friends in the past, but not so much lately. He was konked on the head and stabbed with Elle's letter opener."

She took a breath and continued, "Then we have Raphael wandering around your parking lot, dizzy and confused. I thought he was on something. Turns out he was poisoned. Nick said he had traces of digitoxigenin in his system."

"And that's important because?" Amy asked.

"It's from the oleanders that grow around here. You'll see them everywhere. The flowers are pretty. Just wear gloves if you pick them."

"Raphael and flowers?"

"Who knows? He remembers eating and drinking at Ruby's the night before and that morning. Someone could have slipped him something. Hmmm." Jade said, staring at the wall.

"What?" Amy asked, leaning forward to see what Jade was looking at.

"I remember Ruby talking about Elle picking her flowers." Jade jotted a note to remember to ask about them. "Anyway, Ruby was upset about the murder. And then she was freaked out that the police were taking samples from her kitchen and pantry."

"Todd said that he heard that the police even took her garbage to test. They weren't taking any chances. Did they figure out how Raphael got poisoned?"

"The last time I talked to Nick, he said he was still waiting on full toxicology reports. Not everything shows up in the preliminary screens. But the flowers would be an easy way to get it in the B and B without people noticing or being suspicious."

"Only if they know what oleander looks like," Amy said, Googling on her phone. "Oh, I've seen hedges of this stuff."

"It's all around the coast, especially in the south," Jade added. "We know the reporter didn't poison Raphael."

"Oooh, what if it was the new boyfriend to get rid of the actor or the reporter? Or maybe it was the understudy to get rid of Raphael to get his part? Or Raphael was too much to deal with, so one of the execs wanted him knocked off? Maybe he had some gambling debts, or it was a mafia hit. Nah, I'm going with some jealous husband or boyfriend who didn't like him fooling around with their girl." Amy wiggled her eyebrows up and down like Groucho Marx.

"All possible, but it's starting to sound like a TV show." Jade laughed.

"You don't think it was one of the townies, do you? Ruby and her daughter were easy targets."

Jade shook her head. "This was supposed to be a boon for the local

154

economy. Why would anyone want to jinx that?"

"And we don't know if Olivia's disappearance is a crime yet. That may be a coincidence, and if it is, then we're back to everything revolving around Raphael."

"Maybe I should talk to him again. There's got to be something either he's not telling anyone or that he doesn't realize is an important detail." Jade tapped her bottom lip with her index finger.

"What do you want to do tonight? Jade asked, cleaning up the empty food containers on the table.

Amy shrugged. "I'm having fun playing real-life detective with you. Let's see what else we can find after clearing the table."

Jade returned with two notebooks, a handful of pens, and a stack of colorful sticky notes.

After stopping for a quick ice cream break, the pair scoured all kinds of movie and gossip sites for anything related to Raphael and Elle.

"This has been fun," Amy said. "Thanks for letting me hang out and play with your suspect board. You know what would be fun? I should plan one of those mystery parties at the store. That would be an evening to remember. Wanna help? We could all dress up in cool costumes."

Jade nodded, still staring at the wall.

Amy stood and gathered the dirty dessert dishes. "I need to head back soon. I'm gonna swing by Todd's, and then I have to do inventory."

"I'll get that. Don't worry about cleaning up. Chloe and I will take care of it. Thanks for bringing dinner."

Amy opened the Fat Dragon bag and made a face. "I forgot I ordered cheesecake from the restaurant," Amy said, pulling out two plastic containers from the paper bag.

"I'm still full from dinner and ice cream."

"Do you want me to leave it here?" Amy asked.

Jade shook her head. "No, I'd eat it."

"That's the point. Well, okay. I'll swing by and see if Todd wants to have cheesecake on the beach when he gets off work," Amy said. "You sure you don't want me to help clean up?"

"I'm good. Tell Todd I said hey. I'm glad that it's working out for y'all."

Amy packed up her stuff as Jade cleared the table. She waved over her shoulder. "We're doing a murder mystery night at the store, and I'm counting on your skills to help me," she called, pulling the door shut behind her.

On a whim, Jade pulled out her phone and tapped a text to Raphael. **Hope you're doing well. Any thoughts on the reporter or the poisoning?**

About two hours later, as Jade was climbing into bed, her phone dinged. **Nope. But something bad's happened to Olivia.**

What? She replied. But there was no reply.

Chapter Twenty-Seven

J ade tossed and turned and checked her phone repeatedly to see if Raphael had texted any additional information. Exhausted from the restlessness, she got up and showered.

After a long walk on the beach, she and Chloe headed for the office to get a jump start on the online orders. Maybe when the sun came up, she could wander over to the campers to see what else she could uncover. *Somebody had to know something.* Her thoughts kept coming back to Olivia. Could she really be in danger? Jade fired off a quick text to Nick to make sure it was on his radar, too.

As Jade affixed labels on the three boxes on the counter, Lorelei and Neville strutted in. The cat did his best to annoy Chloe, who growled from behind the dividing door.

"What's new?" Lorelei asked, heading to the coffee maker.

"Not much." Jade scratched Neville behind the ears. More growls from Chloe. "The production manager left, and no one has seen her."

"Which one is that?" Lorelei asked.

"The shorter gal with the long brown hair."

"Oh, the one with the clipboard. I haven't seen her. In fact, I haven't seen any TV people in a while."

"All the orders are packed. I'm putting these bins out front for the delivery guy." Jade dusted her hands on her jeans. Grabbing her puffy parka, she said, "I'm off for a quick walk around the campers. Be back in a bit."

"No problem. We'll have a staff meeting here while you're gone." Her aunt reached for the creamer and a mug.

Jade took two steps out the back door and heard a piercing scream. She looked around, and another scream echoed from the campers. She ran down the rows and followed some of the crew toward the trucks and vehicles near the privacy fence.

Dante, standing next to an open van, pointed at the vehicle and screamed like a little girl. Four large nylon bags sat at his feet.

The van's back doors hung open, revealing a cargo area covered with a pile of bins and bags. Jade stepped closer for a better look. A pale hand with a French manicure lolled out from the bottom of the pile of stuff.

Sucking in a mouthful of cold air, Jade fished her phone out of her pocket as two of the gaffers started pushing things inside the van aside.

Jade called 911. When it connected, she said, "I'm Jade Hicks, and I'm in the lot next to 'Tis the Season. The TV crew found a woman in the back of a van. I can't tell what state she's in, but we need an ambulance."

"Any idea what happened to her?" the dispatcher asked.

"No. I can't see what's happening right now," Jade said.

The burlier of the two men interrupted, "She's breathing. There's a slight pulse. Tell them to hurry."

"She's breathing," Jade repeated. "But it doesn't look like she's conscious." She stepped closer to the back of the van. The woman lay on her side. Brown hair covered most of her face. "It's Olivia Morton. She works on the show."

Jade's heart raced. *No blood in sight.*

"An ambulance and a deputy are on their way. I'll stay on the line with you until they get there. Can someone direct them to where you all are?" the dispatcher asked.

"Can one of you run to the road and send the ambulance over here?" Jade yelled.

One of the sound guys said, "I will," and he trotted toward the curb.

Jade took a series of deep breaths. *Please, not another dead body.*

A pair of sirens grew louder on Neptune Road. "I see them. Thanks for your help," Jade said to the dispatcher as she disconnected.

The ambulance, followed by a Sheriff's Department SUV, bumped over the grassy area and pulled in next to the small crowd around the van. Three

EMTs pushed their way in and went to work on Olivia as Sebastian started to interview witnesses. Passersby gathered at the perimeter of the property behind the temporary fencing.

Jade scanned the crowd. It felt like being in the middle of a three-ring circus. Most of the people, all dressed in black, were from the crew. Jade sidled up next to Sebastian and Dante as the deputy asked, "Are you okay?"

The tall stylist shook his head slowly. "I dunno anymore. There's too much freaky stuff going on here. This was a shock to the system. I didn't expect to find this." Jade patted his shoulder, and he continued, "I came out here to drop off some bags that we'll need for today's shoot. And after this, who knows if we'll actually shoot today. That will send Ezra into an eruption."

"Was the van unlocked?" Jade asked.

"It's always unlocked. We load stuff for the day, and one of the guys drives it over to the set for us."

"Same driver and same van every day?" She pressed as Sebastian gave her a sideways glance.

Dante cracked a smile. "What, you working for the police now?"

"No, sorry. Just curious."

"Yes, it's usually the same van. I dunno about the driver. Lexi and I came over yesterday and got our stuff before dinner. We like to keep our equipment organized and ready to go on a moment's notice." He wiped his eyes with both hands.

"Anything else you remember?" Sebastian asked.

Dante shook his head. "No. We all thought she took off somewhere. We should have known that's not like Olivia."

Sebastian nodded and made his way around the perimeter of people, giving statements. On the other side of the van, Paige stood alone, shifting her weight between her legs. Some of the crew sat nearby in the grass.

Before Jade could corner Paige, Sebastian ambled over to where Jade stood. "Hey. Start from the beginning and tell me what you saw. I know you made the 911 call."

"I took a break, and when I came outside, I heard screaming. I followed it back here, and Dante was pointing to the van. By then, a small crowd had gathered, and I saw a hand sticking out of a pile of bags."

"Anything else?"

"No. I hope Olivia's okay," Jade added.

"Let me know if you think of anything else. Or if you hear of anything useful." Sebastian winked and moved on to the next cluster of people.

The EMTs bounced a gurney over the sand and grass. Olivia looked tiny on the stretcher. Within seconds, the three guided the gurney to the ambulance and sped off with lights flashing and sirens blaring.

Paige's constant fidgeting caught Jade's eye. The tall woman shifted from foot to foot. Then she moved her arms around like she was doing some kind of workout. By the time she started stretching her neck and rolling it around like a relaxation exercise, Jade edged closer to her.

The woman froze. Before Jade could get close enough to speak, Paige turned and hurried toward the next row of campers. Jade picked up her pace as Paige ducked in between two of the campers on some erratic path. As she neared Neptune Road, Paige paused and looked around. Then she turned and ran back toward the campers.

Not wanting to lose her, Jade ignored her aching muscles and sped up. The production assistant ran in a zigzagged path like she was trying to escape from an alligator. Paige slowed near the fence and looked in both directions. Then she ran toward 'Tis the Season.

"Paige, wait," Jade yelled. *This is getting ridiculous. What is wrong with her?*

Ignoring Jade, Paige jogged toward the front of the store. She hesitated at the porch steps, and Jade finally caught up with her.

Jade gulped in air before she spoke. "Paige, wait. What is wrong?"

"Everything," the woman whined, looking over her shoulder.

"But they found Olivia. You should be happy," Jade said. "Doesn't that take some of the pressure off?"

"Not really. She looked dead on that gurney. And now, I'll be stuck doing her job forever."

"Olivia will be back soon. She was breathing when they found her. That's a good sign."

"I dunno. The way that cop talked, it sounded like she was on the way out."

CHAPTER TWENTY-SEVEN

She continued to look around.

Before Jade could reply, Ezra and Brian strode around the side of the store. "Paige!" Ezra bellowed. "I've been trying to reach you for the last twenty minutes. This is unacceptable. Why don't you answer your phone?"

The color drained from Paige's face. She patted her pockets. "I must have left my phone in my camper. I heard screaming and ran out to see what was going on," she whispered.

"I don't care. We've got to get everyone together under the tent. Send out a message. Then we've got to figure out if there is anything that we can salvage from today's schedule. Move it. Get your phone and be at the tent before I am." The veins in his neck bulged. He turned and said something to Brian that Jade didn't catch. Then, the two men strode off toward the campers.

Paige gritted her teeth and took off running again.

At least she still has a job. For now. Instead of returning to work, Jade wandered toward the big tent. The crew had already started to assemble. Clusters of people sat at tables or stood around the perimeter. A guy in black wheeled out a large box and a portable microphone. He handed it to Brian, who thunked it with his large gold ring. "Thank you all for coming on such short notice. There are plenty of chairs up front here. Come on in. We'll get started in a minute," Brian said.

Jade tried to be inconspicuous behind some tables with boxes stacked on them. People filed in like a row of ants headed for a discarded sandwich. Jade recognized a couple of faces. By the time she had ticked off all the facts in her head about Olivia's disappearance, Ezra approached Brian. He nodded, and Brian turned on the microphone. "Hello. Thanks everyone for responding. As many of you know, we found Olivia this morning. They rushed her to the hospital."

The audience rustled in their folding wooden chairs, and some of the onlookers gasped. Paige slipped under the tent. She positioned herself in Ezra's line of sight, but not close enough to talk to. *Interesting. Olivia would have been front and center. Paige wasn't even within striking distance. Maybe that was on purpose.*

Brian handed the mic to Ezra. "I talked to the doctors a few minutes ago. Olivia is going to be all right. They're holding her for observation. She sustained some injuries, and they want to monitor her. But we're glad that she's awake and talking. She'll be back with us soon. I know everyone misses her." A scowl crossed Paige's face when she glanced at her phone as Ezra continued, "And we're able to figure out who attacked her." He scanned the crowd and paused when he spotted Paige. *More fidgeting.* The crowd noise increased, and applause continued for several minutes.

When the noise died down, Ezra pulled out a folded sheet from his back pocket. "Lunch service will start at eleven-thirty. The plan is to be back on the beach near the pier for a twelve-thirty start time. Be on time. We'll follow the afternoon schedule. Stay tuned for the rest of the week. We need to figure out how to play catch up. Any questions?"

Low murmurs spread through the crowd. Someone yelled, "What's for lunch?"

Ignoring the question, Ezra turned off the microphone and made a beeline toward Paige. Jade scooted closer to block her path when it looked like the production assistant was about to bolt again.

Ezra and Brian cornered her and fired off tasks like they were bullets from a semiautomatic rifle. Then they turned and disappeared into the crowd without waiting for a response from the assistant. Jade felt sorry for the young woman, who would never fill Olivia's shoes. The men didn't seem to be the least bit concerned about her or the myriad of tasks they had demanded. Before Jade could come up with a plan to help, someone grabbed her shoulder, and she let out a little whelp.

"Sorry, girl. I thought you heard me," Dante said.

"I was just—"

"Eavesdropping," Dante whispered. "I would have done the same thing. It's like a train wreck, but you have to stare. What'd I miss?"

"Ezra announced the schedule for today, and when the meeting broke up, they cornered Paige, who looked overwhelmed with everything. Lunch is at eleven-thirty. Ezra said not to be late."

"Well, at least we know she didn't try to kill Olivia for her job. If I were

Paige, I'd be wishing they would have kidnapped me instead. She'll be lucky to have a job after all this. I'd be doing everything in my power to get Olivia back to work. I know Ezra and Brian are dying for Olivia's return."

"Maybe I can help," Jade whispered.

"Gotta love your sweet southerness. The rest of us Left Coasters would have hightailed it for the mountains. Don't make eye contact. Don't get involved," he whispered as he followed Jade over to where Paige stood, tapping on her phone.

"Hi," Jade said as she approached. "Can we help you with anything? It's promising news about Olivia, huh?"

"Yes, I guess. I'm uber busy. I don't have time to talk." She turned and jogged toward the area where the trucks were parked.

"Some people," Dante muttered. "Lexi and I will find out the deets on Olivia, and I'll text you later. I need to get moving if I plan to be ready for filming and lunch. Take care."

On her walk back to the store, Jade pulled out her phone and texted Nick. **Got time for dinner tonight?**

Not sure yet. Lots of stuff going on. Can I let you know this afternoon?

Hope your day gets better. She followed it with a pink, sparkly heart emoji.

Olivia, what did you get yourself into? And who was trying to sabotage this production?

Chapter Twenty-Eight

Lorelei, Chloe, and even Neville almost tackled her when she returned to the office.

"Okay, spill it. I'm dying to know what was going on over there," Lorelei said.

Jade patted the cat and the dog. "They found Olivia unconscious in the back of one of the vans. The EMTs took her to the hospital, but they said she should be okay."

"I saw Sebastian walking around." Lorelei glanced at her phone, which continued to ding. "Maybe when she's well enough to talk, she can shed some light on her attacker. Nick and Sebastian need a break in this case."

"He and the forensic team will be busy for a while. The van seems like an odd place for Olivia to end up."

"I'm dying to know what's going on, and so is the rest of Mermaid Bay. They keep blowing up my phone. Let me know what you find out," her aunt said.

Jade nodded and printed the overnight order report. She and Lorelei divided the pages and spent the afternoon packaging the requests.

When the final bin was ready for the delivery driver, Lorelei dusted off her hands. "Whew. That was a workout. Glad to see your business thriving. Your grandmother would have been so proud. This store was her world. And you've helped it grow in ways she'd never imagined."

Jade smiled. "After we get through this adventure, I'm planning events through Christmas. It's our season and time for Bernie to make his regular appearances. After that, I need to come up with some winter ideas for the new year. Gotta keep the people coming back."

Lorelei patted her shoulder. "You're doing a fine job. Just don't be an all-work kind of gal."

Jade's thoughts flashed to Olivia. "Speaking of that, I wonder how Olivia's doing. Got any contacts at the hospital?"

"Maybe." Her aunt pulled out her phone and tapped away with her pearly nails.

"Hmm. My friend is a volunteer at the information desk. She confirmed that she's a patient. They moved Olivia from the emergency room to a step-down floor. She's not in ICU, so that's promising."

"It is. I was planning to take over a gift basket with the hopes of getting in to see her, but it might be too early for that."

Lorelei nodded. "Yep. She's not able to have visitors. My friend said that the police are there at the hospital."

"Nick said he would be busy today when I texted him."

"My friend hopes that Elle and Raphael come by to visit her." Lorelei tapped a reply into her phone. "So, dinner with your hunky beau tonight?"

"Not sure," Jade replied.

Lorelei's perfectly manicured brows almost merged.

"He's working. And this didn't help his already busy schedule. I guess I'll see him sometime this week."

"You both work too much. You need to plan a vacation somewhere."

Jade nodded and headed for her desk. Scouring the online news sites, she didn't see any mention of Olivia. Nothing on the gossip sites either. You'd think the paparazzi would be all over this. If Nell was listening to her scanner, she'd be front and center. "Any other tidbits of news from your sources?" Jade hollered through the door to the lobby.

"Nope. Everyone's on Raphael's watch. They're placing bets on where he'll visit next."

"They're filming at the pier next if that helps," Jade said.

After a restless afternoon without many in-person shoppers and no new information on Olivia, Jade packed up and did her store closing routine after Lorelei left. *No news from Nick either.*

"Come on, Chloe. It looks like we're on our own tonight. Let's go see what kind of trouble we can get into."

The Frenchie's head pivoted ninety degrees and then another one-eighty to the other side. *"Go" must have been the magic word. It couldn't have been the promise of "trouble."*

Jade leashed up the dog, and she followed her out the door. Chloe darted toward the campers and away from their bungalow. The tiny village looked empty. Not in any hurry to be anywhere, the dog waddled down the sidewalk toward the Pirate's Chest and the realty office. A "coming soon" sign was in the window of the former CPA's office. "That's interesting," Jade said, stepping closer to see what was coming. "We're getting a pizza parlor," she squealed.

Chloe's ears flew up, and she sniffed around the brick planter with the dead stalks in it.

"It's Pizza D'Action. Hadn't heard anything, but I can't wait. I don't ever remember a pizza place in Mermaid Bay." She tugged lightly on Chloe's leash and led her across the street to Hot Diggity Dogs.

Todd looked up from a spreadsheet when they walked in. "Hey, guys. What's up?"

Jade smiled. "Thought we'd stop by and pick up dinner. May I have a chili dog with an iced tea and a pretzel?"

"Unsweetened, right."

Jade nodded and handed him her debit card. "Hey, did you see the sign up in Claude's old office window? We're getting a pizza place."

"Here? I mean over there," he pointed out the front window. "I hadn't heard anything about it." His mouth formed a straight line as he grilled her order. "Your order'll be right up."

She tapped a quick text to Vivian Turner, the business council president. If anyone would know the details, it would be the one with her finger on the pulse of Mermaid Bay.

By the time Todd handed her the paper bag and a cup, Vivian texted a response. **New family in town. It just happened.**

Looking up from her phone, she reached for the bag. "Thanks. Vivian said it happened quickly. It's some new folks."

"Maybe we'll get to meet them soon. We can handle another restaurant in MB. It'll be good for the hood. Maybe more folks will eat here instead of going over to Seaport," Todd said. "You had a bit of action over at your place today. I fed a bunch of cops when they finished up. You're ground zero for most of the action recently." He wiped his brow with his T-shirt sleeve.

"Not by choice. They found Olivia in one of the vans, and the EMTs took her to the hospital."

"The one in charge of the production?"

"That's her. They're keeping her for observation. We're all hoping for a quick recovery. Thanks for dinner."

"See ya around. We'll have to try the pizza place when it opens," he called out as she and Chloe headed toward home.

Jade and her Frenchie settled on the couch to eat dinner and catch up on their binge-watching. During the second episode of *Vera*, a knock at the door woke Chloe.

Nick stood on the porch with a drink tray and plastic bag. "Hey, I thought you'd be tied up for the evening," she said.

"I was. I needed a break. And I wanted to see you. I brought coffee and apple pie, courtesy of the Busy Bean."

"Come on in. It's cold out there." Jade shivered and shut the door behind him.

The pair snuggled on the couch, and Chloe wiggled her way in between them in case there was a chance for any pie.

Hopping up for forks and napkins, Jade returned with the silverware and settled in again beside him and her dog. He had changed the channel to ESPN to an NFL highlights show.

After a couple of bites of pie," she said, "Yum. Any news on Olivia?"

Nick wiped his mouth with the napkin, and Chloe looked longingly at his plate. "They're still holding her for observation. But she's awake and talking."

Jade leaned forward, waiting for additional details.

When she stared at him, he continued, "She remembers walking on the beach one evening. Right after she hung up a call with her sister, she hurried across the street to the campers. Someone in a hoodie approached, and she said she woke up later in the dark. Everything hurt. But she didn't know if it was real or a dream. Olivia didn't know if it was a guy or a girl. She didn't see a face or recognize the voice." Nick put the last bite of pie in his mouth. Chloe turned to stare at Jade, who still had some left.

"She was attacked?" Jade said, sitting up straight.

Nick nodded. "Someone hit her and knocked her out."

"Why?"

"Still trying to find that out. She doesn't remember the person saying anything to her."

"Where was she? And the person dumped her in the van? Nobody noticed anything weird happening? And no one noticed her in the work van?"

"We're not sure yet. Sebastian is scouring the neighborhoods to see if anyone caught anything on camera. She said she remembers crossing the street and walking by the campground. She was heading to Ruby's, but she couldn't remember exactly where the encounter happened. She kept saying near the beach."

Jade pulled out her phone, tapped on the app for her store's outdoor cameras and skimmed through the feeds. After a few minutes, she said, "She must have been across the field, out of the range. My cameras didn't pick up anything."

"I'll let Sebastian know. He and the team will be out hitting the pavement again tomorrow."

"If she was dumped in the van all that time, how come none of the crew noticed? They use those vans all the time, right?"

"You'd think. But it was full of stuff. Paige couldn't remember when the vans were last used."

"Somebody's got to know or have seen something. She was missing a long time."

"I don't think anyone was really looking that hard to find her," Nick said, lowering his voice.

Chapter Twenty-Nine

J ade and Chloe headed for the store before sunrise. Not knowing what really happened to Olivia dominated her thoughts all evening and kept sleep at bay for most of the night. After brewing the strongest coffee she could find in the bin, she settled in at her desk to see what was out there on the world wide web about Olivia.

Most of the information came from her biography on the show's website and her long list of credits on the TV movies. Olivia had been with the Love Channel for twelve years. "Olivia, you've been in the business for a long time. This is all the information?" Jade said aloud, causing Chloe to stir in her bed.

On a whim, she pulled up a site of digitized yearbook photos. She found two Olivia Mortons that were about the right age. "Bingo. There you are in 2004. The hair's blonder, but that's you, and there you are again in 2008 at Pomona College in Claremont, California. And you majored in Gender Studies and Theatre. Let's see what else you did."

Jade spent the next hour perusing through Olivia's yearbooks. Her extracurricular activities focused mainly on the theatre department, but she also volunteered at the college's radio station. "Hmmm. That's interesting. She produced two radio shows and did an internship with a TV station.

Chloe hopped up to see what Jade found. "It seems Miss Olivia was also an activist. She attended protests, mainly for environmentalist causes." She rubbed Chloe behind the ears until she fell asleep.

"Wow," Jade said when she read about Olivia's arrests at protests during college. Her outburst caused Chloe to stir. Jade set Chloe on the floor and stood and stretched. "Come on, puppy. The sun's warming up the outside a little. Let's go take a walk."

Chloe sprang into adventure mode and danced at the back door until Jade opened it. The pair walked across the dewy grass, and Chloe led the way to the shrubbery at the back fence line. The blooms on the oleanders were starting to wither. Colder temperatures and overnight frosts were on their way.

The grass around the base of the hedges had gotten taller since the TV crew had arrived. Jade made a mental note to schedule the lawn crew one final time for the season after the campers left. The end of the season always felt bittersweet. On the one hand, it was a much-needed rest after all the tourists had gone home, but cooler temperatures and the shorter days created a feeling of emptiness that she couldn't shake. Even though Christmas was her favorite holiday, she would always be a summer beach girl.

A bird fluttered in one of the hedges. Jade jumped, and Chloe darted after it. She sniffed around in the grass and started to paw at something. Jade tugged gently on her lead, but the dog continued to dig in the mulch and grass.

"Chloe, what's got your attention? Please tell me it's not a critter. The bird already gave me a heart attack." Jade leaned forward and moved the grass. A small hammer that looked like a miniature version of a sledgehammer and a long screwdriver lay under one of the bushes.

"What's that doing here?" Jade picked them up with both hands and turned them over. The hammer's wooden handle had a crack in it. An "EBB" was scratched at the bottom. The hammer part looked like it had been rubbed in the dirt. A dirty stain had dried on one side. Jade scratched her hand on the screwdriver's damaged plastic grip. The screwdriver sported a faint "EBB," too.

"I doubt if these are Bernie's. He's usually meticulous with his tools. I wonder if anyone is missing anything?" Chloe had lost interest and moved on to the next fascinating scent.

She set them back in the grass, snapped a couple of pictures, and sent them to Nick. **This might be important. Chloe found them near the fence,** she added for context.

Her phone dinged seconds later. **Stay there. I'm sending Sebastian over.**

Jade's heart fluttered. *He thinks it's serious enough to check out. Great. And now my fingerprints are all over them. I shouldn't have touched them.*

By the time Chloe had chased a bug and plopped down in the grass, Sebastian walked around the side of 'Tis the Season.

"Morning, Jade. You're up early," he said as he approached.

"You, too. Chloe found something on her walk. It may be discarded junk."

"I heard. Nick asked me to swing by and check it out." He pulled out a pair of gloves from his utility belt as Jade pointed at the flowerbed with the toe of her boot.

He took a series of pictures with his phone and pulled an evidence bag out of his back pocket. "The hammer's heavy enough to do some damage. Know where they came from?" he asked.

She shook her head. "It's not mine. And I'm sure it's not Bernie's. I don't know who EBB is. Uh..."

"What? he asked, raising an eyebrow.

"It thought they may have belonged to someone, so I kinda picked them both up."

"We'll see if they turn out to be useful. If you see or hear anything else that looks out of place, give us a call."

"Okay," she said as he turned and hiked back to his vehicle. "Let's do one more loop, Chloe, and then we'll get to work." The white dog trotted behind Jade toward the craft tent. Voices near one of the rows of trailers drifted toward them in the still morning air. The pair ducked around the corner to see who it was.

"How are y'all?" she said as she approached Dante and Matilda, who sat in plastic chairs with their morning coffee.

"You're out and about early this morning," Dante said. "Ezra has us on a tight schedule this week. He wants us to make up for lost time. That usually means long hours and no fun." Dante wrinkled his nose.

Matilda took a sip of her coffee and smiled. Before she could speak,

Dante continued, "And poor Tilda here can't get any sleep. Her obnoxious roommate Paige is up at all hours, talking on the phone, and playing video games. Girl, you may have to come over and bunk with Marius and me. I think that table thing folds out into another bed. It's got to be better than what you're rooming with now."

"Thanks, dear," she replied. "But I'll get through it. Paige has a lot on her now with Olivia being out of commission. It's just for a little while. Plus, if we ever get caught up, we'll be almost done with the gig here. I think I can bear it for a little while."

"I'm sorry that it's been trying," Jade said. Chloe pawed at Matilda's shoe. The costume designer reached down and picked her up. "Now, aren't you a cutie." Chloe made herself right at home in the woman's ample lap.

"Chloe found something interesting on our walk," Jade said.

"On the beach? Do you ever find money or treasure?" Dante interrupted.

"Sometimes things wash up. Nothing valuable. This was a hammer and a long screwdriver with the initials EBB on it. Any idea who it belongs to? I'd like to get them back to the owner." *I'll save the bag of bones story from the beach for another time.*

Dante's brow furrowed. "No. Not really. You get lots of tourists around here. It could be anybody's."

"There's no telling how long it's been out there. I thought I'd check with y'all first in case someone had asked about it," Jade said.

"Hmm," Matilda said. "I don't remember the names of all the maintenance folks, but you may try over there. There's a big camper and some trucks near that tent. One of the guys on that team may be able to help you."

"Thanks. Come on, Chloe, let's go see if we can catch them before they start their day."

Matilda set the round dog in the grass, and after sniffing Dante's snakeskin shoes, she followed Jade toward the maintenance area.

Men in flannel shirts and jeans milled around the equipment trucks like ants on a popsicle. At first glance, it looked chaotic, but they were all loading and stacking equipment. One guy with a bushy, graying beard paused. "Can I help you?"

"Hi, I'm Jade, and I found some tools over there in the grass. I wanted to see if you all were missing anything?"

"You'll need to talk to Eddie. Over there in the Dodgers ball cap." He pointed to a figure hunched over a black box near a utility van.

"Thanks." Jade trekked over to a white van. "Excuse me. I'm sorry to bother you. My dog and I found some tools this morning, and I wanted to see if they belong to the crew."

The short and stocky figure turned. A forty-something woman with tight silver curls under her ball cap replied, "Whatcha got there?"

"Hi, I'm Jade. We found these." She held up her phone for the woman to see.

The square-shouldered woman moved closer and pulled Jade's extended arm closer to her face. "Yep, those are mine. Had a bunch of stuff go missing since we've been here. Some stupid prankster or some sneaky thief, I guess. The hammer and screwdriver were the latest things. The wrenches disappeared when we first got here. We never did find those."

Before Jade could comment, the woman pulled the phone closer. "How in the devil did they get in your flowerbed? Let's see, that's the hammer I needed yesterday and my screwdriver. I carve my initials in all my stuff for just this kind of situation. But where are my two hefty wrenches? If I find out who's pilfering my stuff, I'll bean someone in the head. They need to keep their hands to themselves. And be respectful of others' property. So where are my things?"

"The police took them as evidence."

The woman paled. "Why would you call the police?"

Before Jade could explain, Eddie muttered, "Great. Now, I'll never see them again." She turned her back and trudged over to a large black storage box.

On her walk back, she texted Sebastian. **Eddie in maintenance said the tools are hers. She said two wrenches are also missing.**

Chapter Thirty

J ade's stomach rumbled as she stepped onto the sandy sidewalk of the
Busy Bean. "Come on, Chloe, as soon as we get the store opened, we'll
have some breakfast. And I think James slipped you some turkey bacon
in the bag."

The enthusiastic dog danced in circles around Jade's feet. As the pair hiked
over the dune toward Neptune Road, Paige stumbled down the sidewalk
with an armload of clothes and folders. The tall woman stopped several
times to pick up the garments she'd dropped.

"Hi, Paige. Do you need some help?"

The production assistant let out a heavy sigh that almost sounded like a
guttural growl. "No. I've got to find Matilda. That troglodyte isn't answering
her phone."

Jade trotted along beside her. "You sure? I don't mind carrying some of
that." Chloe sniffed Paige's work boot.

The woman recoiled. "Eww. Don't bite me. Get away."

"She won't. Come here, Chloe." Jade picked up the dog. "She works at the
store with me. She's my Christmas ambassador."

"Whatever," Paige said. "I don't like dogs or cats. Or birds. Never mind. I
have stuff I need to get done before Ezra has a coronary."

"How's Olivia?"

"Who knows. I don't have time for the feels. There's too much going on
with management breathing down my neck. Elle's costume didn't fit. Seems
like someone gained a little weight recently, and I need Matilda to do her job.
But I can't find her. She has an aversion to technology and the twenty-first

century, and those idiots took all the golf carts." Paige dropped what looked like a blouse and skirt.

Jade picked up the clothing, and Paige snatched it with her free hand. "Thanks. I'm in a hurry. And it's not enough that they made me room with the old bat who smells like mothballs, but now I'm her keeper, too. This is all too much. It's not worth it."

"I guess you'll be glad when Olivia's back," Jade said, picking up her pace to keep up with the woman's long strides.

Paige stopped abruptly. "That won't make my problems go away. But at least I won't have Brian and everyone else calling me at all hours to do stuff that's not important. They are impossible. Toxic."

Ignoring Paige, Jade prodded for any other bit of information, "I hope Olivia's feeling better. Did they say what happened?"

"Listen, I'm busy. And I really don't care. Surely, she pushed someone too far. She's a pain. Olivia's demanding, and someone had had enough. I gotta go before I get fired. Maybe that would be a relief."

"Do you want me to give you a ride back to the set?" Jade asked.

"No." The woman hustled off with her arms loaded. *I wonder how she even sees over that pile of stuff.*

Jade stopped and took a breath. "Wow. Let's go eat our breakfast before it gets cold." She put Chloe down on the sand, and the Frenchie scampered toward the store.

After sharing a bite of her biscuit with Chloe, Jade settled in at her desk. *Some of these Hollywood folks are something else. I don't think I'd want to work with them every day in that high-octane environment.*

On a whim, she texted Dante, **How're you doing? Any word on Olivia? Saw Paige today, but she was super busy.**

Seconds later, he responded with, **Girl, it's been a circus here. I'm over here rolling my eyes all the way back to last Tuesday. I will be sooooooooo glad when Olivia's back. Soon can't come soon enough.** He followed that with another text full of circus animal emojis.

Hope things calm down. Paige was on a costume errand, Jade replied.

I thought Matilda was going to sock her in the nose when she blamed

her for the boo-boos. Lotsa drama, he replied.

Jade laughed and dove into the overnight orders that took longer than she had expected to fill. For some reason, there was a run on football team ornaments and penguins. She made a note to add them to her next restocking order.

She shifted in her chair to ward off the twinge in her back. Chloe had the same idea. She stretched out on the floor in what looked like a doggie yoga pose. Jade's text alert interrupted their little exercise break.

Had lunch yet?

Nope, she replied to Nick.

I'm at Todd's. I'll bring food in a bit.

Jade replied with a series of heart emojis and a smiley face.

When footsteps scraped across the wooden porch, Chloe turned into an attack dog. She stopped barking and rolled over on her back when Nick stepped through the door with hot dog-scented take-out bags.

"Hey there," Nick said, reaching down to pet Chloe. "I brought lunch."

"Come on back. Do you need something to drink?" Jade asked.

"Water's good. How're things going? Sorry, I've been the invisible man."

Jade handed him a bottle of water and kissed him on the cheek. "Missed you. You look tired."

"A lot's been going on, and we're nowhere close to solving any of it. And Olivia doesn't remember much about her attacker." Nick pulled out a chair at the work table.

Jade sat across from him and pulled out a hot dog and tater tots. "Thanks for bringing lunch. I've been tied up with orders and inventory this morning."

"The news is that we think the hammer you found was the one used on Olivia Morton. Maybe the reporter, too. There's DNA on it, and we're hoping it's traceable."

Jade made a face. "Sorry. I know my prints were all over it. I picked it up to see it better. I didn't think about it being a weapon. And how did it get there? My back fence is not on the way to Ruby's place."

"Maybe someone was looking to get rid of the evidence."

"But there's a really big bay right across the street. Most people would have tossed it into the water," she said, popping a tater tot in her mouth.

"If they were smart or thought about it. It may have been a convenient place to toss it. I'm waiting for the forensics to come back on that, too. The reporter also had blunt force trauma to the head. The stabbing happened after he was already dead. And someone attempted to poison Raphael. The second set of tests came back and indicated the presence of…" He pulled out his phone and scrolled. "The presence of digitoxigenin and oleandrin."

"Sounds like it's from the plant," Jade added.

"That's exactly what it came from. And Olivia was hit with that heavy-duty hammer. It was a good thing they found her when they did. She was severely dehydrated and concussed."

Jade took another bite of her hot dog while thoughts of the three crimes bounced around in her head. *It had to be someone with the Love Channel. Who would want to harm a reporter, Raphael, and Olivia? It doesn't make sense that it's a random person or separate events. My gut feeling is that there's some connective tissue between the three events.*

Nick took one final swig of water and balled up the hot dog wrapper. "I've got to get back. We have a task force meeting this afternoon. Not sure when I'll be free. Can you do dinner maybe Friday or this weekend?"

She stood and hugged him. His warm embrace, mixed with the spicy scent of his aftershave and shampoo, made her want to extend lunch a little bit longer. "Sounds like a plan. Thanks for the food. I've missed you."

"Hey, we've only got a week and a half before these folks leave town. We're redoubling our efforts to make some progress on this. Gotta run." Nick kissed the top of her head and strode out to the front of the store.

Jade waved, and Chloe followed him to the door.

When the door shut, Jade picked up the trash and recyclables. She pulled out her notes and poured over all of the connections. *What am I missing?*

Chapter Thirty-One

J ade yawned and did another lap of the temporary campground on her walk at lunch the next day. She hoped the exercise would get the endorphins pumping since she stayed up too late looking for any connection between the three incidents and any of the people on her suspect list. When she reached the sidewalk, she turned left and headed toward the bookstore and the pier to check on the filming. Crowds lined the sand behind the plastic fencing as they watched Elle and Raphael film a scene multiple times at the entrance to the wooden pier.

When Jade's legs started to twinge, she stretched and headed back to the store to relieve Patti. Peeking in the front windows of the Busy Bean, she made a detour for two of James's latest offerings, the Peppermint Patti. Hot chocolate would be a nice afternoon treat, and it would warm up her hands.

Balancing the two to-go cups, Jade punched in the code and opened the back door. Chloe yipped, and Jade heard voices in the front. She poked her head through the doorway. Simon, the delivery guy, winked at Patti and hoisted three bins of packages up. "See you tomorrow," he said.

"Let me get the door for you," Patti cooed.

"'Preciate it. And thanks for the cookies. I'll miss our little chats when I switch routes next month."

"Me, too. And congratulations on your promotion," she yelled as he headed down the porch steps.

She closed the door and sighed. "Now, I'll have to break in a new driver, and he'll never be as nice as Simon."

Jade smiled and handed her a hot chocolate.

"Thanks. I will miss him. He's been fun to talk to, and it doesn't hurt that he looks like a Love Channel actor or a romance novel cover model," Patti said, blowing on her cup.

"You should ask him out for coffee or something," Jade nudged.

Patti made a face. "I don't know."

"Or at least get his contact information." Jade raised one eyebrow.

"I'll think about it." Changing the subject, Patti added, "I put the inventory list on your desk."

"Thanks. Always the dedicated employee. But you should think about getting his contact info. You'll be sorry if you let a chance get away."

Jade returned to her desk and picked up the inventory. Lots of new items for her next order. Her phone buzzed, drawing her attention away from Patti's list.

Ruby texted. **Have you seen Wren?** Jade's stomach dropped like she was on a rollercoaster. Not another problem with the TV crew.

Before she could reply, her phone buzzed with a number she didn't recognize. Hoping it wasn't someone inquiring about her vehicle warranty, she said, "Hello," hesitantly.

"Ms. Hicks, please," said a gruff voice on the other end.

"This is Jade. How can I help you?"

"This is Ezra Hopkins with the Love Channel, and I'm in a bit of a pickle this morning. I can't seem to locate Paige Wilson or Wren Pierce. Could you take a minute and check to see if either is at the campers? Neither are answering a phone this morning."

"Not a problem. I'll go check and let you know either way."

"Good," he said, disconnecting.

Jade made a face at her phone and yelled to Patti, "I've got to go check on something for Ezra. I'll be right back."

"Okeeeee dokey," Patti replied.

Pushing thoughts of doom and disaster to the back of her mind, Jade slipped into her puffy parka and out the back door. She hustled across the lot, looking down every row. Not seeing anyone, she trekked over to the big tent. Most of the equipment trucks were gone, and one woman was under the tent, wiping off the tables.

"Hi. Have you seen Paige or Wren?" Jade asked. The woman shook her head and continued with her task.

Jade circled the tent and looped back for another pass through the campers. On a whim, she walked to the camper behind Dante's and knocked on the door. When there was no answer, she tried again, straining to listen for any nearby noise. When there was no response, she trudged back to the store and texted Ezra an update.

Then she texted Nick, **Ezra called. He can't find Paige or Wren.**

Think there's an issue? he replied.

Don't know what to think. Keep an eye out.

Nick sent a string of eye emojis, and Jade laughed.

She focused on her upcoming marketing schedule for Halloween through New Year's while Patti chatted with customers in the front of the store. Thoughts of Paige and Wren kept interrupting and trying to drag her to the dark side. Could someone really be targeting the TV crew?

At four-thirty, Jade locked the front door behind Patti and did a quick walk-through. "Come on, Chloe. It's you and me. Let's go see what we can find."

On their way home, she spotted Marius and Dante and nudged Chloe closer to the men. "Hey, guys. How are y'all?" she asked as she approached.

"Girl, I don't know how much more of this chaos I can take. They're dropping like flies," Dante said.

"What happened?" Jade stepped closer to the pair.

"Paige was late, and Ezra was on a rampage," Marius said.

"And our girl, Paige, wasn't even clever enough to make up a decent story. Her lame, 'I overslept' bit is getting old. We're all taking bets on when the bigwigs will can her hind parts. My vote is for the minute Olivia returns," Dante said, checking his phone.

"What about Wren?" Jade asked.

"Who knows? She works for corporate, so she comes and goes as she pleases. Wren's not afraid of anyone. Her bosses are at headquarters. She may have gotten reassigned to another project. Nobody seemed too concerned."

"Except Ezra and Brian. They both are out of their minds. They bark orders constantly," Marius muttered.

"I hate to say this, but I'll be glad when this one is over. I think we all need a break from each other. I think your beach is cursed," Dante said.

Jade bit her bottom lip and swallowed her original retort. "I hope not. But Chloe found a hammer in the bushes over there yesterday. It belonged to Eddie. Any idea why a hammer would be near my fence?"

"Eddie doesn't like anyone to touch her stuff," Marius said. "She's been railing about misplaced and stolen stuff since we got here."

"I have no idea why someone would throw it away. Unless they used it to bonk someone on the head. This is too much. This show is jinxed. Maybe I need to find a safer line of work." Dante ran his hand through his bleached do that resembled a pompadour from the doo-wap days.

"I think someone's out to get Eddie. She went on a tear recently on some of the camera guys and the gaffers. She got them in trouble for cutting corners. They may be trying to teach her a lesson," Marius said.

"Hey, we're heading out to karaoke night with some of the guys. Wanna come along?" Dante looked up from his phone screen. "We could all use a break from this lunacy."

"Thanks so much, but I need to work on some things tonight at home. Y'all have fun." Jade waved over her shoulder as she guided Chloe through the campers toward the street.

After getting Chloe fed, she made a ham and cheese sandwich and settled in at her dining room table with a glass of milk. Jotting down all the miscellaneous facts she could remember, she added additional sticky notes to her wall. Right now, it was a jumble of brightly colored squares with no pattern or focus. Was she wasting her time? Maybe she should leave this to Nick and his task force.

She pulled down all of the pastel-colored squares and read each one. On a whim, she made a column for each person and put the appropriate notes under each. Olivia, Raphael, Elle, and Paige had the most items under their names.

A knock at the door broke her chain of thought. Chloe tried to push her way out when Jade opened the door for Nick. He scooped up the dog and stepped inside.

"Hey. I left the gym and thought I'd check in on you. I promise as soon as this is over, I will no longer be the phantom boyfriend." Jade hugged him and squished the little dog between them. Chloe wiggled and broke up the embrace.

"I see you've done some remodeling." Nick pointed to the wall.

"I thought maybe a new perspective would help. These seem to be the people that I have the most information on." Jade tapped her bottom lip with her index finger. "Do you know if they found Wren?"

"Nobody filed a report, so technically, she's not missing," he said, staring at something under Elle's column. "Wanna go for a walk? Maybe it'll clear both our heads."

Chloe yipped and galloped toward the door.

"Sounds like she agrees. Let me get my tennis shoes. Be back in a sec," Jade said.

By the time Nick had Chloe leashed up, Jade returned with her shoes and coat. She followed the pair out the door and down the path where the crushed oyster shells had an iridescent look in the twilight. The setting sun backlit the pine trees to the west, and the moon, almost full, looked magical in the gray-purply sky.

The trio walked in silence across the empty beach. Lights in the nearby homes and businesses dotted the shoreline. The red light on the end of the dock flashed in a heartbeat pattern to warn boaters not to stray too close to the shore.

The chilly breeze made Jade shiver, and Nick put his arm around her and pulled her close. "This one is stumping me. All kinds of nefarious things are going on, and it seems like the culprit is a ghost. He or she leaves no clue. They can't be lucky all the time," he said.

"And the crimes tend to vary. They seem kind of random, with different victims. No pattern," Jade added.

"Maybe that's the clue that we're looking for." Nick slowed his pace.

"Maybe there is no grand plan. They could have happened at the moment without any planning. Crimes of passion."

"That would make sense. I have racked my brain looking for the one big string that connects them, and there doesn't seem to be anything," she said.

"You won't believe the tips and clues the task force has been running down. It seems endless. And we have to either prove or discard each one. It's overwhelming. Oh, criminy. Who left all that garbage under the pier? If it's the film crew, I need to speak to the producer." Nick pulled away and sped toward the pylons and the pile of trash bags in the damp sand. Jade trailed behind in the fading light.

Nick grunted and handed Jade Choe's leash. He grabbed two of the trash bags and tossed them away.

Chloe darted for the bags, sniffing and snorting. Jade picked her up as Nick continued to toss bags behind him.

"Call 911," he shouted. "Tell them I'm with you, and we need an ambulance. I think she's still breathing."

Chapter Thirty-Two

J ade juggled Chloe's leash and her phone. When the call connected, she said, "Hi, this is Jade Hicks. I'm with Sheriff Nick Driscoll under Suggs's Pier. We need an ambulance right away. There's an unconscious woman, but the sheriff said she's breathing."

"Suggs's Pier?" the dispatcher asked.

"Yes, we're under the pier. Sort of in the middle."

"Rescue is on the way. Can someone guide them over to where you are?" the dispatcher asked.

"Yes. Thank you." Jade disconnected and stepped toward the trash bags. Leaning forward for a closer view, she gasped and stifled a shriek that came out as a squeak.

Wren Pierce lay curled up in the sand. If she didn't know better, Jade would have thought she was sleeping.

"What's wrong with her?" Jade asked.

"Not sure. There's some blood on her face," Nick said, shining his flashlight app around the scene. "I'm guessing it's blunt force trauma like the others." He straightened up and let out a stream of air. "We'll check the back of her head when rescue gets here."

As a siren approached in the distance, Nick punched in numbers on his phone. "Driscoll here. I'm under Suggs's Pier. We found the body of an unconscious female. Rescue is on the way. Send over the closest deputy and forensics." He disconnected and continued to search around Wren.

Hoping there was some kind of clue about who did this to her, Jade hugged Chloe close to her. The chilly evening breeze and the sense of dread that

184

had descended with the nightfall caused Jade to shiver.

The sirens turned from a whine to a howl, and Jade shook off the pall of another attack. "I'll go wave them over." She trudged through the sand and signaled with one hand at three approaching EMTs. When they were close enough to hear, she shouted, "She's over there with the sheriff."

The trio jogged through the sand and took over the scene. Within minutes, they had Wren strapped to a backboard as Sebastian trudged over in the opposite direction.

Bright flashes caused Nick, Sebastian, and Jade to pause. When the blue dots stopped floating in front of her eyes, she looked around. Nosy Nell hurried across the sand toward the Busy Bean. Her camera bounced up and down as she bustled away.

"What's up? Looks like someone's been monitoring a police scanner," Sebastian said, shaking his head at the reporter's quick exit.

"We spotted a bunch of trash under here. When I came over for a closer look, I found the publicist. She was breathing, so maybe she can tell us what happened when she's stabilized," Nick said.

Sebastian nodded and started to surround the area with crime scene tape. He wrapped the perimeter and tied off his yellow tape around the pylons.

Jade pulled out her phone again and dialed Ezra. After a couple of rings, she heard a gruff "Hello."

"Mr. Hopkins, this is Jade Hicks. I'm at the pier with Sheriff Hobbs and his team. They found Wren unconscious."

The producer interrupted with a string of curses. When he paused for a breath, Jade continued, "They took her to the hospital."

"Which one?"

Jade looked at Nick and asked, "Hospital?"

"Riverside," he replied.

"They're taking her to Riverside Hospital," she repeated to Ezra.

"Same one as before?"

"Yes."

"I'll get Paige on it. Or maybe I should do it myself. Thanks for the update." The producer disconnected.

When Nick moved closer to her, Jade whispered, "Ezra or someone from his team is headed to the hospital."

"Thanks. I'm gonna be here for a while. Sorry," Nick said. "The forensic guys are bringing in the generator and the lights. Looks like a long night. Sebastian, I'm heading to the hospital."

"Do y'all need anything?" She asked, stepping closer.

"No. I promise a real date soon. One that doesn't end with a police investigation." He kissed her on the top of her head and returned to where Sebastian stood near the trash bags.

"Come on, Chloe." Jade hiked home through the sand. For all the police and rescue activity, the beach was fairly empty. She was surprised not to see more reporters or gawkers. Nell must have landed the scoop on this one.

After firing up her laptop, she made a list of the key players and sent an email to Todd, hoping his contact from last summer could help. One of his gamer friends who ventured into the underbelly of the internet assisted him with a barrage of negative reviews. It was worth a shot. Maybe she could dig up some dirt on the cast and crew that mere mortals don't have access to.

Jade paused and stared at her wall. She hopped up and added a sticky under Wren's name. *Everyone seemed to be a target.*

Jade picked up her phone again and put it down. Changing her mind about calling Ruby, she grabbed her purse. "Chloe, I'll be back as soon as I can. I need to check on something."

The white dog rolled over in her bed with all four stubby legs in the air.

Jade hurried out to the lime-green Jeep and took the long way to the Pearl to avoid the people gathered on the nearby streets. Flashing red and blue lights gave an eerie view of the faces in the gaggle that had gathered at the dunes. The crowd that had materialized out of nowhere and had expanded like a floating jellyfish. People covered the area from the back of Mermaid Books and the Busy Bean to the sand, where they watched the police action under the pier.

Jade inched forward around the crowds, and about fifteen minutes later, she found parking near Ruby's and hurried to the front door. Light spilled out from all the front windows of the B and B, creating an inviting glow.

"Hi, Jade," Ruby said when she opened the door. Her voice sounded softer, but she let out a sigh.

"Hi. You doing okay?" Jade stepped inside the foyer. "I was with Nick when he found Wren under the pier tonight," Jade whispered. She glanced around to see if any of the Love Channel folks were nearby.

"This whole filming thing has been a fiasco. I'll be lucky to get out of this with my reputation intact. My establishment has been drug through the social media muck more times than I'd like to think about. Now, I'm counting the days until they leave town."

"I know it's been tough. The EMT said they took Wren to Riverside Hospital. Where is everyone?"

"Paige was here for a while. She said she was going back to her camper. She had a headache. Ezra and Brian rushed out without saying anything, and Olivia's in the library resting. I haven't seen Elle and Raphael. They were both acting cagey, and they slipped out before the rest of the group got word about Wren. Eleven more days, by the way. I may take a vacation after all this is over. Somebody can wait on me and bring me tall, pink drinks with fruit spears and colorful paper umbrellas." Ruby brushed a stray strand of gray hair that had slipped from her ponytail off the side of her face.

Jade patted her shoulder. "You deserve a vacation. Go somewhere fun. I want to see Olivia before I leave. You need anything?"

"No, just for you and Nick to figure out who's trying to sabotage this show. I feel like I'm always checking that the doors are locked and constantly looking over my shoulder. It's taxing being on high alert all the time." Ruby turned on her crepe-souled shoes and headed toward the kitchen.

Jade followed her partially down the foyer and paused at the entrance to the library. Olivia, dressed in black yoga pants and an orange hoodie, lounged in one of the side chairs near the fireplace. A large hardback rested upside down in her lap. The production manager looked ten years younger with no makeup and her long, straight hair pulled back in a ponytail.

Jade knocked lightly on the wood trim of the doorway. "Hi, Olivia. I thought I'd stop by and check on you." She chided herself for not putting together a basket for her.

"Oh, hi," the woman said, straightening her back and setting the book on a side table. "I think I dozed off."

"How are you doing?" Jade stepped closer to where the woman sat.

"It's nice to be back." Her voice was barely above a whisper. "It felt like it was touch and go for a while. I'm hoping to head back to work tomorrow. I should have been there today, but I've been a bit lightheaded. I hate this out-of-control feeling."

"Can I get you anything?" Jade asked.

She shook her head slightly. "I'll hang out here for a bit, and then it's time to turn in."

Jumping at the chance to probe a little about the attack, Jade asked, "Any idea who did this to you?"

"No. Like I told the police multiple times, I was walking back here after having a heated conversation right after I had had one with Paige. I guess I was a little distracted about the altercation, and I didn't really pay attention to what was around me. I remember someone with a hooded sweatshirt approached. And then it's all a blur after that. I couldn't even tell the officers if it was a man or a woman. The person was tall. Taller than me." She braced her hand on the side of her head and paused. "I woke up a couple of times in a dark place, but I might have been dreaming. I remember being hungry and thirsty. And then I woke up at the hospital."

"I am so sorry this happened. Your coworkers were really concerned, and they've missed you. My dog and I found a mallet-like hammer under the bushes behind the store. Not sure if it has anything to do with your case, but we turned it over to the police."

"Hey, anything at this point could help. I'd like to find out why I was attacked. My purse and wallet weren't stolen. I can't believe it was some random person. And robbery obviously wasn't the reason." She rose and steadied herself on the chair.

"Can I help you to your room?" Jade asked. "Or have Ruby bring you anything?"

"No thanks. I'll be fine. I need to lie down." She walked slowly toward the staircase in the lobby. "On second thought, could you ask her to bring me a ginger ale and some saltine crackers? Thanks." Olivia climbed the stairs one step at a time.

Jade knocked and pushed open the kitchen door. "Hey, Ruby. Olivia returned to her room. She wanted to know if you had any ginger ale and saltine crackers?"

Ruby nodded and pulled a box of crackers from a nearby cabinet. After arranging them on a plate, she went to the industrial refrigerator to retrieve the drink. "Not a problem. Be back in a flash."

"Call me if I can do anything." Jade waved over her shoulder. Jade picked her way down the driveway. The light from the streetlamps cast yellowy halos on the street that almost look like puddles. When she rounded the corner to retrieve the Jeep, she noticed the reporters gathered in clusters. The flock of paparazzi rushed at her like gulls after a French fry as she neared the Jeep. Each peppered her with questions.

"What can you tell us about what happened tonight? Are the Love Channel folks huddled at the inn over there? Will filming get delayed? Is someone trying to sabotage the show?"

"I was here visiting my friend Ruby. What have you heard?" Jade asked, pasting on her best-surprised look.

The taller guy with the camera said, "They found someone under the pier. After the ambulance left, we rushed over here to see if anything was going on. Who's inside back there?"

Jade shrugged her shoulders. "I was there to talk to the owner. Sorry, I can't help you." She unlocked the Wrangler's door. The nearby photographers had to step back quickly as she swung open the door and climbed in. She rolled down the window and called out, "You may check with Nell Jones, our local reporter. She always has her hand on the pulse of what's going on around here." Jade put the Jeep in gear to head home and scour the internet for anything new.

Chapter Thirty-Three

If Jade didn't know better, she would have thought it was the middle of summer in Mermaid Bay based on the crowd size on Neptune Road. She picked up Chloe and dodged elbows and people on her way to the store. It felt like a life-sized game of Frogger with people because no cars could get through.

Around her vacant store, throngs of people congregated near the hurricane fencing. One of the guards from the production company patrolled in a golf cart behind the orange plastic fence. He kept repeating his path up and down the barricade like he was mowing grass. One golf cart wasn't going to stop that mob from surging.

Jade scooted around the edge and hurried to the back door of her store. She flipped on her laptop and added a pod of strong coffee to the machine. Today, she needed the strongest brew she could find. Maybe two. While waiting for the machine to come to life and heat up her caffeine, Jade scrolled through her phone. Vivian had sent out a congratulatory business council group text to Nell, who sold some of her photos to a Hollywood publication. *Good for her. She's been waiting for a big break for a long time.*

As she settled in at her desk to print out the overnight orders, a knock at the back door caught Chloe and Jade's attention. Jade took a swig of her coffee and opened it. "Hey there. Oh, sorry. With all those people out front, I didn't unlock the front door."

"Oh, no problem," Patti said, bustling inside. "I couldn't get through them anyway. I had to make a detour. It's crazy out there. I parked in the neighborhood and hoofed over. What is going on around here?"

"Nick and I found Wren under the pier near a bunch of trash bags. And Nell sold the story to some Hollywood gossip site."

"Yay for her. I mean Nell, not Wren," Patti said, pulling a mug from the cupboard. "If this keeps happening, they'll run out of people who can fill in for each other. It seems like everyone is getting attacked. Does Nick have any leads? The Love Channel's not all that lovey-dovey. And what was Wren doing under the pier all by herself? She didn't seem like the outdoorsy type."

"I haven't talked to Nick since last night. I know he didn't get much sleep. I left as the forensic unit arrived. I don't know how long the police stayed at the scene," Jade said.

"This whole filming thing has been crazy. It's not like how I imagined it. Maybe a true crime network needs to come to town next. We haven't had much luck with the romance."

Jade made a pruny face. "It's not as glamorous as I thought it was. Oh, I saw Olivia at Ruby's. She's ready to return to work. Speaking of that, I didn't get very far this morning. I ran the report of the previous night's orders." Jade held up the papers.

"I'm on it. It'll keep me busy. Be back in a flash to start boxing them. That is, after coffee. It's been loco today. I feel like I've already had my workout with my jaunt over here." Patti loaded her mug with creamer.

"Thanks. I need to poke around and see what I can find out."

"Let me know if any of it's juicy," she called over her shoulder. "We haven't heard much from Raphael and Elle. They must be trying to fly under the radar, which is weird because they always seem to be battling for the headlines."

"Now that you mention it, I haven't heard a peep about them."

"And the gossip sites have been focused on bigger stories. Some K Pop band broke up," Patti called from the lobby.

Jade brewed a second cup of coffee and pulled up her spreadsheet. She had reordered her sticky notes in the dining room twice. Was she looking at this all wrong? Jade pulled up a blank workbook and started listing all the love/hate connections. She scoured all of her notes and jotted down anything pertinent.

When she was done, she sank back into her chair and stared at the screen. Raphael had the most love connections with Elle, Britt, a ton of starlets and models, and even a fling with Paige. She couldn't find any love interests of the dead reporter. But Elle and Raphael were upset with him about the photos and extortion attempts. Elle had been linked through the years to rock stars, directors, and more than her fair share of her leading men. Right now, her latest tete-a-tete was the security guard, even though she rendezvoused occasionally with Raphael.

Now, where Olivia and Wren weren't linked romantically with anyone Jade could find, they did have quite the list of altercations with actors, staff, and crew. They were tied with a long list of enemies if you didn't count all the wacky fan comments that Raphael and Elle received. Brian, the director, had been happily married for years, and Jade couldn't find any dalliances or naysayers.

Ezra liked young actresses and had been connected to a long string of blonds through the years. He'd been married and divorced three times, and before Elle became a Love Channel sensation, they had a summer fling during a filming of a rom-com early in her career. Interesting. Lots of overlaps. Jade decided to transfer this information to color-coded sticky notes to add to her board when she got home this evening.

Letting out a heavy sigh, Jade turned when Patti entered with a cart full of glass and pop culture decorations. On the top, Jade spotted some heart and film-themed ones she had ordered for the Love Channel's visit. The cart's second shelf, filled with mermaid and beachy ornaments, almost spilled when she stopped abruptly by the desks.

"Here we goooooo," Patti said in a singsong voice. "I love filling the orders. It's a cross between a scavenger hunt and shopping excursion."

"Let me help you wrap those." Jade stood and stretched.

Patti and Jade set up an assembly line-like production on the worktable. Within an hour, everything was boxed and labeled.

"There," Patti said. "All done. The beachy ornaments seem to be doing well. You may want to order some mermaids and starfish."

Jade nodded. Her phone buzzed with an incoming text. Glancing at her phone, she said, "It looks like Vivian's calling a business council meeting this evening at five to talk about security and ways we can stay safe." She set her phone down on the desk. "I guess I should go."

"At least the people-watching should be entertaining. You should bring popcorn." Patti pulled out her phone. "I've got to head straight home. It's book club night at my house. Let me know if anything interesting comes out at the meeting. We may need to practice our personal security moves." Patti did a karate chop that made Jade laugh.

On days like today, Jade was grateful for the website orders, especially when there was no foot traffic in the store. She and Patti had everything buttoned up by four o'clock. "Time for a walk and to get Chloe settled." The dog's ears shot up, and she danced next to Jade's desk.

"I'm leaving, too." Patti picked up her jacket and purse. "I need to pick up some food trays and dessert for tonight. If you don't have anything for me, I'll see you this weekend."

The crowds around the store and campers had dissipated since this morning. Chloe was able to walk without the fear of being trampled by tall humans.

After freshening her makeup, Jade grabbed her purse and jacket. "I'll be back as soon as I can, and we can work on our murder wall later." Chloe was ears deep in her food bowl to have any relevant feedback on the suspects.

Jade had to dodge jaywalking visitors and those who chose to avoid the crowded sidewalks by driving almost in the middle of Neptune Road. When she finally found a parking spot in front of the government center, she let out a sigh. "That took way longer than it should have," she said to herself.

Falling in with the line of people headed to the front doors, she entered the already packed library and found an empty spot next to the back wall. The air in the conference room seemed stuffy. Jade wiggled out of her jacket and leaned against the cool cinder block wall.

Flocks of people flooded into the room as Vivian popped her head in the doorway and proceeded to count the audience. Her finger bounced up and down, and her lips moved as she completed her task. She paused and frowned. Vivian opened the two doors to the conference room and kicked the doorstops into place. Then she turned and pushed her way through the standing crowd to the lectern. After thumping the microphone several times, a high-pitched squeal echoed through the speakers, and a groan radiated from the audience. Vivian scowled at the AV technician in the back and then blew into the microphone.

"Thank you all for coming to our business council meeting to talk about safety. But before we get started, I want to remind you that we are almost at the fire marshal's count for capacity in this room. Overflow guests can be accommodated in the lobby area outside of the doors." Vivian pointed with both hands toward the doors that opened into the main part of the library. She looked like a flight attendant demonstrating emergency features. "Remember, safety is everyone's concern."

The crowds moved around, and some people stepped outside the conference room. Jade glanced around at those near her. Most of the people who lined the back and side walls looked like reporters with multi-pocketed vests and large cameras. Vivian's AV tech propped open the back door, and the blast of coolness offered a slight reprieve from the stagnant air.

"Thank you all for coming. We will start momentarily. Is Deputy Sanchez here? If he's in the back, y'all make room for him," Vivian said, scanning the room.

"Coming. Sorry. My meeting ran late." Sebastian made his way through the crowd with his uniform hat in his hand. When he took the lectern, Sebastian raised the microphone. "Hello, everyone. I'm glad to see so many of you concerned about security. I'm Deputy Sebastian Sanchez, and I wanted to take this opportunity to review some safety tips that are good for everyone to practice." He nodded toward the AV guy in the back, and the lights dimmed. Sebastian proceeded to step through a presentation that he must have prepared for school kids. The audience yawned and fidgeted in their seats, but no one left in case there was something more interesting at the end.

When the slides dimmed and the fluorescent lights popped back on, Sebastian asked, "Are there any questions?"

A loud roar rose in the room as photographers and reporters rushed to the front with hands waving.

Vivian pushed Sebastian away and banged on the lectern with her gavel until the audience settled down. "Excuse me. We need to be civil. One at a time. There is no reason for chaos or yelling. Deputy Sanchez can answer one question at a time. Puh-leeeze." Vivian stepped back and tapped the gavel on the palm of her hand repeatedly as Sebastian stepped forward again.

"I'm here to take questions about the safety presentation. The sheriff's task force will have a press conference tonight at seven o'clock in front of the building next door to address the situation that happened under Suggs's pier." Murmurs and rustling filled the room.

The reporters started to pour out of the room like bugs headed toward a discarded popsicle. Sebastian waited until the room emptied.

"Thank you, Deputy Sanchez, for your patience and that wonderful presentation on how we can all be safer and look out for each other. I like the buddy system you recommended," Vivian added, stepping back from the microphone.

"Any questions?" Sebastian asked, looking at the remaining audience members.

Kelly Jamison, owner of the Pirate's Chest antique store, raised her hand. When the deputy nodded in her direction, she cleared her throat. "Is there reason for alarm? I mean, it seems like the crimes have amped up around here."

"Everyone should be cautious and alert," Sebastian said. "Always be vigilant of what's around you, and report anything that looks odd or strange. And look out for those around you."

"It's kind of disconcerting that we've had a rash of attacks in a short amount of time." Kelly played with the rings on her hand.

"Again, please report anything that looks suspicious. We know that we have many guests in town. Totals recently have rivaled our tourist numbers in the height of summer. Don't hesitate to call the sheriff's office if something looks out of place."

"Thank you, Deputy." Kelly glanced around the room.

Tish Taylor, standing near the doorway with two of her realtor cronies, raised a perfectly manicured hand with blood-red nails. "Excuse me, Deputy. At the press conference today, do you know if anyone will address all the bad publicity this filming is bringing to our community?"

Sebastian tipped his chin slightly in Tish's direction. "I'm not sure if it will be called out specifically, but the sheriff and the task force will address the issues and the progress of their investigations."

Amy stood in front of her seat next to Todd and waved her arm in the air. When the deputy called on her, she said, "Hi. I had a comment about what she said. Um, not all publicity is bad. I know no one likes bad reviews or negative stories, but it isn't always horrible." She patted Todd's shoulder. "People tend to have short attention spans before they move on to the next hot topic. By the time this show airs, all of this chaos will be a footnote. I suggest that we all wait it out. We'll roll into summer, and this will be a distant memory."

Tish and her posse glared at Amy, who took her seat. Todd stretched in his chair and draped his arm around the bookstore owner.

Tish cleared her throat, and all eyes focused on her with laser precision. "You may be right. But that doesn't change anything now. We're still in the middle of a crime spree. And the media is blaming us. They'll pack up and go back to Hollywood, and we'll have to clean up the mess." She raised one eyebrow and glared at Sebastian.

After a long pause, the deputy scanned the room and said, "Again, there will be specific information at the press conference at seven. If you're interested, I suggest that you attend or watch it on the local news. Any more questions?"

When no one spoke, the deputy continued. "Then thank you. Be careful out there." He picked up his hat and exited the room.

Vivian banged the gavel again. "Any business council items to discuss?"

When no one replied, she banged her gavel again. "Then meeting adjourned."

Jade filed out with the crowd. On the sidewalk, where it was shoulder-to-shoulder people, she felt a tug on her sleeve.

Chapter Thirty-Four

"Hey," Amy said, slightly breathless, catching up to Jade on the sidewalk. "You flew out of the meeting like your hair was on fire. Todd and I are planning to grab something to eat at his place and then head back in time for the press conference. Do you want to ride to the hot dog stand with us?"

"Thanks," Jade said, following Amy and Todd to the parking lot. Jade let out a deep breath, relieved when she spotted his blue FJ Cruiser and not his hearse. She piled in the back seat, and Todd bumped through the grassy area, avoiding people wandering around outside the government center.

A few minutes later, they pulled into the back of Hot Diggity Dogs near the dumpsters. Todd hopped out and unlocked the back door.

"Let me wash up, and I'll be ready to grill whatever you ladies want for dinner. Come on in," Todd said.

"Lobster?" Amy yelled as he walked down a dimly lit hallway.

"Funny," he replied from somewhere inside. "That's not on the menu yet."

Jade and Amy found a table near the front window where they could watch streams of people wander around town.

"Lisa's doing okay by herself at the bookstore. I'm hoping some of this traffic turns into customers," Amy said. "There's been tons of browsing and not a lot of buying."

"What can I get you?" Todd yelled from the grill as his part-timers waited on the growing line of customers.

"What do you want?" Amy rose and looked at Jade.

"A turkey dog with mustard and a Coke. Thanks."

"Be back in a flash." Amy bypassed the line of customers and stood near the counter closest to the grill.

She returned with three drinks. "It pays to know people," Amy said with a wink. She slid onto the bench across from Jade.

"Looks like he'll be busy for a while. That line appeared out of nowhere." Jade stared out the front window. The queue of people now extended from the counter out onto the sidewalk.

"Amy, you're up," Todd yelled.

She popped out of her seat again and fetched the tray of hot dogs and onion rings. "Dinner is served," Amy said, returning to her seat.

The two ate in silence as Todd and his staff kept the line moving.

"I love to watch him work," Amy said. "He's got this down to a science." She leaned forward and whispered, "And I'm glad business has picked up for him since that fiasco. We have to head back soon if we want to get a good spot for the press conference. Let me see what he wants to do." Amy wormed her way closer to the counter.

Jade popped the remaining bite of hot dog in her mouth as Amy talked to Todd, who continued to grill orders.

Amy slid into her seat. "He doesn't want to leave his part-timers in a lurch with this crowd. He said I could take his car and drive us back."

"Or we could walk," Jade added. "My Jeep is there, so I can bring you home."

"Sounds like a plan." Amy gathered up the trash and returned to the counter. She handed Todd his car keys, and he leaned over the counter to kiss her. "Y'all have fun and stay out of trouble."

"We'll try, but we may call you if we need bail money," Amy yelled over her shoulder.

The women waved and made their way past the line of customers and out onto the packed sidewalk. Jade and Amy threaded their way through the throngs and found a spot where they could see most of the glass entryway to the Sheriff's Office, where a lectern and three flags stood nearby on the sidewalk. Nick, two state troopers, and the town administrator approached the lectern, and the noise level increased as the crowd jockeyed for the best viewing spot.

The town manager stepped forward and adjusted the microphone. "Thank you all for coming out tonight. I'm Charles Winters, Town Manager for Mermaid Bay. This evening, the joint police task force led by Sheriff Nick Driscoll and our state trooper partners will have a statement related to recent events in our community. There will be a few minutes for questions, so hold your items until the end. In the meantime, I'd like to remind everyone to stay alert and vigilant. If you see something out of the ordinary, please report it to the authorities. And now, I'd like to turn it over to the sheriff."

"Thank you," Nick said, stepping closer to the mic. A tingle of excitement shot through Jade as all eyes were on her handsome boyfriend. "Over the past weeks, we've had a string of incidents affecting members of the TV cast and crew from the Love Channel who have been filming all around town. The task force, made up of our staff, the state police, and the state police's forensics unit, has been investigating this and pursuing hundreds of leads. Over six hundred of them have been from calls to our hotline. We have stepped up patrols and have worked closely with the Love Channel executives in their effort to increase their private security details." Nick paused and scanned the faces in the audience. "The task force is pleased to announce that we have made an arrest. This morning, Eddie Bailey was arrested for assault, kidnapping, and murder." A murmur arose from the audience. Nick paused, and when the noise subsided, he continued, "I don't have any details at this time. The investigation is ongoing. I'd like to thank all of our partners, especially Trooper Mark Evans from the Richmond field office. We will have another briefing when we have more details to share."

Jade's eyes widened. *Eddie, the owner of all the missing tools? Why would she kill the reporter?*

"Thank you, Sheriff." A slim officer in a blue uniform stepped forward. "I am Mark Evans, the state police liaison on the task force, and I facilitate information sharing and resources. We would like to thank everyone who called the tip line and all of our partners who helped make today's arrest possible."

The town manager looked around and then stepped up to the microphone after a long pause. "We'll take a couple of questions in the time remaining, but please know, Sheriff Driscoll and his team won't address anything that is currently under investigation."

Hands flew into the air. And it seemed like every reporter within earshot took two steps forward and yelled out a question.

The town manager tapped on the microphone, and the thunks bounced off the nearby buildings. "One at a time. We'll try to get to as many folks as we can, but the task force members do need to get back to their work. You, in the pink coat."

"Hi, I'm Corinne Mathieu with WRIC out of Richmond. Can you give us anything else on the man you have in custody?"

Nick leaned forward, "Her name is Eddaline Bailey, and she is a member of the maintenance and construction team for the TV crew that is in town filming."

People in the audience shuffled and rustled, and some made gasping noises.

Someone in the crowd yelled, "Could you say the name again and your name, please."

"It's Sheriff Nicholas Driscoll of Mermaid Bay, and this is Trooper Mark Evans with the Virginia State Police. The suspect in custody is Eddaline 'Eddie' Bailey."

"Did she act alone? Or are you still looking for additional suspects?" A guy with a beard yelled.

"At this time, this is our only arrest," Nick said.

Reporters called out questions, and it was hard to hear anything over all of the loud voices.

The town manager stepped forward. "We need to get back to work on the investigation. We will have another update when there is something to share." As he, Nick, and Trooper Evans slipped inside the glass doors, the AV technician from the library approached the lectern and started to disassemble the equipment. When the reporters realized there was no one except the AV guy to shout questions at, they headed toward the parking lot.

"Well, that was fun. Sort of not," Amy said. "I'm marking press conferences off the old bucket list. Did you know this Eddie person?"

Jade nodded as the pair walked to her Jeep. "Chloe found a hammer near my back fence after the murder. It had 'EBB' carved into the handle. After the police took it, I asked around. That's when I found out Eddie was Eddaline. She said that the hammer, a screwdriver, and some wrenches had gone missing recently."

"Interesting. It's a good thing you didn't give her the murder weapons back." Amy gritted her teeth.

As the traffic cleared, Jade drove slowly toward Mermaid Books. Amy said, "I'm going over to Todd's. I've got to catch him up on all the news."

Making a quick right turn, Jade pulled into the Hot Diggity Dogs' lot next to the hearse.

"Thanks for the ride. Tonight was more fun than reruns on TV." Amy hopped out and hurried toward the front door.

I guess I won't have to add all those new sticky notes to my dining room wall after all. But why does Eddie's arrest bother me so much?

Chapter Thirty-Five

J ade couldn't keep thoughts of Eddie's arrest out of her head. She tossed and turned all night. It didn't make sense. How was the carpenter linked to all the incidents on the set? Jade racked her brain to try to remember if Eddie was even around when most of the problems occurred. Wouldn't someone have noticed her at the B and B?

On her walk to the store, she dialed Nick's cell before she lost her nerve. He said, "Hey, what's up?" before she could chicken out.

Jade cleared her throat. "I was thinking about Love Channel stuff this morning." She paused and cleared her throat again. "I mean, are you sure about Eddie?" she almost whispered.

"Why?" It sounded like he was chewing something.

"She doesn't seem to fit any of the motives or scenarios."

"The DNA and her fingerprints came back on that hammer and a coffee cup from one of the scenes. We can link her to two of the crime scenes."

"Oh," Jade said, her thoughts bouncing around her head like ping-pong balls. "Let me know when you can stop by for dinner."

"Will do. I'm headed to the office now. See you." He disconnected, and Jade stared at her phone. *But it still doesn't make any sense. She just popped out of nowhere.*

Chloe interrupted her thoughts as she darted toward the campers instead of the store. Jade followed to see what caught the Frenchie's attention.

A golf cart bounced along the grass. It slowed down as the pair approached.

"Hi, Olivia." Jade waved as Chloe tried to climb into the cart with the production manager. Jade picked up the pudgy dog and hugged her close.

"It's good to be back, even if I have to spend all my time cleaning up disasters." She reached over and patted the wiggly dog. "I told Ezra I still wasn't a hundred percent, but I'll give him what I can."

"He's thankful to have you back. I heard about Eddie. I was surprised." Jade watched the woman's face.

"I still don't have any memory of the attack except that I thought I remember the person being taller. I guess it could have been Eddie. I didn't recognize the voice. But maybe she was disguising it. I'm glad this mess is over."

Before anyone could comment, Paige came around the corner carrying a black gym bag. She stopped abruptly when she saw Olivia. Her mouth opened, and then she closed it.

"Hi, Paige." Jade waved.

The woman, dressed in all black with a black raincoat hanging open, shifted her stance like she was about to turn and bolt. "I didn't realize you were coming back today. I have some things I need to take care of for Brian this morning," Paige finally said.

"Like what?" Olivia asked.

"He wants me to call corporate and get a backfill for Eddie for the remainder of the schedule. He also wants changes to Elle's costumes. He wants me to revise the schedule and get him a copy by this morning. And something else that I can't remember right now."

"Well, figure out what the thing was and let me know. Take care of the costume request, and I'll call corporate. Meet me at the craft tent in ten minutes to go over the schedule before you send it to him. I don't want any more screw-ups. Brian and Ezra have been fussing about what's been going on around here." Olivia paused and stared back at Paige, "And I would have thought you would have jumped at the chance to show your skills. You showed everyone something. And you left them talking. Don't look at me like that. You had to know you were in over your head." Olivia made a harrumphing sound. "Oh, by the way, I have a list of things I need you to take care of this morning, too. The tent in ten." Olivia pointed over her shoulder and then back at Paige.

Paige pasted on a cheesy smile, but the burning look in her eyes told another story.

Olivia nodded to Jade and put the cart in gear. She pointed her index finger at Paige. "Nine minutes now."

Paige turned and ambled between two nearby trailers.

"Come on, Chloe." The little dog snorted and followed Jade to the store.

Jade busied herself until the front door slammed, and Patti barged in. "Can you believe it? The crowds are back out front. They are so interested in the arrest. This show will be infamous. It's now linked to a true crime story. And we're trending again on social media." Patti paused and took a breath. "This is soooo exciting."

Looking out the front window, Jade could see hundreds of people along the plastic fencing near the campers. "I guess it's great publicity for the show."

"I heard that there were some of those true crime podcasters in town. We could be in the news for days." Patti's eyes sparkled. "Maybe they'll even do a documentary on it. Mermaid Bay may never be the same. They will want to talk to you since you found the weapon."

"Oh, I hope not. I'm done being in the spotlight," Jade said. "I need to do some work around here. Let's see what kind of orders came in overnight." Jade booted up her laptop and opened her application. "Wow. This is incredible. The last time I checked, we were well ahead of previous years, and that doesn't include our Christmas numbers yet. Whoo hooo!" She handed Patti three pages from the stack that spewed from the printer.

They each took a cart and spent the rest of the morning filling and shipping orders.

When Jade plopped down in her seat for a quick break, her phone rang. "Hi, Amy. What's up?"

"It's time for some fun. Todd forgot to tell you that he has a retro band on the patio tonight. Wanna come? Is Nick working?"

"Probably. But I'll check. Chloe and I'll be there. When?"

"I'll save you a seat. It starts at seven. Be prepared for all the eighties' hits. I need to go find my banana clip and legwarmers. See ya tonight." Amy disconnected.

"Hey, Patti, do you have plans for tonight?" Jade yelled through the open doorway.

"I'm having drinks with friends. Why?"

"Todd's got an eighties cover band on his deck tonight."

"Totally tubular!" Patti yelled from the lobby. "We're off to Tequila Mockingbird. If we're done early enough, we may swing by."

Jade tapped a quick invitation to Nick on the off chance he might be free. Her phone dinged with two frowny face emojis. **Sorry. Wrapping up stuff here. We have a meeting with the DA that will go late.**

If your plans change, I'll be with Amy and Todd on the HDD deck rockin' out to rad 80s tunes, she replied.

Gnarly, he texted back with a smiley and a heart.

The list of suspects and their relationships kept tickling at Jade's thoughts and pushing out the ones she had about tonight's concert. *Eddie still made no sense as the perpetrator. She wasn't even on anyone's radar.*

Did she totally miss the mark on this one? Nick's team had better information than she did. She tapped her pen on her desk. Opening the file, she scrolled through the names and relationships. Love and hate were a thin line apart, and there were quite a few of these on her list. Jade stared at all the associations on her list. Eddie's arrest didn't fit with anything she knew about the attacks. The carpenter wasn't linked to anyone. Why would someone flying under the radar go on a rampage?

She spent the next three hours scouring the internet for anything on Eddie Bailey. Not surprisingly, all the hits about her arrest had appeared overnight and in the wee hours of the morning. There was very little about Eddie's past. Her name and title were mentioned on the Love Channel page, and she had a brief bio on the IMDb page. "Hmmm. Fifteen years with the Love Channel, and she'd been crew on Hollywood productions since 1982. What would send a career person off the deep end? And what did Olivia say about her attacker?" Jade said aloud.

Chloe raised her ears and listened for any of her favorite words. When she didn't hear anything else interesting, she stretched out on her bed for an afternoon snooze.

Jade shook off the odd feeling and started to pack up her stuff. She wandered into the lobby. No, Patti. She followed snippets of "Karma Chameleon" into the rainbow room, where Patti dusted ornaments on the trees.

"Oh, hi," Patti said, turning off the music blaring from her phone. "Just tidying up and spending some time with my favorite ornaments."

Jade smiled. "I like all the colored lights in this room. Most of the showrooms have white twinkles. This one always reminded me of Oz. And that's always been my favorite movie." She brushed her hand across the decorations on the pink tree. "I hope you have fun tonight."

"I'm looking forward to it. We'll see if a good night becomes a fantastic night." Patti's dimples showed on her round cheeks when a smile lit up her face.

Jade crinkled her brow.

"I invited Simon, our old delivery guy, to join us. We'll see what happens." Patti giggled.

"Keep me posted on all the details. How exciting!" Jade winked at her friend.

"I hope there's news to tell. But right now, it's friends hanging out for drinks." Patti gave the tree with the pink ornaments one last swipe with the feather duster and said, "I'm headed out, too. I need to find something spectacular to wear."

"Have fun," Jade yelled as Patti retreated to the office. Jade did her walk-through and checked all the doors and windows. After setting the alarm, she said, "Come on, Chloe, we need to go find something retro to wear tonight."

At home, Jade found a thick sweater and pulled out fuzzy socks in case the wind off the water was chilly. She grabbed a poufy neon bow on a headband from her Halloween bin and pulled her hair up in a ponytail. She floofed the bow and touched up her makeup.

"You need something to represent the decade of excess," she said to Chloe. The dog side-eyed her and walked into the hall.

Jade rummaged through Chloe's costume collection and pulled out a spiked dog collar and a leather jacket. "I'll be the pop princess, and you be the hard rocker." Chloe raised one eyebrow and headed toward the front door for her leash. Jade grabbed a beach blanket and joined her French bulldog.

After a quick walk along the path to the beach, Chloe slowed her pace and sniffed everything in sight. Jade pulled her jacket closer around her and picked up her speed as they approached Todd's back deck. A small crowd had already gathered on chairs and blankets in the nearby sand.

She spotted Amy waving with both arms near the edge of the crowd. Jade tugged on the leash, and the pair trudged closer. "Hey. Glad you could make it. I saved you a seat. Where's your beau?" Amy patted the sand chair next to her.

"Working again."

"I thought he'd be out partying after arresting the bad guy. Or gal, in this case," Amy said.

"He said he had stuff to wrap up."

Todd interrupted and handed each of the women a brown bottle. "Hey, lovelies. Glad you could both make it." Not to be left out, Chloe jumped in his lap when he plopped down in the sand chair.

The dog curled up as the band started with a string of Cyndi Lauper, Adam Ant, and Culture Club covers. Amy and Jade danced in the sand to some of the hits from the Big 80s.

When the band took a break, the pair plopped down in their chairs. The stage lights lit up the area. Jade scanned the crowd and recognized some of the townies and film folks. She waved to Dante, who sat near Marius, Matilda, Lexi, and Olivia. Dante nodded and yelled, "Hey, you guys. Love this retro stuff."

Paige drifted through the crowd and stood a short distance behind the movie crew folks. No one seemed to notice her, and she made no effort to talk to anyone. Even in the dim light, Paige's scowl looked menacing, like she was harboring some big secret. *If looks could kill.*

Before Jade could get up to walk over to where the production assistant stood, she looked around and disappeared into the crowd.

Jade waved to the crew and stopped in the sand next to Olivia. "How are you feeling?"

"Back to normal. It's nice to hang out for a change," the production manager said.

"What happened to Paige? I thought I spotted her over here."

Marius made a throat-slashing gesture with his finger, but it was too late for Jade to retract her question.

Olivia paused. "She better not be. She needs to be back at work finishing all the stuff she didn't get done earlier. Work first. Then play. She's on thin ice."

The band blasted out a Van Halen medley, and Jade swallowed her comment about Paige. When the music drowned out their conversation, Jade waved and trotted back through the sand to her seat.

Paige and Olivia seem to be at each other's throats constantly.

Chapter Thirty-Six

Cuddling under a fuzzy blanket on the couch with Chloe, Jade zoned out from her television show. Thoughts of Eddie's arrest kept banging around in her head. She hopped up and pulled out her list of relationships. *What is bothering me so much about this?*

Grabbing a marker and two stacks of sticky notes, she dashed off all the names. She jotted romantic encounters on the magenta ones and sworn enemies on aqua ones. After putting them on the wall, she stepped back and looked for anything relevant. Paige and Raphael had the most problem relationships. *And they'd also had a fling at one time. Nick and his team are sure they have the right person. The Paige and Raphael thing seemed so out of place with all of his other supermodel and starlet flings. But so was Eddie's arrest. Something that I can't quite put my finger on keeps tickling at the back of my brain.*

Before Jade could explore her love/hate idea any further, her phone dinged with a series of alerts. The cameras behind the store showed two or maybe three people in the shadows. The grainy footage made the figures look shadowy as they darted in and out of the picture. Then, as quickly as they appeared, they were gone.

Bats bounced around in Jade's stomach. Everything looked okay, but she needed to double-check. She didn't want to be that crazy lady who called the police every time something moved outside. She'd go take a peek to see if it was really an issue. Stuffing her phone, keys, and pepper spray in the pocket of her jacket, she patted Chloe on the head and slipped out the front door.

She jogged down the street and slowed her pace as she neared the store. Nothing moved near the porch. Jade tiptoed around the side and poked her head out. The only sounds were an occasional tree frog and a car passing by. She stood and stared into the darkness. Nothing moved near the campers. Her heartbeat pounded in her temples. Little lights dotted the horizon from the camper windows.

Just as she moved around the back, she heard a twig snap and footsteps. Jade froze and listened. The rustling continued. She pulled out her phone and retreated around the corner. Fumbling to dial 911, she finally connected. "Hi, this is Jade Hicks at 'Tis the Season. I'm outside the store. I caught some intruders on the camera, and I need the police to come out," she whispered.

"How many intruders? And are you in a safe place?" The dispatcher asked.

"I'm fine. I think it's two. Maybe three. I can't tell. They're prowling around the back of my store."

"Can you give me any description of them?"

"No. They're all in dark clothing. I need to get closer. Hang on." Jade said. She nimbly walked through the grass, trying not to make a sound. She spotted two figures behind the store. One was lying in the grass.

"There are two of them," she whispered hurriedly into the phone. "And one's on the ground for some reason."

Using the shadows from the edge of the building as her cover, she picked her way around the store's back door to get closer.

"What do you want from me?" a female voice quivered.

Jade crept closer and gasped. She hoped the pair didn't hear her. Someone in a dark hoodie stood over the person on the ground. Jade couldn't identify either one. The standing person had his back to Jade. It looked like he was hunched forward. The person on the ground had curled up into a tight ball and inched away from the standing figure.

Jade scooted closer. The standing person kicked the one on the ground in the ribs. She groaned, clutching her stomach. She sat up and faced Jade. *Olivia!*

The standing guy kicked at the figure again. "Shut up. You've done enough damage. It's over. I can't take any more. You have ruined my life."

"I didn't ruin your life. I gave you a chance, which by the way, you managed to royally screw up all on your own." Olivia gritted her teeth and spat out the words.

"I'm tired. Overworked. Stressed out. You people are brutal. And nothing ever meets your standards. You have to control everything."

"If you can't take the heat, get out." Olivia snarled. "You should have been let go a long time ago. I defended you, and look where it's gotten me."

"Shut up. You did no such thing. I've heard how you talk about me, and I've had enough of you. You're always Miss Perfect. Everyone loves you. We can't live without you. We'll see about that."

"So, you framed Eddie? You hate the show that much?" Olivia asked, her voice cracking.

"I don't hate the show. Just most of the people. I had a chance here. A real chance. I thought you were my mentor. Ha, was I wrong. I was the grunt who got all the dirty work. And you couldn't just be the boss of me at work. You had to stick your nose into my private life and ruin that, too."

"Oh, Paige. That thing you had with Raphael was never a real thing, and everyone knew it. You can't blame me for that. You know how he is. You were another notch on his conquest list. There wasn't anything there. I did you a favor."

"Some favor. You messed up everything. You really wanted him for yourself. Admit it."

"What? Are you crazy? I don't mix business and pleasure. And you should have known better. He is so not my type."

"You don't even know how to have fun. All you do is work and run the rest of us ragged. Raphael and I had something, and you butted your way in and ordered him to stay away from me. You can't stand to see me happy, can you? You can't stand to see anyone happy."

"You signed a contract like the rest of us that there's no fraternizing with your coworkers. He needed to focus on work, and so did you. I was trying to help save your job. You've been on thin ice for a long time."

"No, you saw that I was in a good place, and you can't stand for anyone else to succeed. I hate you. I hate you all." Paige wiped her cheek with the hand holding a gun.

Jade sucked in a breath of air. *What is taking the police so long?*

"I've had enough, and I don't care what happens. Plus, the police think it's Eddie. It's perfect. Maybe they won't find you this time," Paige added.

"And like everything else you do, it's half-baked. Did you not think this through?" Olivia sat up. "They have the person in custody, stupid. If you kill me, they'll know she didn't do it. And it's low tide, you moron. You didn't even bother to check the details as usual. You always fly by the seat of your pants."

"She'll get blamed for the rest of the stuff. And I'll be long gone before anyone finds you. There's a huge ocean out there. Everyone'll think it was an accident. Get up! We're going for a walk."

"I'm not going anywhere with you. You're crazy," Olivia said, gritting her teeth.

Before Paige could reply, a noise caused them to turn their heads toward the fence. When nothing moved, Olivia looked in Jade's direction.

Jade motioned a shhh signal and hoped Olivia got the message. It was a little hard to see.

"I said get up. Let's go see the water. I will be free of you finally. And who's stupid now? They won't know it's a murder if they can't find the body. Fish and crabs will take care of you for me." Paige waved her arms around wildly. "It's not so much fun when someone's barking orders at you, is it?"

Jade hoped the gun wouldn't go off accidentally as Paige continued to wave her arm around.

What is taking Nick's guys so long? Jade couldn't wait for the police. She had to do something to save Olivia before Paige got her across the street and near the bay. She took a deep breath, shoved her phone in her pocket, and let out the loudest banshee yell she could muster.

As the two women turned to see what was happening, Jade launched herself on Paige's back, and the pair landed hard on the ground, where they wrestled for several minutes.

A crack echoed through the quiet night. Jade's ears rang. Paige dropped the gun and bucked like a bronco. The taller woman wriggled free of Jade's grip and tried to find the gun in the tall grass.

Jade shook her head to try to dim the ringing in her ears. Not spotting the gun nearby, she launched herself again toward Paige, who crawled around, feeling her way with her hands.

After some finger jabs and unconventional wrestling moves, Jade ended up on top of Paige. When she paused to catch her breath, Paige reared back and punched her in the face. Stars flashed in front of Jade's eyes.

"Get off me. You'll ruin everything. And why does everyone want to help her?" Paige whined.

"Because they like me," Olivia yelled.

Paige went to say something, but she paused, reaching forward. Jade used the opportunity to distract the production assistant from getting the gun again by elbowing her in the back.

This time, Paige reared up with Jade on her back. She swung around, trying to shake off her attacker like a bucking mechanical bull. Jade's head and back ached as Paige bounced around.

"Freeze," a man yelled. "Now!"

Someone grabbed Jade's waist and pulled her off of Paige. Nick set her down on the ground several feet away. "We'll talk later," he said as he and Sebastian cornered Paige.

Sebastian cuffed Paige and escorted her toward one of the police vehicles in Jade's lot.

Nick checked on Olivia, who had the gun at her feet. "Are y'all okay? After the EMTs check you out, we'll get your statements." Turning toward Jade, he said, "You're gonna have quite the shiner there, slugger. I wish you had waited for us to arrive."

"I didn't know what she was thinking. She threatened to kill Olivia and dump her in the bay. And she had a gun. I had to do something."

"I know. We heard the whole conversation. You didn't hang up with dispatch."

"I got distracted." Jade pulled out her phone and disconnected the call. Quite a crowd had gathered on either side of the plastic fencing. Ezra and Brian skirted the barrier and headed toward Olivia.

A nearby EMT handed Jade an ice pack and cleared her after a checkup. They transported Olivia to the hospital for some tests.

"Come on," Nick said, draping an arm around Jade's shoulders. "We can talk in my vehicle."

Jade settled in the passenger seat after Nick moved some files, a clipboard, and his water bottle. "So, what happened?" he asked.

"I saw something weird on my camera app, so I came over to check it out before I called you. I thought it was someone casing the store, but it was Olivia and Paige arguing."

"We've got it all on tape, thanks to you. She's an angry woman," Nick said, jotting something in his notebook.

"Paige felt she was mistreated, and I think the root of it was that Olivia had broken up her relationship with Raphael and dismissed it as a casual fling. She was really enraged."

"The lead actor?" Nick asked.

Jade nodded. "He's, let's say, cavalier with his relationships. There have been many, and those were the ones that made it to the tabloids. Paige and Raphael didn't seem to go together, but she thought they did. The cast and crew are thrown together so much, maybe they found a common bond. It was a thing in Paige's mind," Jade said.

"Enough to set her off with Olivia. And it seems once her revenge started, she acted out against anyone who caused her grief. I'm not sure how premeditated some of them were. We'll find out the details when we question her. You okay? I'm gonna be here a while. You can stay in the vehicle, and I'll take you home when we're done."

"I'm fine," Jade said, sitting up straight in the passenger seat. "You do what you need to do. I'm headed home for some aspirin and bed. I'll catch up with you tomorrow. I love you. Be safe." Jade kissed him and climbed out of his SUV.

"I should say the same to you." Nick smiled.

Back home after two aspirin and a glass of milk, Jade settled on the couch to process the evening's events. Chloe was more interested in finishing her snooze.

214

Jade's cheek started to throb, so she fished out a bag of frozen lima beans from the bottom of her freezer as a make-do ice pack. She glanced at her stickies in the dining room. Her hunch was right. Eddie wasn't the one.

Ignoring the throbbing in her cheek that seemed to be in sync with her phone's constant beeping, she padded down the hall to her bedroom. She'd deal with the ton of emails and texts later. After all the chaos, it was time for a hot shower and some mindless TV.

Chapter Thirty-Seven

Jade glanced at her phone and the texts and emails about her encounter last night. Not having the energy to deal with it this morning, she poured her coffee in a to-go cup and gathered her things. Maybe work would take her mind off her throbbing cheek and the large purplish bruise around her eye that makeup wouldn't cover.

"Come on, Chloe. Let's see what's shaking at the store."

When the pair rounded the corner, she heard the crowd before she saw it. People had surrounded the store and the lot next door, while TV news vans blocked part of Neptune Road.

She picked up Chloe and hurried around to the back. Once inside, she peeked out the front window at the growing crowd. Letting out a heavy sigh, she headed to her desk to boot up her laptop and answer the ever-growing number of emails.

Sharp rapping on the back door sent Chloe into a barking jag. Jade opened the door, and Patti bustled in. "Sorry. I couldn't get through to the front porch. Again! Girl, you have caused a sensation."

"Me? Paige was the killer. I just helped detain her," Jade said.

"That's not what the internet says." Patti waved her phone in front of Jade. "You captured the killer and had time for romance. Watch out. You may be the heroine of the next Love Channel production. And I knew her when. There's a picture of you hugging the sheriff." Patti winked at Jade.

Jade steadied Patti's hand that she was waving around so she could see a video that featured a picture of her twirling around on Paige's back, and then there was a picture of her kissing Nick in his vehicle. *Who had time to*

216

snap pictures instead of helping me stop Paige?

"You're famous," Patti gushed. "And the buzz of Mermaid Bay and all the gossip sites. You better hurry up and post something on social media or answer your texts before Vivian calls a special council meeting to make sure you're okay. And that's quite the black eye. You look like one of those M and M fighters."

Jade cracked a smile. "MMA. Yep. I look so attractive."

"Enjoy it. You're what everyone is talking about this morning. Maybe we could get you one of those fedoras that you could pull down low to cover it up for your press conference this afternoon. On second thought, sport it with pride. You're a hero."

"Press conference?"

"Wren announced it this morning at the press conference the police had. You really haven't been checking your phone, have you? Nick made a quick statement about releasing that other woman and the arrest of Paige. Wren credited you with saving Olivia's life and the show. Now, you're the hero of every Love Channel fan on the planet. She said you'd be joining them for this afternoon's Love Channel press conference." Patti's eyes sparkled, and she waved her arms for effect. Then she scrolled through her phone to find the video clip.

Jade closed her eyes for a minute to ward off the headache forming behind her eyes. *How did this happen again?*

Before she could fish any aspirin out of her desk, another string of loud knocks interrupted their conversation.

Patti breezed over, stepping in front of Chloe to let Wren in.

"Did your phone get damaged in that melee?" the publicist asked as she barged in. "I've been trying to get in touch with you for hours."

"Sorry," Jade said, rising. "I was a little sore and tired, so I went to bed to try to sleep it off."

"Wow. That is some bruise. Our fans will eat it up. I can't wait to show you off," Wren said.

Jade furrowed her brow until it caused her face to hurt. She rested the side of her head on her hand.

"I need you to join Olivia and Ezra for a press conference today. We wrap up filming this week, and we thought this could be a kick-off for our media blitz. It's at three o'clock in front of the Sheriff's office."

"I did what anyone would do," Jade said.

"Uh, no. You saved Raphael from being poisoned and Elle from being framed for murder. You saved Olivia and me, and Eddie will be eternally grateful for finding the real culprit. Ezra is so pleased that all of this behind us, and he wants to invite you to Hollywood for the premiere of *My Coastal Valentine*."

"Oooooh, how thrilling," Patti said, hugging herself with excitement. "Great job, Jade."

"So, we're okay with three o'clock? We want to have the video ready to hit the afternoon news cycles. And don't cover up that eye. Stay away from Dante and Lexi. They'll pull out the heavy theatre makeup. I want you just the way you are. Our viewers will love that you risked life and limb for the Love Channel."

Jade opened her mouth and closed it again. The two women stared at her. "Three o'clock is fine," she finally said.

"Great. See you this afternoon. Be there early. And wear a dark, solid color." Wren zipped out the back door.

"You get busy answering your fan mail, and I'll take care of the overnight orders," Patti said.

Jade turned toward her laptop and printed the report. "Six pages. Even with all the trouble, the on-location filming has been profitable for local businesses. Hey, wait. You didn't tell me about your date with Simon."

"It was just a group of friends. But we had fun. Our real date is this weekend," Patti giggled and loaded bins on her cart. She winked and grabbed the handful of pages. "I may need two carts today," she yelled over her shoulder as she disappeared into the display rooms before Jade could probe more about Simon.

Jade had enough time to plow through hundreds of texts and emails and countless social media comments before she headed home to freshen up and get the Jeep.

"I'll lock up here and see you at the government center," Patti said. "Break a leg. I need to make a scrapbook to commemorate all that happened this fall."

Jade smiled, but it turned into a cringe when her cheek started throbbing again. About a half hour later, Jade found on-street parking near the government center and hustled to the sheriff's office. The crowd spilled over into the parking lot, where a line of news trucks sat nose to tail for three blocks. Jade pulled her gloves out of her coat pocket and wriggled her fingers inside. The temperatures had dropped as a storm threatened off the coast.

Jade scooted closer to the front of the building and stood next to a group of reporters. She felt a tug on her shoulder, and she turned to see Elle's security guard trying to get her attention. "Hey," he said. "Wren wants you up front. Follow me." He bulldozed through the crowd, and Jade followed in his wake of annoyed people.

The AV guy adjusted the sound system as Nick, Charles Winters, two state troopers, Wren and Ezra, made their way to the lectern, and the crowd noise dissipated.

Charles Winters stepped forward and tapped the microphone. "Thank you all for coming out on this chilly day for the joint press conference from members of Mermaid Bay's sheriff's office, the Virginia State Police, and the Love Channel. Sheriff Nicholas Driscoll, head of the task force, has an update."

"Thank you, Charles." Nick stepped forward. "The Mermaid Bay Sheriff's Department made an arrest in the murder of reporter Seth Davis and the recent attacks on members of the cast and crew of *My Coastal Valentine*. The person we have in custody is Paige Wilson, a former production assistant for the Love Channel. We have also released all other suspects in the case."

Nick looked left and right, and when Wren nodded, he continued, "And I'd like to turn it over now to Wren Pierce, publicist for the Love Channel."

Wren stepped forward in a full-length, puffy white coat and matching hat. Her red leather gloves matched her bold lipstick. "Hello. We at the Love Channel are deeply saddened that one of our own has been arrested for murder and poisoning, kidnapping, and assault. But we would like to thank the Mermaid Bay Sheriff's Office, the state police, and the task force for all the work they put into capturing the responsible party. I would also like to thank local business owner, Jade Hicks, for her quick thinking in stopping the killer from attacking again and holding her until the police arrived. We are eternally grateful for her quick action and risking bodily harm in the process." Wren pointed to Jade.

Suddenly, all cameras and eyes were upon her. Jade hoped she didn't have a deer-in-the-headlights look.

Wren didn't miss a step. She continued, "Filming in Mermaid Bay will wrap up this week. Despite all the attacks, we have enjoyed our stay here, and we look forward to sharing *My Coastal Valentine* with you all and the world next year." When she paused, the reporters shouted questions and waved arms.

"We'll take a few questions," Charles Winters said.

"Has Raphael Allard made a full recovery? And Sheriff, was Elle Valentine ever a suspect?"

"Raphael is fine. He has made a full recovery and is back to his old self," Wren said. "And no, Elle was never a serious suspect. The reporter died from a head wound, and the alleged murderer tried to frame Ms. Valentine. Thankfully, it was easy for law enforcement to see through the ruse."

The barrage of questions, mostly about the filming, lasted for another half hour. Jade breathed a sigh of relief when none of the questions were directed at her.

Finally, Charles Winters raised his arms. "Thank you all for coming. Our law enforcement officers need to get back to work. Good day."

Jade felt another tug on her elbow. Nick patted her arm and tilted his head toward the glass doors. She followed him to a spot near the front doors.

"You doing okay?" he asked.

She nodded. "But one thing's bothering me," she said. Nick frowned, and she continued, "All the attacks make sense except one. Why did Paige kill the reporter?"

"When she confessed, she said she thought the guy was Raphael. When she entered the room, it was dark and he was seated in the chair. Paige flew into a rage about how their relationship ended and how he didn't stand up to Olivia. She said he kowtowed to whatever she said. Paige didn't realize the guy wasn't Raphael until he was already dead. Then she got the not-so-bright idea to frame Elle."

Jade's hand flew to her mouth. "Oh, how awful. Did you ever find the murder weapon?"

"It was a wrench. We found it in her trailer. What about you? You feeling okay?"

"I'm fine. I've looked better, but this will heal quickly."

"You look fine to me. I wish you hadn't put yourself in danger. Dinner tonight at the Red Herring? A real date with no police calls. I have a couple of things I need to wrap up here. How about I pick you up in an hour at your place? I owe you a night out."

"See you then." Jade did a little wave and melted into the crowd.

Now, to start making plans for the show's premiere and Mermaid Bay's debut on the world's stage. Chloe may need her own Instagram account and agent after all of this.

Patti's Cherry Sparkles

Ingredients:

- 2 ½ cups of all-purpose flour
- ¾ cup of sugar
- 1 cup butter (cubed)
- ½ cup chopped, maraschino cherries
- 12 ounces of white baking chocolate (chopped)
- ½ teaspoon of almond extract
- 2 teaspoons of shortening
- Coarse sugar and edible glitter/sprinkles for decorating
- Waxed paper

Directions:

Preheat the oven to 325 degrees F.

Combine the flour and a ½ cup of the sugar. Add the butter, cherries, and 2/3 cup of the white chocolate. Then add the extract. Mix together and roll the dough into balls (quarter-sized).

Place the balls on an ungreased cookie sheet. Flatten the balls. You can use a glass dipped in sugar to flatten the cookies equally.

Bake for 10-12 minutes. The cookies should be slightly brown. Cool the cookies on a wire rack.

In a microwave, melt the shortening and white chocolate. Stir until the mixture is smooth.

Dip half of each cookie into the shortening/white chocolate mixture. Add the coarse sugar or sprinkles to your cookies. Place on waxed paper to cool.

Jade's Raspberry Jams

Ingredients:

- ¾ cup softened butter
- ½ cup sugar
- 1 large egg yolk
- 1 ½ cups all-purpose flour
- 2 tablespoons of raspberry preserves
- Confectioner's sugar

Directions:

Preheat the oven to 350 degrees F.

Combine the butter and sugar. Add the egg yolk and mix thoroughly. Add the flour.

On a lightly floured surface, knead the dough for 2-3 minutes. Roll the dough into one-inch balls. Place about two inches apart on a greased baking sheet. Use a spoon handle or a pill bottle to make an indention in the center of each cookie ball. Add about ¼ teaspoon of raspberry preserves in the indention.

Bake for 13-15 minutes until the cookie is browned. Cool the cookies on a wire rack. Cover the cookies with confectioner's sugar while they are warm.

Note: You can roll out the dough and use a small heart-shaped cookie cutter for more Valentine's Day fun.

Chocolate-dipped Hearts

Ingredients:

Cookie:

- 2 cups of all-purpose flour
- ½ cup of sugar
- Dash of salt
- 1 cup of cubed butter
- 1 tablespoon of cold water
- 1 teaspoon of almond extract
- ½ pound of dark chocolate candy coating (melted)
- Waxed paper

Directions:

Preheat the oven to 325 degrees F.

Combine the flour, sugar, and salt in a large bowl. Add the butter. Stir in water and the almond extract. Mix all ingredients well.

On a lightly floured surface, roll out the dough and cut with a heart-shaped cookie cutter. (A ¼-inch cookie cutter is best.)

Melt the chocolate candy coating.

Put the cookies about one inch apart on an ungreased baking sheet. Cover and refrigerate for 30 minutes.

Bake the chilled dough for 13-16 minutes until the cookies are lightly browned. Cool on a wire rack. After the cookie has cooled, dip half of the cookie in the candy coating. Let the cookies dry on the waxed paper.

Crème Brule Sugar Cookies

Ingredients:

Cookie:

- ¾ cup softened butter
- ½ cup brown sugar
- ½ cup granulated sugar
- 1 large egg
- 1 tablespoon of vanilla extract
- 2 cups of all-purpose flour
- 2 teaspoons of cornstarch
- 1 teaspoon of baking soda
- ¼ teaspoon of kosher salt
- Parchment paper

Icing:

- 1 8-ounce block of cream cheese (softened)
- 1 ¼ cup of powdered sugar
- 1 teaspoon of vanilla extract
- ¼ cup granulated sugar

Directions:

Preheat the oven to 350 degrees F. Line two cookie sheets with the parchment paper.

Mix the butter and all the sugars together. Add the egg and vanilla.

In another bowl, mix the flour, cornstarch, baking soda, and salt. Mix the contents of both bowls and stir until smooth and thick.

Create table-spoon-sized balls of dough on the lined cookie sheets. Flatten each cookie ball slightly.

Bake for 9-10 minutes until the cookies are brown. Cool the cookies on a wire rack.

Beat the cream cheese until it is smooth. Add the sugar and vanilla for the icing. Spread about a tablespoon of the icing on each cookie.

Lorelei's Cookie S'mores

Ingredients:

- 1 ¼ cups of all-purpose flour
- ½ teaspoon of baking powder
- ¼ teaspoon of baking soda
- ¼ teaspoon of salt
- 8 tablespoons of unsalted, softened butter
- ½ cup of sugar
- 8 graham crackers (crushed) – This should be about one cup full.
- 1 large egg
- 1 teaspoon of vanilla extract
- 12 large marshmallows (cut in half)
- 24 Hershey's Kisses (unwrapped)
- Parchment paper

Directions:

Preheat the oven to 350 degrees F. Line two cookie sheets with the parchment paper. Mix the flower, baking powder, baking soda, and salt together. Then using a mixer, beat the sugar, butter, and half of the crushed graham crackers on medium for about 3 minutes. Add the eggs and vanilla. Reduce the mixer speed to low and add the flour.

In a dish, pour the rest of the crushed graham crackers. Roll the dough into 1 ¼ inch balls and roll them in the dish of crushed graham crackers for coating. Bake for 10-12 minutes. Cool the cookies on a wire rack for about

5 minutes.

Heat your oven's broiler. Put a marshmallow half in the center of each cookie. It looks better if you put the cut side face down. Broil cookies for 30-45 seconds until the marshmallows are brown. Put the hot cookies on a wire rack and put a chocolate candy in the center of each marshmallow. The candy and marshmallow should melt on top of the cookie.

Patti's Peppermint Fudge

Ingredients:

- 3 cups of white chocolate chips
- 1 14-ounce can of condensed milk (sweetened)
- 1 teaspoon of peppermint extract
- ¼ teaspoon of sea salt
- Crushed peppermint candies or candy canes

Directions:

In a large bowl, mix the chocolate chips and the condensed milk. Microwave for about a minute. Stop it every 15-20 seconds to stir the mixture. Add the peppermint extract and salt.

Pour the mixture into a greased 9x9 pan. You may want to line it with foil for easier cleanup. Smooth out the mixture in the pan and sprinkle the crushed candy on the top.

Allow the fudge to cool and cut into squares for serving.

Acknowledgements

I want to thank my family and friends who provided all the wonderful support for me and this book: Stan Weidner, thanks for always being there, my parents who instilled in me a lifelong love of reading, Cortney Cain for always providing early morning sanity checks, Meagan and Jocelyn Cain, my social media gurus, and Bill Cain for always giving me the giggles. And I appreciate all the encouragement, love, and support from my Bethia UMC family.

I am so grateful for my talented Sisters in Crime, Guppy, Virginia is for Mysteries, International Thriller Writers, and James River Writer friends. Your support is invaluable! K. L. Murphy, Mary Burton, Jayne Ormerod, thanks for all your encouragement!

Many, many thanks to my fabulous agent, Dawn Dowdle for all her help and hard work and her team at Blue Ridge Literary Agency. And a huge thank you to Shawn Reilly Simmons and the infamous Dames of Detection, and everyone at Level Best Books for letting me share Mermaid Bay and all the antics of Jade, Amy, Chloe, Neville the Devil Cat, and Peppermint Patti.

Many thanks to Dom, Jennifer and Ms. Bruin Bear Cristello for all of your expert advice on French bulldogs. And thanks to Matt Heath for answering all my theatre and film questions.

About the Author

Through the years, Heather Weidner has been a cop's kid, technical writer, editor, college professor, software tester, and IT manager. She writes the Delanie Fitzgerald Mysteries, The Jules Keene Glamping Mysteries, and The Mermaid Bay Christmas Shoppe Mysteries.

Her short stories appear in the *Virginia is for Mysteries* series, *50 Shades of Cabernet*, *Deadly Southern Charm*, and *Murder by the* Glass, and she has nonfiction pieces in *Promophobia* and *The Secret Ingredient*.

She is a member of Sisters in Crime–Central Virginia, Sisters in Crime–Chessie, Guppies, International Thriller Writers, and James River Writers.

Originally from Virginia Beach, Heather has been a mystery fan since Scooby-Doo and Nancy Drew. She lives in Central Virginia with her husband and a pair of Jack Russell terriers.

SOCIAL MEDIA HANDLES:
  Blog: http://www.heatherweidner.com
  Twitter: https://twitter.com/HeatherWeidner1
  Facebook: https://www.facebook.com/HeatherWeidnerAuthor
  Instagram: https://www.instagram.com/heather_mystery_writer/

Goodreads: https://www.goodreads.com/author/show/8121854.Heather_Weidner

Amazon Authors: http://www.amazon.com/-/e/B00HOYR0MQ

Pinterest: https://www.pinterest.com/HeatherBWeidner/

LinkedIn: https://www.linkedin.com/in/heather-weidner-0064b233?trk=hp-identity-name

BookBub: https://www.bookbub.com/authors/heather-weidner-d6430278-c5c9-4b10-b911-340828fc7003

TikTok: https://www.tiktok.com/@heather_weidner_author

YouTube: https://www.youtube.com/channel/UCyBjyB0zz-M1DaM-rU1bXGA?view_as=subscriber

LinkTree: https://linktr.ee/heatherweidner

AUTHOR WEBSITE:

http://HeatherWeidner.com

Also by Heather Weidner

The Jules Keene Glamping Mysteries
  Vintage Trailers and Blackmailers
  Film Crews and Rendezvous

The Mermaid Bay Christmas Shoppe Mysteries
  Sticks and Stones and Bag of Bones

The Delanie Fitzgerald Mysteries
  Secret Lives and Private Eyes
  The Tulip Shirt Murders
  Glitter, Glam, and Contraband
  Male Revues and Subterfuge

The Mutt Mysteries (Novellas)
  To Fetch a Thief
  To Fetch a Scoundrel
  To Fetch a Villain
  To Fetch a Killer

Short Stories
  The *Virginia is for Mysteries* Series (Volumes 1-3)
  Murder by the Glass
  Deadly Southern Charm
  50 Shades of Cabernet

Nonfiction
  The Secret Ingredient, The Mystery Writers' Cookbook
  Promophobia